SCENE AT THE COFFIN MAKER'S.

MYSTERIES OF

Old Saint Paul's.

A TALE OF THE PLAGUE.

SEVENTEEN BEAUTIFUL ENGRAVINGS

BY THE AUTHOR OF "LEGENDS OF LONDON," "CHRONI-
CLES OF OLD LONDON WALL," &c.

LONDON: G. VICKERS, 28, HOLYWELL STREET, STRAND.
AND ALL BOOKSELLERS.

1841.

MYSTERIES OF

Old Saint Paul's.

A TALE OF THE PLAGUE.

Vide page 2

CHAPTER I.

It was on a bright sunny morning in May, some centuries back, that streams of well-dressed citizens, accompanied by their wives and daughters, were bending their steps in the direction of Old Saint Paul's. From the Chepe, Watling Street, Ludgate, and Dowgate, the footway was scarcely passable, in consequence of the throngs that were advancing with hasty steps towards the Cathedral. The occasion for this great movement was to offer a public prayer to Heaven to avert and allay the devastating horrors of the plague, which was now making rapid strides into the City of London, having completely hemmed it round from Rotherhithe to Bankside, from Bankside to Westminster, from Westminster to the Long Acre ; and from thence it stretched out its death-dealing snare down Holborn, eastward, as far as Great Turnstile ; and St. Andrew's was now infected. As yet the great City had

1.

escaped:—the destroyer not having passed the bounds of Ludgate or Aldersgate; but watched, as it were, like a secret enemy in the night, to effect an entrance by stealth.

It was upon this momentous occasion that this great public worship was to be celebrated: all business had been entirely suspended in the City for the day, and the devout and timid inhabitants were fast filling the chapel, galleries, and aisles of Old Saint Paul's Cathedral. The great or middle aisle (commonly called Paul's Walk), was at this time a public lounge, and generally thronged with the gallants of the town, bullies, alsatians, and rogues of all descriptions, no one in decent apparel being denied access to so public a meeting place: and, in short, it was a place where the devout christian and the cut-purse, the hypocrite and the gallant, lovers and their mistresses, jealous rivals, watchful duennas, rich widows, and suspicious fathers, mingled in one dense cluster; yet all pretending to be upon visits of devotion and worship.

The bell had ceased tolling, and the inner chapel was now crammed to excess; still one or two stragglers less expert than others were seen hurrying up the steps and proceeding to the folding doors, between which some forced an entrance, whilst others, less persevering, contented themselves with pacing to and fro with the crowd in the middle aisle, which now assumed a goodly muster, partly composed of persons too late for the service, and yet too devout to leave the sacred edifice entirely; and partly of the variety previously alluded to. It was at this moment that a female, closely enveloped in a mantle and hood, came hurrying across the stone pavement of the side aisle, as if in earnest expectation of meeting with some one; she gazed round in various directions, and by this means attracted the general gaze of the gallants who were carelessly strutting to and fro, playing with their silver headed canes, and turning the points of their moustache; two or three had even approached towards her with the appearance of curiosity and familiarity, and had just closed round her, when one more bold and free than the others, rather rudely lifted the hood which hid her features from view. He had, however, scarcely raised it, and betrayed a pair of beautiful blue eyes and long brown tresses to the gaze of his simpering companions, than he was roughly grasped by the collar, his intruding arm knocked up, and himself instantly whirled round on his heel against a pillar, by the arm of a dashing young gallant who had just approached, and, who, taking the female by the hand, instantly entered into conversation with her in a familiar tone, and slowly led her away.

A loud laugh from his companions echoed the sound of his head's concussion against the stones, and the young man boiling with rage, and forgetting for the moment the sanctity of the place, drew his sword, and before any one could prevent him, rushed after his opponent. A word and a blow was all that preceded an attitude of defence and attack; when the clashing of swords brought crowds to the spot. The young gallants had crowded round their companion, and forcing his sword from his grasp hurried him out of the cathedral by a side avenue, thus averting the serious consequences that might await so flagrant an act in a place of worship, and on such a solemn occasion, whilst the young man who had rescued the lady from their rudeness was roughly chidden for his boldness by the bystanders.

" Be pacified, and let us away, dear Arthur," said the lady in evident agitation; at the same time urging her partner towards the centre door of the cathedral.

" Oh, a plague on such cowardly hounds !" muttered the young man, as he sheathed his sword. Then placing one arm round the waist of his fair companion, he led her towards the door, pausing as he went, and looking over his shoulder, as if anxious to catch a glimpse of some of his opponents in the crowds who were gazing on in apparent surprise and horror at what had been but the work of a moment.

Having now brought the two principal parties, who form the heroes of our story, before our readers, we must introduce others closely connected with them, and thus come to the important development of our tale :—

Master Matthew Elliot was a citizen and stationer, who lived in an old-fashioned house in Cheapside, carrying on a very extensive business, and was much respected by all his fellow-citizens and neighbours. His family consisted of an only daughter Constance, who was at this time just eighteen, and who possessed charms of extraordinary attraction ; causing her name to be a standing toast with all the city gallants, ravishing every heart, and being beset by a whole troop of despairing admirers in secret, not one of whom received the slightest favourable recognition in return, except one Master Arthur Latymer. Master Elliot, moreover, had a son, a promising youth of sixteen ; the family circle being completed by his amiable wife. In addition, however, we must not forget Lawrence Wood, an orphan, a youth arriving at manhood, living under his protection, and performing the duties of an assistant in the warehouse. The domestics in a family so regularly conducted, were few ; there being but Dame Trivet, an old housekeeper, who filled the various offices of cook, nurse, and servant of all work, assisted by her grandson, Scrubb. Master Matthew was a very pious man, and it was his custom every morning and evening to assemble with his household to pray to Heaven, to shield them from the ravages of the enemy that was now dealing death so plentifully around. It was, therefore, considered by him as an imperative duty to be present with his whole family at the service in the cathedral mentioned at the commencement of the chapter, and our readers will doubtless by this time have concluded that it was no other than his daughter, Constance Elliot, who was the cause of the fray between the gallants in the aisle of Old Saint Paul's.

Amongst the numerous admirers, or we may say lovers, of Constance Elliot (for no one could admire her without loving her) was Lawrence Wood, the orphan protected by her father ; they had been brought up together from childhood, first regarding each other as brother and sister, but by degrees as the youth grew towards manhood he could not remain unmoved by her exquisite beauty. He had just turned his twenty-first year, and having amassed a tolerable sum of money in his kind benefactor's employ, his hopes and intentions were to return and settle in his native town of Gloucester, whither he thought the fair Constance would accompany him as his bride. Yet he had never revealed his love to her, or even received sufficient encouragement from the maiden herself to warrant such a hope ; but being, as he considered himself, in every respect worthy of her, and his personal appearance much in favour of him, he had reckoned it as a matter of course that no one else could have had opportunity, or chance if they had, to out-shine him—but Lawrence was mistaken, as we have already introduced his rival in the person of Arthur Latymer.

It was some days after the adventure in the cathedral that two richly-dressed young gallants were walking up the Chepe, and had arrived opposite the door of our citizen and stationer, Matthew Elliot, when they were both violently jostled against by a bullying alsatian of Whitefriars, who came reeling along from one side to the other, and, coming in violent contact with the two gallants, sent them sprawling in the mire. The younger of the two was the first to regain his feet, and, approaching the bully, demanded an apology for the unjustifiable insult.

" Apology—me !" roared the bully. " By St. George, and I like that, too. Will Browden to ask forgiveness of such a silk and velvet tassel as thee ! Bah ! beg of me rather not to make worm's meat of thee !" And placing his .

hands on his hips he looked the enraged young gallant in the face—"by my good steel," he continued, "but you are as pretty a golden butterfly as one need try to snap at"—and saying this, he gave the youth a smart blow on the chest with his herculean fist, and reeled on, laughing aloud.

"Then if you will not apologise, ruffian, defend yourself," answered the gallant—and drawing his sword in an instant he made a pass at the bully, who was thus compelled to draw.

"Ha, ha, ha!" laughed the alsatian, as his short sword glittered in the sun, "'twould be a pity to spoil such a pretty face, so I will be content with one of those little fingers covered with such shining rings:—Ah! there! steady! you're too quick"—this was said as he parried the blows of the gallant, which were dealt with the fury of a madman.

By this time the clashing of swords had drawn a crowd round the combatants; some were loudly cursing the bully as a coward, and cheering the gallant, who, being but a youth, was no match for his more powerful antagonist. Others tried to pacify them; amongst whom was Master Elliot, who being attracted by the noise, had now joined the crowd. "Part them, or there will be murder done! call the serjeant," he cried aloud. Yet no one dared to approach near enough, till the second gallant, who had now recovered himself, drawing his sword, rushed in between them, and after several severe struggles, beat down the weapon of his companion, and at this moment the bully taking advantage, passed his blade through the sword arm of his opponent, and fled.

All was confusion and uproar; several of the bystanders gave chase to the bully, who, however, after several windings and turnings escaped into Thames Street, and got clear off. Those of the crowd who remained behind now busily engaged themselves in attending upon the wounded man. His companion, after binding up the wound to stay the blood, which was fast oozing from beneath his silken vest, begged of Master Elliot to allow him to be placed in his house, while he ran for a surgeon, as the youth had swooned.

Master Elliot was anything but an unfeeling man, but still under existing circumstances, he hesitated on this point, and considered inwardly of the trouble and inconvenience he should be put to: if the youth should die, he must be a principal witness in a case of murder, and all the horrors and anxiety of a court of trial rushed upon his mind—he dared not refuse for humanity; he feared to accede for his wife; and in this state of mind he ran to a legal friend of his close at hand to ask advice. During his absence, the youth was carried into his shop, and the first restoratives that could be obtained were applied. In a few minutes his eyes opened; he spoke, looked round, and smiled. He was then led into an inner room, and was there attended by Dame Elliot and her daughter Constance, who, upon recognising the features of the young gallant, uttered a loud shriek of surprise; which was instantly checked by a penetrating look from the young man; Constance at the same time, with a great effort, construing the cause of her terror into the sight of the blood which had besmeared his dress. The young gallant, after this, seemed to recover most miraculously, and also to be over grateful to his young nurse for her attentions to him. He gently pressed her hand, which was not withdrawn, and the mutual looks of recognition which passed between them would have created suspicion in the minds of more susceptible persons than Matthew Elliot and his wife, who never for a moment dreamt of any one loving their daughter.

The fact, however, stood thus. The affray previously mentioned as having taken place was preconcerted and arranged, and the wounded gallant was no other than Arthur Latymer himself, who had undergone all to be blessed by an interview, and hold a conversation with the idol of his affection. His wound was, in truth, but a scratch; his indisposition was more feigned than real; and, being rather off his guard by the success of his stratagem, he began to converse freely with Constance, and his conversation became so animated and tender, that Dame Elliot thought it best to desire her daughter to retire. This mandate, however unpleasant, Constance could not openly disobey, and casting on Arthur one of her tenderest glances, she was about to leave the room, when he caught her by the hand.

"You must not leave me, thus; dear lady," he exclaimed. "Suffer me at least to return you my sincere thanks for your kind attentions, to which alone I may owe my speedy recovery." Saying this, he seized her hand, and passionately pressed it to his lips.

Dame Elliot, who had hitherto considered Arthur's looks as more free than welcome, was now completely astounded by his words, and wrenching her daughter's hand from his grasp, she would have forced her from the room, but Arthur now commenced a sally upon the dame, whom he overwhelmed with thanks and favours.

"I need no thanks for a good deed, sir," replied Dame Elliot to his courtesies. "We are but middling people, and I am sure no objects of compliment from people of your stamp, if we may judge by your dress; so good day to you, sir, and may you mend speedily."

"Nay, do not leave so abruptly," replied Arthur; "allow me, at least, to present you with some tribute of my regard;" and taking from his neck a beautiful miniature he presented it to Constance, who, blushing, accepted it.

"I desire you not to take it," cried her mother; "and I must request you, sir, to leave the house instantly."

"But first say, lovely angel, is that present acceptable to your sight? will you preserve it for the sake of the giver?" exclaimed Arthur, as he once more grasped Constance's hand, and knelt before her.

Constance looked not, spoke not, but her face and neck were dyed in crimson as she tremblingly placed the miniature in her bosom, and tried to free her hand from his grasp.

"Nay, you must not leave me," he exclaimed, "one word only, and I am answered. Am I objectionable in your sight?"

"Answer him not," shrieked the dame; "he deceives you, as do all these Court gallants. Tell him you despise him, and bid him begone."

"I despise no one, dear mother," replied Constance artlessly. "But I will bid him begone, if *you* wish it."

"Then you would not do so of your own accord," exclaimed Arthur passionately, at the same time catching her in his arms. "I am not, then, an object of scorn to you?"

Dame Elliot having somewhat recovered from the surprise into which this interview had thrown her, seized Arthur by the arm, exclaiming in an authoritative tone, "Begone, sir! I will not allow these familiarities; such conduct as this evinces on your part evil intentions!"

"By my life, none!" replied Arthur. "I love her, and would possess her."

"No doubt," replied the dame, "for a week or a month, and then turn her ruined and broken-hearted upon the world!"

"No; for life, for death, for ever!" responded Arthur fervently.

Dame Elliot was for the moment staggered at the apparent frankness of the young man's assertion; but fearing the result she replied, "Why, then, if you really esteem my daughter, and your intentions are indeed honourable, this is not the manner to evince them. You should have first consulted her father before you dared to address his child. And, till he has given you leave to do so, I must request you to cease your intrusions."

"And I too, indeed," rejoined Constance. "I will never consent till my father does."

" Dutiful girl !" muttered her mother in an under tone. Then, turning
to Arthur, she said, " Besides, you are a stranger ; you appear rich and a
gentleman, but for aught we know might be nothing more than some swaggering cut-purse—no, no, we must know something more of young men then
a mere interview, before we let them pay their addresses to our daughter.
This latter part of the speech was uttered in a dignified tone, and the old
dame tossed her head in disdain, to think of an anonymous son-in-law !"

" It is not for me to praise myself, I know," replied Arthur. " I am but
a private citizen ; and what faults I seem to possess now would all disappear
should chance endow me with such a lovely partner as the fair Constance."

" That may be true ; but I am sure that a person of your strange de-
meanour, without any other recommendation than your gentility, will never
meet with Master Elliot's consent to wed his daughter," observed Dame
Elliot. " So you waste your time, sir, I can tell you."

" I hope it is not so," replied Arthur. " But should I make my claim
good with him, shall I stand in hope of obtaining your's, dear madam ?"
inquired Arthur of Dame Elliot ; his eyes constantly changing from the
countenance of the daughter to that of the mother.

" I shall give no answer to such questions," replied the dame tartly ;
" and let me tell you, sir, that I am not at all prepossessed in favour of one
who thus thrusts himself so unceremoniously and so unasked into the
privacy of a family. I would you were gone, sir !"

" Yes, Arthur, leave us for the present," rejoined Constance hastily, and
evidently off her guard ; but it was too late for her to recall her words—she
had betrayed herself.

Arthur Latymer bit his lip with vexation, and fixed his glance upon the
countenance of the dame to watch the effect of the disclosure thus inadver-
tently made.

" Hey-day ! and likely, too. Arthur, Arthur, indeed !" re-echoed the
dame, in a shrill voice ; " then you know something of this pretty peacock,
eh, simperer ; dost hear me, Constance ?" Here the dame grasped her
daughter's arm, and looking angrily into her face exclaimed, " Tell me, de-
ceiver, have you known this flatterer long ? who is he ? and how dare you
plan this meeting, for 'tis no other. But your father shall know all—every
thing of his daughter's artfulness and duplicity."

" Mother, dear mother, hear me ! I am not the deceitful girl you think
me. I can explain all." Constance's utterance, however, failed her, and
she gave vent to a violent flood of tears, and sank back in a chair.

" Constance," exclaimed Arthur, " my own, my dear Constance. Be
composed ; I will reveal all, and obtain pardon for us both."

Constance being somewhat composed by this soothing appeal, Arthur
Latymer addressed himself to her mother, and informed her in a brief
manner as follows :—" You cannot wonder that I should love your daughter,
my dear madam, for who could see her once without loving ; especially with
myself, who had to endure the grief of seeing her, and debarred from the
opportunity of speaking to her. I had regularly met, watched, and followed
her, but until the solemn day of public worship at St. Paul's, last week, we
had not spoken ; it was then that I told her I loved her, implored her to
forgive me, and asked permission to visit her, but was positively denied, as
she would hear of no proposals unknown to you ; this, madam, is the deceit
for which you blame her ; rather condemn me."

To say the truth, Arthur's appeal at first produced a rather favourable im-
pression upon Dame Elliot ; but she was invulnerable. She had made a
charge, given her sentence, and could not now think of being talked out of
her opinion by any one.

" Young man, or Master Arthur, as your lady-love would style you, it is not thus that you will win our consent, by practising deceit at first, and then making a long confession when all is discovered by your lady's simplicity. This instant quit the house, and dread to enter it as you would one smitten with the plague."

" Say, rather, as one smitten with the plague would enter a house of cure ; which, as this does mine, contained his only hope of life !" rejoined Arthur, penitently.

" Constance shall not even say adieu !" rejoined the dame ; and she would have forced her daughter from the room had not Arthur stepped forward and seized her hand.

" Do not leave me, Constance," he said imploringly.

" This is presumption, indeed, to my face !" exclaimed Dame Elliot.

" I would not willingly give you cause for offence, my dear madam," replied Arthur, " but I request you will allow me to explain to your husband, with whom my influence may doubtless prevail."

" I shall do no such thing," answered the dame pettishly.

" Then I remain till his return," replied Arthur.

" We will see to that, indeed," replied the now enraged mother ; and hastily leaving the room she called for aid in a loud tone. " Here, Lawrence ! John ! Scrubb ! all of ye ; help, help !"

" Oh, Arthur, quarrel not, I implore you !" exclaimed Constance, her words nearly drowned in her tears."

" Fear not, my love ; I will only defend, not attack," replied her lover.

As he spoke, Dame Elliot re-entered the room, followed by her son John, and Lawrence Wood, armed with stout cudgels. Pointing to Arthur, she ordered them to put him from the house. The son contented himself, however, in merely repeating his mother's commands to the youth, who stood whispering into Constance's ear, not heeding them. But the manner and conduct of Lawrence was far different, for he saw in the person of the stranger his rival—a rival evidently gaining a firm possession of that heart he thought so entirely his own, and burning with rage he rushed upon Arthur, who, not being prepared for so violent an attack, staggered and fell to the ground, and with him Lawrence Wood.

" Ruffian, unhand me !" shouted Arthur, as Lawrence pinned him to the ground in his grasp.

" Lawrence ! would you murder him ?" shrieked Constance, as she endeavoured to extricate him from her lover.

" Nay, then, if you plead in his cause he is free," exclaimed Lawrence; " Let him leave the house."

In an instant Arthur gained his feet ; his hand grasped the hilt of his sword, and he would have dared it in defiance had not a look from Constance stayed him, and taking her hand he would have pressed it to his lips to have breathed a fond farewell upon it, but Lawrence, contemplating his motive, seized him by the waist, gave one herculean spring, and both rolled headlong down a flight of stairs.

Neither of them were much injured, but upon trying to regain himself Arthur was firmly caught as in a vice by Lawrence, who, throwing both his arms round him, rendered him utterly helpless. A long, loud shriek from Constance echoed through the house as Lawrence disappeared over the balustrade with his rival, and being anxious that Arthur should not convey to Constance the nature of any injury he might have received in his hasty descent, he touched a small door with his foot, which opened into the Old Jewry, and pushing his companion through it, followed after him. The young man, now at liberty, occupied the first few moments in recovering a sufficient quantity of breath to commence a new attack. Arthur was armed with his sword, Lawrence with but a stout oaken cudgel, which, however, in his hands, would have proved the most formidable weapon of the two. He now broke silence by addressing his rival.

"We have met strangely, young man," he began, in a lowering tone, "but we cannot part so. May I ask your name, and your warrant for this intrusion upon that fair damsel you have so unceremoniously insulted in her father's house?"

"You shall have neither," replied Arthur, "or if I had even insulted her would I make amends to you—a serving-man, indeed! But harkee, my well-paid young bully, you may consider it part of your duty to carry to your master and mistress's ear all you may learn concerning them; from me then learn, for their instruction, that I most ardently love their daughter, and I swear that she as true loves me, and whether they will give consent or not, she is mine. I'll have her in their spite: say this, and I forgive the usage you have dealt out to me; and so adieu!"

Arthur Latymer now turned suddenly upon his heel, and in another instant would have been out of sight, but Lawrence, who during this speech had been motionless as a statue, darted after him, and seized him by the arm. "Treacherous villain, stay!" he exclaimed; "is it not enough that you have by cheating and artifice obtained possession in our house, but you must basely rob and plunder that house of a jewel more costly than thy own life? Speak, thou quivering caitiff, speak, or by my soul I'll wrest it from thee!"

"I understand you not, fellow," answered Arthur.

"You have to-day, for the first time, entered that house?"

"I did so."

"You saw—his—Elliot's—*my* Constance there?"

"Your Constance!" exclaimed Arthur in surprise.

"Ay, mine, and wholly mine, ere you saw and poisoned her youthful ears with thy infernal speech. Villain, hear me! I have treasured up the love of that fair being from my very boyhood; I had no other dream but her, no other hope or wish but to unite my life with hers, and end our days as happy as we first began. I now find you crossing my path, coming betwixt my life and me; but take heed! and rather attempt to snatch the food from the jaws of a hungry tiger, or struggle with a fellow man to see which one shall live, than rob me of my heart's best hope. I have no other motive to live but for her. If you proceed, you die!"

As Lawrence uttered the last expression, he drew from under his vest a small dagger, and with this emphatic menace disappeared. Arthur laughed at his entreaties and injunctions, and puzzling his brains what device he should adopt to obtain another meeting with Constance, he walked merrily along, and soon mixed in the crowded streams of Cheapside.

CHAPTER II.

It was late in the day before Master Elliot returned home; and upon being informed of the result of his hospitality to the young gallant, he was much disconcerted, though he tried to conceal his meditations on the subject. After making a few observations, he retired into his counting-house, and remained there till business had ceased. His principal motive was to watch for Arthur, but he not returning, he considered it as a frolic played by some city gallant; for, to speak truly, he would have been seriously alarmed at the idea of any thing like an affection existing between his daughter and a person totally unknown to the family.

Vide page 4.

From the evening of Lawrence Wood officiating as cudgeller extraordinary, and ejecting Arthur Latymer from his master's house, a great change took place in the behaviour of Constance towards him. She had hitherto been merry and friendly with him, but she now seemed pensive and sad— scarcely tolerating his presence, and barely returning answers to any questions he might put to her. This was not lost upon Lawrence, and after one or two attempts to draw her into something like a familiar conversation, he let the trial drop. He was, however, determined to watch her, since, if he could not win her affections for himself, he vowed that Arthur Latymer never should supplant him. Her mother, too, had often detected her in deep study, and then heavy sighs would follow, and it was evident that the young gallant still retained a place in her memory. Mrs. Elliot, however, declined informing her husband of this circumstance till some more fitting occasion.

Things remained in this state for several days, and Master Elliot and his wife had settled down comfortable in the opinion that the gay young spark had lost all recollection of their daughter, and that the affair had totally dropped. Differently, indeed, judged Lawrence. Arthur might, it is true, manage to blind the eyes of a doting father and mother, but not one who loved the same being as himself, one who watched every look, sigh, or movement that she made. He had conjectured that there were letters passing to and fro, as he had seen Constance reading slips of paper when alone, and folding them up hastily when she thought she was discovered. He had never tried to possess himself of one: he considered it would be a dastardly action, and a mean advantage. But Lawrence was determined to watch for the messenger who fetched and carried the epistles, and ultimately succeeded in his object.

It has been before mentioned that the family of Master Elliot was not complete without the persons of Dame Trivet and her lacquey-boy, Scrubb; and what family in those days was or could be considered perfect without an ancient-looking portly dame for a housekeeper; one who could either brew

2.

or bake, make syllabubs and mince-meat, confections, &c., and mix a sack-posset with any innkeeper in the City. Even such a one was Dame Trivet. Moreover, she was a clever nurse; the children of the family had looked upon her as a second mother; added to which she was viewed in the light of a skilful apothecary, who would whisp a case of instruments from her pocket, and take out a raging tooth, or bind up a wound with any medical student in the kingdom. She was a perfect calendar of old and rare receipts for scalds, burns, coughs, &c.; all of which she invariably undertook to cure. She had been with Master Elliot ever since his marriage, was a hale dame of sixty, with but few infirmities, and much less of temper than is generally found in servants of her age and class.

Her boy Scrubb, who was in relationship a grandchild, was a thick-built lad, with short cropped carotty hair, a blear eye, immense long arms, and an inconceivable great head. He was excessively timid and suspicious, and ten times more so than ever since the plague had broken out in London. No sort of diversion could drive this plague question out of his head, and it was in vain for him to try and struggle with it; he would often start up in the night, fancying he heard shouts of "the plague! the plague!" by myriads of voices (as he would describe it to be): if any person met their death by ordinary or accidental circumstances, it was set down by Scrubb that the plague must have had something to do with it. He read and purchased every bill, paper, book, or recipe concerning it, that his slender funds would allow; he would eagerly walk miles every day to peruse the bills of mortality, and would return with the cheering information that deaths were decreasing—only eight deaths in one parish; one of them an infant, only two months old, or a man and boy who had been in the habit of attending on the dead cart. Sometimes he would put on a most melancholy appearance, on hearing it announced that the number of deaths had increased, and were approaching nearer the City. He would talk for hours upon the particulars of individual cases, argue upon the extent of the patient's sufferings, watch daily and hourly the spread of the disorder, and calculate at so many houses a day when it was likely to reach Cheapside; then how many hours would elapse before it reached his master's house, and when there which of the inmates was most likely to be the first victim, and which stood the best chance of recovery when stricken. By Dame Trivet's advice he took strong decoctions of herbs, such as wormwood, rosemary, rue, &c., doctoring it up with other mixtures, till it was so repulsive he could scarcely swallow it. He constantly chewed and smoked tobacco, whenever he came within half a mile of any infected house or district. He always wore under his vest a dried pig's ear, as a famous safeguard against the plague. Every new dose or mixture that came out was sure to find a patron in Scrubb, provided his pocket allowance would meet the demand; he had even sold a favourite spaniel to raise the price of a bottle of " Newly-invented, sure-restorative, and positive-preventive plague-water." His also being of a very superstitious nature caused him to dwell much more on the vague and foolish prophecies which were then prevalent: among the most prominent was one that " Cheapside should be a pasture;" that " London should become a second Babylon, and its inhabitants rooted out from the face of the earth;" and that " the living should perish by the number of dead surrounding them." He trembled at the ravings of ignorant and deluded preachers who occupied the corners of most of the streets and lanes, dealing out death and torment to all the land, and proclaiming " that the hour was come!" " death was triumphant!" and that " the day of retribution was at hand!" He had had his nativity cast, and it was there predicted that he would be in great danger at the end of June, and he had made up his mind that he was to die of the plague at that period. Previous to his having fallen a victim to the plague-terror, he had formed an attachment for a young tavern wench hard by, who used to visit Dame Trivet on occasions of great dinners and routs, to take a lesson or two in the culinary art, and as Scrubb always came in for a share of the sundry pickings after the feast, a sort of cupboard or board-and-lodging affection had sprung up between him and this damsel of the Fleece, in the Old Jewry ; but latterly the idea of the plague had so absorbed his mind that he neglected to pay his regular visits to the Fleece pantry, lest the infection might have found its way there also : in fact, he had given way so much to the absurd notion, and become so wan and ghastly, that it would have been quite easy to persuade him that he was seized with the first symptoms.

It was one of the two persons whose various peculiarities have just been described, that Lawrence suspected to be either confidant or messenger between Constance and Arthur Latymer: he was certain that she did both receive and send letters, and he therefore fixed his mind upon Scrubb, and determined to watch him.

Not many days had elapsed before Lawrence, happening to enter rather suddenly into a room occupied by Scrubb, found him busily engaged at a rough sort of toilet, combing away at his fiery mane ; his dress had been newly put on for the first time, and he wore a short sword or dirk, as was the custom among servants and plebeians in those days, who tried to ape the manners of their superiors. Scrubb was so busily engaged on his personal decoration, that he did not perceive the intrusion of Lawrence, until he popped his head over Scrubb's shoulder, and displayed two heads in the glass instead of one. This so frightened Scrubb, that he started back into the room, and by this means had not the presence of mind to hide a letter which lay on the table, and which had been entrusted to him to deliver to Arthur Latymer. Lawrence immediately recognised the hand-writing of Constance !

"Ah ! you must not read that," shouted Scrubb, rushing to the table, and making a snatch at the letter. But he was too late : Lawrence had seized the letter, and now held it firmly in his grasp.

"So, so, master Scrubb, I see you are the sly messenger and traitor in this business, are you ? Fear not; it is all at an end now ! Master Elliot will be glad of this discovery to discharge so unworthy and disobedient a rascal as you are from his service."

" 'Tis but a note from Miss Constance," replied Scrubb ; regaining the letter before Lawrence had noticed the whole of the direction. " I guess it ought to have been there by now."

" Been where ?" eagerly inquired Lawrence.

" Promise to return the letter again, and you shall see," cunningly replied Scrubb.

" On that you may depend," answered Lawrence ; and eagerly snatching the letter from Scrubb's hand, his eye glanced on the following—" Arthur Latymer, at the Swan, Bankside." "So, so," replied Lawrence, in an under tone, "I now know where to meet my rival. Scrubb," he resumed, " you shall have this letter again on one condition only, and that is, let me know the precise answer returned to this letter; it shall not affect you in any way : to that I pledge my honour. What say you ?"

" Why, as you promise not to bring me into trouble in the affair, I don't mind," answered Scrubb ; " its no matter to me who knows it, so as Miss Constance does, and Master Elliot does not. But I must be moving. I should have been back again ere this ;" and so saying he made for the door, Lawrence at the same time dropping a small coin into his hand, and bidding him be true to his word they separated : Scrubb on his mistress's errand, and Lawrence to ponder on the result.

It was some days after this event took place that a grand fete was announced between the London 'prentices and the students of the Temple in the shape of a boat-race on the Thames. High stakes and wagers were laid on the occasion, and every one, from the boys of Paternoster-row to the shipbrokers' clerks in the Minories, was expected to be there. Master Elliot had promised a holiday to his workpeople and his household in order that they might be present, and it was on this day that Arthur was to meet with Constance. This information Lawrence obtained from Scrubb, in answer to his mistress's letter, which was a verbal one ; accompanied, however, with a small piece of gold to keep it in the holder's memory for a sufficient time to be accurately delivered.

The morning of the race was on the 29th of May—a day celebrated in the annals of the reign of King Charles. Long before the appointed hour, swarms of boats were gliding on the Thames, each decorated with colours and awnings of every description, filled with watermen, tradespeople, and worthy citizens and their families. The bells of all the neighbouring churches were sending forth loyal and merry peals (it being the anniversary of the Restoration of Charles to the throne of England) ; the Tower guns had been firing salutes since daybreak ; every house on London Bridge was decorated with banners, flags, and loyal mottos, and by ten o'clock, the appointed hour, the Thames was so completely covered, that, to use a modern writer's expression, " it would have been possible to cross it by stepping from boat to boat." Master Elliot, being the Warden of the Stationer's Company, the worthy citizen had obtained possession for the day of one of the company's small barges, which accommodation was also enjoyed by the rest of his household ; the barge being splendidly decorated with flags, and emblazoned with the arms of the company, and guided by eight rowers in scarlet dresses.

To high and low, young and old, the boat-race was a scene of unparalleled attraction. But there were two persons among that vast assemblage who took no more interest in its result than if it had not been—these were Constance Elliot and Lawrence Wood. Constance, ever since the affray in her father's house between Lawrence and Arthur, had maintained a strict and cool behaviour towards him ; vastly different to the previous light and merry pastime that was formerly spent between them. Lawrence, on his part, was equally reserved, partly from pride, and partly from a desire to watch her actions unobserved, and wreak vengeance on his rival. A profound silence was therefore maintained on both sides. The sports on the river being concluded, Master Elliot resolved upon calling on an old friend of his in the Temple—a Mr. Briefwell, and for this purpose he requested Lawrence to accompany his daughter home ; and it was not till this request had been made that any thing like a conversation ensued between them. Lawrence knew that he was near the spot where Constance had promised to meet Arthur after the boat-race, and he could plainly see that she would gladly have had any companion but himself. Upon nearing the shrubbery belonging to the Temple Gardens, which was rather a secluded spot, Lawrence observed a number of young Templars among the trees, and wishing to give Constance an opportunity of meeting with Arthur, he feigned surprise at the absence of an expected companion, and politely requesting Constance to wait for him, he disappeared by the water side.

No sooner, however, had Lawrence parted from Constance, than Arthur was at her side ; having observed the stratagem of Lawrence at a distance. We will now leave the lovers to themselves for a short time, while we return to Lawrence and his companions. Upon reaching the banks of the river, Lawrence entered one of the booths fitted up for the amusement of the various visitors to the regatta, and there found many of his old companions and apprentices to the number of two hundred, principally consisting of the boys of Ludgate and Paternoster-row; then the most formidable class of any in London. It appeared by the conversation going on that the boys had fairly won the race, but that the Temple students had raised a quibble, withholding the wager, and taking the credit of the feat to themselves. Finding a sensation prevalent so favourable to his own designs, he took good occasion to fan the flame. He calculated that Constance would be joined by Arthur immediately upon his quitting her, and he now thought if he could gain the apprentices' assistance, he might be enabled to wreak upon his rival's head that revenge he had so ardently desired. Accordingly, in the midst of the noise, jumping to the top of a bench which stood in the centre of the booth, he called aloud for a hearing, which was soon obtained.

"Apprentices of London!" began Lawrence, emphatically; "You appear to me at this moment to be writhing under the different feelings of both injury and revenge for the usage you have, as a formidable body, received from the hands of these powdered caterpillars, these worse than locusts; but I, one of yourselves, have this instant received a deeper blow, and one, too, that will affect the honour of all the apprentices in the City of London; especially those who have fair maidens whom they prize, and love to think of as their own."

"Speak, Lawrence! Tell us! What is it!" was now re-echoed by at least a dozen voices, as Lawrence paused for breath to continue his address.

"I will," he replied. "You are all acquainted with good old Master Elliot, the stationer of Cheapside; and of course are also aware that he boasts, without denial, of the fairest damsel in the City's gates for a daughter; but, however, you who have other hearts to treasure will not, I dare say, deny that she is no common beauty. Now I have presumed so far as to enjoy certain opinions concerning that fair maid and myself—but be that as it may—to the purpose. Master Elliot and his family came here to-day to witness the race; after it was over, the care of his daughter Constance was bestowed upon me, to see her safe to a friend's house in the Temple, hard by. The crawling hounds, however, have dogged our steps—have laid wait for the fair prize I conveyed, and have dragged her from me; thus violating the trust reposed in me, and inflicting a deeper wound in the honour of the London apprentices! Fellows! Brothers! will you join in the rescue!"

"All, all!" was immediately responded to in answer, by the excited young men, who eagerly grasped each one his club, and whirling it over his head, seemed eager for the conflict.

"Then follow me!" exclaimed Lawrence, leaping down from his elevated position; "one and all—come on! and let our cry be the well-known shout, "'Prentices and Clubs!"

So saying he bounded from the booth, hat in hand, followed by the whole of the apprentices, who came down in one stream after him; waving their clubs, and with loud menaces shouting "'Prentices and Clubs!"—Down with the Templars—down with the cut-purse villains!"

On they sped through Whitefriars, where their number was increased by some idle blacksmiths, butchers, bear-baiters and their dogs, who were lounging in the neighbourhood, joining in their cry, and rushing on with them towards the Temple Gardens.

The gardens were situated on the immediate banks of the Thames, occupying a space of ground of about four acres, which was tastefully decorated with flowers and summer-houses, and formed the principal retreat of all the gallants of Fleet-street and the Temple. It was in these gardens that Arthur Latymer had tarried for Constance; and immediately on perceiving that Lawrence had left her, he rushed to her side, and placing her arm within his, led the way to another part of the gardens. Here, seated in one of the summer-houses, which were entirely covered with the creeping ivy, he told his tale of love in the ears of the beautiful Constance, till he had almost made her consent to a clandestine elopement, by presenting to her the inflexible objections of her father, and the prejudices of her mother.

The lovers were, however, suddenly interrupted by Lawrence Wood appearing before them. He stood at the entrance of the bower, and fixing his angry eye upon Arthur, exclaimed—"So this, then, is the way that citizen's daughters are way-laid by you perriwig-pated coxcombs, is it? Villain! There are odds between us which must sooner or later be paid—Constance, will you with me, or shall your father know in whose company I have left you?"

"Doubtless you intend to inform him, or you would not have watched and betrayed me," answered Constance; without, however, turning her face towards him.

A pause of a few moments here ensued, which was broken by Arthur rising to his feet, and with one spring seizing Lawrence by the throat, forced him backwards to the earth; then placing his knee upon his chest, and drawing his sword, Arthur held him in his power.

"Hold, Arthur! for Heaven's sake!—pray release him!"

"He will do it himself," shouted Lawrence, as with an herculean writhe of his body he twisted off his antagonist and regained his feet, though not without being slightly wounded in the neck by the point of Arthur's sword.

"He requires no help, but fair play," exclaimed Lawrence; and dealing Arthur a severe blow on the head with his cudgel, the combat was renewed.

Constance ran to the extremity of the gardens screaming for help, and her cries were immediately answered by about a dozen of Arthur's fellow students, who rushed to the scene of action. Here, perceiving how matters stood, they seized upon Lawrence, and having forced away his grip from Arthur's throat, hurled him into the river.

"Oh Heaven's! you have drowned him!" shrieked Constance.

"Then he will tell no tales!" rejoined Arthur, as he hurried out of the gardens with Constance, at the same time pointing out the necessity of their immediate flight.

To return to Lawrence. Being a good swimmer, after two or thee plunges, he had struck out and succeeded in gaining the shore, when his first thought was to rejoin his comrades, who were waiting his return at some distance, and inform them of the discovery he had made. He bid them follow him; and it was not long before the apprentices met with the students in the centre of a large paved square, after passing through a long dark passage.

"Clubs, clubs!" was the signal cry, and each man took his foe. Lawrence fought his way to Arthur Latymer, in whose arms Constance had fainted, and, as to gain possession of her was his sole object, his attack was slow and considerate. After vainly endeavouring to obtain a parley with him, by the aid of a companion he was disarmed and bound, and Lawrence took his fainting charge in his arms, and left the scene of the fray.

Those of the students who could disengage themselves from the grip of their adversaries fled. Arthur Latymer was led, bound, with his hands behind him, as far as the conduit in the Chepe, where the boys, after having deluged him with water, hunted him back again as far as Ludgate-street.

Immediately upon leaving the conflict, Lawrence had seated Constance upon a stone bench; and after a few moments she recovered; gazing wildly round she rose up, and beckoned him to follow her, and they made their way to the house of Master Briefwell, the friend on whom Matthew Elliot had appointed to call.

"I suppose," began Constance after a long silence, "you will lay all you have witnessed before my father?"

" On one condition, Constance, I will not," answered Lawrence。

" Name it," she replied.

" That you will not meet Arthur Latymer again ; at least you will let me know of it."

After a pause Constance replied—" I promise." By this time they had arrived at the residence of Mr. Briefwell, and found Master Elliot and his wife holding a conference with Briefwell's housekeeper from the second-floor window. On approaching nearer, Lawrence perceived a large cross on the door—it was an infected house, and contained the plague !

The fact was Master Briefwell had been plague-stricken, and, according to custom, the house was closed, and all correspondence checked: with a heavy heart at such unlooked-for tidings, Master Elliot and his family returned home. The fatigues of the day (for it had been scorching hot), and the dismal news he had learnt of his friend Briefwell, cast a gloom upon all, and by eight o'clock the household were summoned to meet in the parlour at the usual family devotion.

Master Elliot offered up a long and fervent supplication for protection against the devouring pestilence with which the City was scourged. He acknowledged that this visitation had been justly brought upon it by the wickedness of its inhabitants; that, like the dwellers in Jerusalem before it was given up to ruin and desolation, they " had mocked the messengers of God and despised his word." He concluded by exhorting those around him to keep constant watch upon themselves ; not to murmur at God's dealings, but so to comport themselves, that " they might be able to stand in the day of wrath, in the day of death, and in the day of judgment." This produced a powerful effect upon its hearers, and they arose,—some with serious, others with terrified looks.

As Constance was about to leave the room, she beckoned to Lawrence ; as he approached to obey her mandate, she softly whispered in his ear, " Arthur Latymer comes here again ; I keep my word !" and in an instant she was gone.

Lawrence remained in a state almost of stupefaction, repeating to himself, as if unwilling to believe them, the words he had just heard. Master Elliot noticing at the time his bewildered looks, kindly inquired if he felt unwell. Lawrence returned an evasive answer, half determined to relate all he knew ; but the next moment he changed his intention, and, influenced by the chivalric feeling which always governs those, of whatever condition, who love profoundly, resolved not to betray the thoughtless girl, but to trust to his own ingenuity to thwart the designs of his rival, and preserve her. Acting upon this resolution, he said he had a slight headache, and the subject was not again resumed.

At ten o'clock, the whole family assembled at supper. The board was plentifully though plainly spread, but Master Elliot observed that Lawrence, who had a good appetite in ordinary, ate little or nothing. He kept his eye constantly upon him, and became convinced from his manner that something ailed him. Not having any notion of the truth, and being filled with apprehensions of the plague, his dread was that Lawrence was infected by the disease. Supper was generally the pleasantest meal of the day at the stationer's house, but on this occasion it had passed off cheerlessly enough, and a circumstance occurred which threw the whole of the family into confusion and distress.

As the family were about to separate for the night, and Dame Elliot had risen to quit the room, she staggered, and complained of a strange dizziness and headache, which almost deprived her of sight, while her heart palpitated frightfully. A dreadful suspicion seized her husband. He ran towards her, and assisted her to a seat. Scarcely had the good dame reached it, when a violent sickness seized her ; a greenish-coloured froth appeared at the mouth, and she began to grow delirious.   Strengthened by his suspicions, Master Elliot examined her tongue, when the fatal spots appearing, he exclaimed she was plague-stricken, and sank into a chair !

CHAPTER III.

THE appearance of the plague in his own house was indeed a terrible blow to the courage and fortitude of Master Elliot.   However, he had in some measure made up his mind to the attack ever since he noticed the disease so near the city walls ; and which now, step by step, had stalked on from house to house till it reached his own.   Where it would end, and at what period, the great Mover of all things only knew ; and in him did the honest citizen place all his hopes.   He had studied the first symptoms of the plague, and was tolerably well acquainted how to prescribe for it, and to that task he now busied himself.   First giving special orders to dame Trivet to allow no one to enter his wife's chamber, he desired Constance to repair to her own apartment, and would on no account allow her to pass the night with her mother, though she eagerly implored it.   Locking each one in their respective rooms Matthew Elliot retired into a little back apartment, and calling to him his assistant, Lawrence Wood, closed the door upon them.

"Lawrence," said he, sorrowfully, as he entered the room, "the monster has fastened his claws upon us at last."

"I know it, master—I know it," replied the youth.   " But it is not fear that will save us from his fangs ; I am ready and willing to do anything to avert the calamity, however perilous, that you may command me ; and to assist in the recovery of my dear mistress I will risk my own life."

" I know it, Lawrence," answered Master Elliot, gratefully.   " So let's begin our task, there, reach me that bag, and the green box next to it," said he, pointing to a little shelf above their heads ; "it contains precious medicines, which must be immediately put into vigorous action.   Kindle a fire quickly, whilst I mix the decoction."

Lawrence speedily set about obeying his master's orders, and whilst the flames were playing round a copper pan placed on the fire causing its contents to boil, the worthy husband was throwing into it his various ingredients, which consisted of marsh mallows, lily roots, spirit of sulphur, and a few burnt figs ; these were to prepare a strong draught to promote perspiration, and thus allay the ravages of the disease.   An ointment compounded of Venice treacle, canary, and other stimulating doses completed the prescription, about which every pains was taken, and not a moment wasted in the preparation.   Although provided with these remedies, which he was well aware were the best that could be applied at the present stage of the disease, he resolved to dispatch Lawrence for medical advice, in case they should not prove efficacious, and accordingly commissioned him to fetch Doctor Calder, a physician, residing in Watling-street, who had recently acquired considerable reputation for his skilful treatment of those attacked by the plague, and who afterwards gave to the medical world a curious account of the ravages of the disorder, as well as of his own professional experience during this terrible period.   He likewise told him to give notice to the Commissioner of Health (for there were two or three such officers appointed to every parish at this awful season by the City authorities), that his house was infected.

" Dear master, you may depend upon my utmost speed," replied Lawrence ; and both immediately left the apartment ; Lawrence upon his melancholy

Vide page 22.

errand, while his master bent his steps to the apartment of his afflicted wife, to administer all the aid it was in his power at present to afford her.

Endowed with a thorough knowledge of the distemper, and acquainted with the mode of treating it prescribed by the College of Physicians, Elliot was at no loss how to act, but, rubbing the parts affected with a stimulating ointment, he administered at the same time doses of the medicine he had prepared, and other powerful stimulants prepared by dame Trivet. He had soon the satisfaction of perceiving that his patient became somewhat easier; and after swallowing the posset-drink, a moisture broke out upon the skin, and appeared to relieve the sufferer so much, that but for the ghastly paleness of her countenance, and the muddy look of her eye, the hopeful and attentive husband would have indulged a hope of his wife's recovery.

While preparing to set out, Lawrence again considered within himself whether he should acquaint his master with Arthur Latymer's meditated visit. But conceiving it wholly impossible that Constance could leave her room, even if she were disposed to do so, he determined to let the affair take its course; trusting to his own ingenuity to thwart the evil designs of his rival. On his way to the surgeon's, he entered a small room occupied by Scrubb, and found him seated near a table, with his hands upon his knees, and his eyes fixed on the ground, looking the very image of despair. The atmosphere smelt like that of an apothecary's shop, and was so overpowering that Lawrence could scarcely breathe. The table was covered with pill-boxes and phials, and a dim light was afforded by a candle nearly burnt to the socket.

"So you have been drugging yourself," said Lawrence, entering.

"Keep off!" cried Scrubb, springing to his feet. "Don't touch me.

3.

Drugging myself! I have taken three refuses, or pestilential pills; two spoonfuls of elixir of vitriol, the same quantity of compound anti-pestilential decoction ; half as much of Sir Daffodill Drenchwell's electuary ; and a large dose of camphor. Do you call that drugging myself? I call it taking proper precautions, and would recommend you to do the same. Besides this, I have sprinkled myself with vinegar, fumigated my clothes, and rubbed my nose with camphor till it smarted so intolerably I was obliged to leave off."

" Well, if you don't escape the plague, it won't be your fault," returned Lawrence, smiling. " But I have something to tell you before I go—a secret !"

" A secret ! what is it—tell me," demanded Scrubb in a breath ; " where are you going ?"

" For medical advice," replied Lawrence.

" Is Mistress Elliot, then, dying ?" eagerly inquired Scrubb.

" No ; she is not considered dangerous. But I have something to tell you, Scrubb, which you must attend to whilst I am out.'

" I can't, I won't, I shall not, I will not, I say, go near her ; I will not touch her, look at her, or breathe the same air that fills this infected house an hour longer if I can help it," ejaculated Scrubb in a voice of terror and agitation.

" You will not be required to see or touch your mistress, depend upon it," replied Lawrence. "But, as to leaving the house, I am much afraid that will be impossible, as I am now going to the Head Commissioner of Health's office to acquaint him that the house is infected ; the mark will be set on the door, and no one will enter or go out, except the medical attendants.

" Oh, horror ! murder ! and shall I be buried alive with the plague ?— Consider me as a dead man," roared Scrubb most vociferously.

" Cease howling, knave, and listen to me," said Lawrence, disturbing his reverie by a sudden grasp at his arm. "You must mind what I say, as you value your life. I shall not be absent long ; keep the door fast, and do not let any one in, except Doctor Calder, upon any account whatever. Do you understand me ?"

" I do," replied Scrubb, terrified by his threatening menaces.

" Then attend to me ; if, when I return, I find you have not obeyed my orders, I will trounce you within an inch of your existence. Come, follow me, and let me out."

Followed by Scrubb, Lawrence proceeded to the windows and doors in the rear of the house, and having made them all fast and secure, he again strictly admonished him not to give any one admittance, except the doctor, till he returned. Scrubb promised obedience, but supplicated Lawrence not to go to the Health Office—" Consider," said he, " what a dreadful thing it is to be pent up in a house with the plague. Besides, you know, I often take a walk of an evening to the Fleece, in the Old Jewry ; I know a friend there, and would not break my engagement for the world."

" 'Tis useless imploring me ; it must be done," answered Lawrence.

" Oh, it's a dreadful thing, though, to be imprisoned for a month. I noticed some houses in Newgate-street, yesterday, locked up ; the watchmen were at the door, but the miserable inhabitants were at the windows ; such faces—Oh, Lawrence ! it has haunted me ever since !"

" Pshaw ! you are a fool !" answered Lawrence ; " it is this that will give you the plague, if you ever have it ; your fears are worse than any contagion. But I lose time ; I must go."

As he was about to close the door, Scrubb held out his hand to him, and Lawrence, taking it for a kindly farewell, grasped it, but immediately found his hands full of strong scented anti-infective lozenges, plague-drops, and healthy-root, which the poor deluded Scrubb had attempted to force upon him as a preventive to infection. Hurling them in the donor's face with a loud laugh, he closed the door and bounded along Cheapside.

We must now direct attention to Arthur Latymer, and to do so sufficiently must retrace our steps back to the evening of the affray in the Temple between him and Lawrence Wood.

Boiling with rage, and writhing beneath the taunts and jeers of his companions, Arthur made bitter and solemn protestations of revenge. He had made an appointment with Constance (which she had divulged to Lawrence, according to her promise), to see her that very evening at her father's house, when he meant to induce her to elope with him. Turning a deaf ear to the raillery of his companions, he suffered himself to be led with them to the tavern of St. Dunstan's Head, which was the resort of all the young gallants and Alsatians of Fleet-street and Whitefriars.

They accordingly entered an apartment denominated the "Dice Room," in which several tables were situated, each table being occupied by persons engaged in the chances and hazard of a throw. They were all so deeply engaged in play, that the entrance of himself and companions was not taken notice of until a loud shout from some of the party announced their arrival. At this signal the players stopped, and those of the fortunate ones fell to the pleasant task of pocketing gold pieces and cracking jokes upon the ill fortune of those from whom they had won them.

At one of the tables sat a group, the most prominent of whom was a dissipated-looking young man, attired in the very extreme of the prevailing fashion, with ruffles of the finest lace, a richly-laced cravat round his throat, white silk hose, adorned with gold clocks, velvet shoes of a brilliant colour, fastened with immense roses, a silver-hilted sword, supported by a silken band, and a cloak and doublet of violet-coloured velvet, woven with gold, and ornamented with gems and ribands. He had flowing auburn hair, and a broad-leaved hat, looped with a diamond buckle, and placed carelessly on one side of the head. His stature was slight but well-formed, and his face might have been termed handsome, but for its licentious expression. He was addressed by those around him as Sir Robert Harlingham.

Opposite him sat one whose name was Moreton, and who was likewise a very handsome young man, though his face was much flushed, partly by the liquor he had taken, and partly by his losses at play. He was equipped in the costly regimentals of a captain in the king's guard. His left hand convulsively clutched an empty purse, and his eyes were fixed upon a sum of money which he had just handed over to Sir Robert, and which that person was transferring to his pocket.

The remainder were mere idle gallants and superior young men of the city, who having no better place of resort had turned into the tavern to watch the chance of the dice. There was one, however, amongst them whose look betrayed his character—that of a sharper and a bully—calling himself Captain Blount, his pretensions to military rank being grounded upon his service—so he stated himself—rendered during the civil wars. He was a man of very ferocious exterior, marked with a number of scars, and destitute of one eye, the place of which was covered with a black patch; his face was of a deep mulberry colour, clearly proclaiming his devotion to the bottle, while his nose, which was none of the smallest, was covered with "knobs and flames of fire" (a true Bardolph of his day.) He was of the middle size, rather stoutly built, though not so as to impair his activity. His dress consisted of a cloak of scarlet cloth, very much stained and tarnished, and edged with silver lace, jack boots with huge tops, spurs, and a rapier of preposterous length. His hair was short and woolly like that of a negro. His hat was fiercely cocked; his manner swaggering and insolent, and he was always puzzling his brain to invent new curses.

Arthur amongst so many was not long in finding a familiar, for a dashing young man rising from his seat at the lower end of the room came towards him and taking him by the hand exclaimed, " Why Arthur, man, what ails thee ? Art smitten by the plague ? Has the fair Constance proved false, and flown with some more favoured swain ? or is it—"

" Pshaw ! you banter me," exclaimed Arthur sharply. Drawer, bring us a bottle of Burgundy," he added, turning to a serving-man at his elbow. " Come with me to yonder table, Vincent, and I will tell you all. I need advice, and that speedily."

" That's brave," replied Vincent Palmer (who was no other than the very friend who seconded Arthur in the fight with the pretended bully in Cheapside), " We can watch what goes on, and gain information at the same time. Here is the wine. I will wager it against any in his Majesty's stores. Come, here's to Constance ; may she prove gentle, flexible, and true !"

" Amen !" replied Arthur, following suit with his friend. This having opened a correspondence between them, Arthur went on relating to his friend what had befallen him since his first visit to Master Elliot's house, of the meeting in the Temple Gardens, spoke of the affray with the apprentices, and grinding his teeth with rage vowed sure and speedy vengeance upon Lawrence Wood.

During this relation the other persons in the room were not idle. Sir Robert Harlingham was the first to return to play, and addressing the somewhat chap-fallen young man who had been his opponent, and whose last coin he had just deposited in his pocket, said, " Do we go on ?"

" I have no more to lose," answered Morton doggedly ; " you have every coin I possess."

" What of that ?" exclaimed the knight, " you are still rich ; at least you possess a prize so rare, that I will stake the whole sum you have lost— nay this purse besides—against it, if you will but throw ;" and adding another to the one he had recently taken from Moreton, he jinked them temptingly before his face.

" I do not understand you," replied Moreton, rather sulkily, and vexed at what he considered a jest.

" You have a mistress—she is beautiful !" said Sir Robert.

" Ha ! what of her ?" answered Moreton angrily. " Do you dare—"

" Nay, man," replied Sir Robert, " I meant nothing—nothing ; only that possessing so fair and lovely a creature as the gentle Estelle, you could not be utterly ruined."

" Slanderer !" exclaimed Moreton, evidently much excited at his mistress's name being mentioned in a public dice-room. " Villain ! you pollute her sacred name by breathing it in this den—you know her not."

" Ah, ah !" sneered Sir Robert, " do I not ! Not know the soft texture of her hand, the lightning of her eye, the honey of her lip. If I did not both know and love her, too. A good joke, truly !"

" Liar !" roared Moreton ; and seizing up a goblet of wine he dashed the contents in the face of Harlingham, drew his rapier, and stood upon his guard.

In an instant passes were exchanged. But the conflict was a short one. Fortune, as in the previous instance, again declared herself in favour of Sir Robert. He instantly disarmed Moreton, who made his way out of the house, uttering the wildest expressions of rage and despair.

A long loud laugh from the knight followed the exit of Moreton, as he exclaimed, " Poor fool ! he would not stay to hear me bid a price for the wench, but he has given her to me for nothing—see here !" and holding up a key, he repeated his laugh, so loud and shrill, that, overcome with its effects, he sank back in his chair.

" But what has that key to do with the lady, Sir Robert ?" inquired Captain Blount.

" Every thing," replied the knight eagerly. " I know his house in the Strand—she lives there: he is away to finish the night in a debauch to drown his losses, and *this*," again holding up the key, " is the way to his fair possessions. Now do you understand me ?"

" Infinitely good," roared the captain ; and both again gave way to a violent fit of laughter.

Arthur Latymer and Vincent had till now been but spectators in the affair, but the wine having been freely circulated between them, they were full of spirits and revelry, and eagerly joined in the triumph of Sir Robert Harlingham and the captain over poor Moreton and his mistress.

After congratulating the knight upon his extraordinary success both in gold and love, Arthur observed, " that he should be careful for the future how he staked his mistress at a throw of the dice with Sir Robert."

" Tut, man !" replied the knight ; " 'tis but a common-place throw ; for handsome mistresses are as plentiful as pebbles."

" Then you reckon their hearts nothing, I suppose, Sir Robert ?" rejoined Arthur, pointedly.

" Not a jot," replied the knight. " I would always have a mistress for each portion of the day, as my friend Colonel Lavender observed in a song I have often heard him sing."

" A song !' re-echoed all present. " By all means let us have it.'

" I have no objection," said the knight, " provided you do not censure. " It runs thus :"—

> At sunrise with Emma I stray,
> And vow I'm all grief when away ;
> But at noon with my Flora I sit,
> Enwrapt by her charms and her wit.
> And pass a sweet hour away.
>
> > Then drink up your glass,
> > Let each lad have his lass,
> > And count each dissenter a loon ;
> > Who'd deny you the joy,
> > In sweet courtship to toy,
> > Yet be changing from night until noon !
>
> At even with Mary I rove,
> And my fervour in love try to prove ;
> But at night with young Kate I am found,
> Or else with young " Sue of the Mound.*"
> > Then drink, &c,
>
> So lovers ne'er give up a plan,
> So true to the pleasures of man,
> But catch all in your net that you may,
> And choose a fair lass for each day.
> > Then drink, &c.

At the termination of this ditty the room re-echoed with the deafening shouts and ringing of glasses upon the tables greeting Sir Robert's melody. Some, indeed, went so far as to demand its repetition, but the night being far spent, Sir Robert declined, especially as he had such an important mission on hand as that of laying siege to the heart of Moreton's mistress in his absence.

---

* A place of low resort near Whitechapel, which existed at this time.

The young gallants getting more noisy than prudent, Sir Robert wrapped his cloak round his shoulders, beckoned to Blount to follow him, made a brief apology for his imperative departure, and took his leave for Moreton's house, accompanied by the captain. Arthur and Vincent were not long in following their example, and slipping out at a side door gained Chancery-lane unperceived.

Bending their steps hastily towards Cheapside, they proceeded along Holborn at a brisk rate, scarcely exchanging words till they reached the house of Master Elliot, before which they halted. The bell of Bow Church at that moment chimed the hour of midnight, which was speedily answered by others in the immediate vicinity.

" Our haste is useless," exclaimed Arthur, surveying the house. " She has retired to her chamber : the signal was to have been a light from that topmost window, but all seems still as death. Little did Arthur know, at the time he uttered his surmise, the true cause of the apparent loneliness of the house. They paced backwards and forwards, crossed to the other side of the street, straining their eyes intently to catch the least glimmer of a signal. The dwelling of Master Elliot was a large old-fashioned house, built in the middle of the previous century, and had projecting stories one over the other, in such a manner as seemingly to overhang the street. The front of the house displayed large oaken planks, covered with pannels of the same material, and the projections supported heavy beams, embellished with carved figures of grotesque appearance. Each floor had three deeply-cut windows, protected by stout wooden bars, and having small panes of glass set in leaden frames, while a similar number of gables, and long leaden spouts, which overhung the street, finished the roof. The name of the owner, upon a huge sign, hung before the door.

A dull light appearing at one of the lower windows of the house, caused Arthur Latymer to dart across the street to the spot, supposing it to be the signal of Constance's approach. But, however, like a deceiving will-o'the-wisp, it immediately disappeared upon his arrival before the window. At this moment, casting his eyes towards the door, how great was his dismay, how unspeakable his horror, when he discovered the red cross, the signal of infection and the plague, pourtrayed upon the door-posts ; he stood trans-fixed to the spot, gazing upon the terrible omen of death, till his sight be-coming strained and dizzy, and his brain confused with the suddenness of the accusation, he reeled backwards and would have fallen, had not Vincent Palmer at that moment caught him in his arms ; having followed him across the street, and stood watching like himself the horrible signal before them.

For several minutes Arthur Latymer was senseless to all around him ; but soon recovering himself again, he awoke to all the horrors of a torturing suspicion. " It is Constance who is attacked with the plague," he exclaimed, as soon as he could articulate. " I knew she would not fail her appointment, unless something positively impossible had betallen her ; yes, it is the plague, but come what will, stay me who may, I am resolved to see her, and this night too !"

" Madness is in such a determination, Latymer," exclaimed Vincent, surprised at such utter recklessness and imprudence. " It would be im-possible !".

" It might be difficult ; but not impossible," replied Arthur. " Besides, I have sworn to see her this night ; sworn it by my love, by my constancy to her, and I will not fail ; no, even though I force myself through a legion of fiends, and grasp her stricken hand clammy and cold in death, yet would I not hesitate. Vincent, we must part ; a good-night to you."

" No, no ; Arthur you must not, you shall not pursue so rash and danger-ous a step. To fight for, or elope with a fair one is perhaps excusable though imprudent; but to enter a house infected with the plague, is the height of madness; 'tis absolute death, suicide, nothing less.''

"I care not," replied Arthur. "My life is staked as it were upon the possession of this girl, and 'tis not the fear of infection that will keep me at bay; so go I will."

"But what good can your presence possibly avail ?" coolly retorted Vincent; "if stricken with the plague, as you suspect, will you be enabled to cure her ? or think you she could listen to one of your high-flown love stories of elopement, constant love, and eternal happiness, when writhing on a bed of sickness—perhaps of death ? Or if she were sensible to your address, think you her friends would permit such an interview, in such a moment of peril ?—Psha! man, you must be mad to dream of such a thing !" Come, I will see you to Temple Bar—"

"Not a step," sullenly retorted Arthur; "if I cannot have your assistance, I will not accept of your advice; so you may even trudge alone, if you will have it so."

"Taunt me not, thus, Arthur," replied Vincent, rather nettled at the somewhat taunting answer of Arthur to his reasoning; " You know I fear not ordinary dangers in matters of this sort, which I have proved to you before now. But this is a step so rash, so utterly void of anything like reason or necessity, that I should consider all partakers in its risks nothing short of lunatics; I hear the watch coming this way; we may meet with unpleasantness if we stay here loitering longer. I am sure your mistress cannot expect you at such a time as this, so she will not be disappointed.

" But I have promised and I have sworn to meet her, to see her this night, and see her I will, if nothing short of sudden blindness on my part prevents me; even if she were a corpse I would not shrink, were it but to clasp her in my arms, press her clay-cold lips to mine, and whisper in her ear 'I HAVE COME !' "

"But, Arthur, let me entreat you," observed Vincent, gently forcing him from the spot by taking his arm; which, however, was suddenly twisted from its grasp by a powerful struggle on the part of Arthur Latymer, who, darting from his companion, rushed down Milk-street, and was suddenly lost to view by entering a dark narrow passage that led into Lad-lane and the back of the houses in Cheapside.

Vincent Palmer stood for a moment undecided how to act or which way to turn; but suddenly communing within himself, he resolved to loiter about the spot till Arthur might return; so wending his way towards Cornhill, he was lost in deep contemplation of the probable issue of his friend's hazardous adventure.

Arthur Latymer was well acquainted with the locality in which he was now groping,—walking it could not be called; for unaccommodated with gas-lamps, or hardly decent pavement, he had to find his way in the pitchy darkness of the night along narrow entries, and using his eye-sight to the best advantage to discover holes, cellars uncovered, and water, from the miserable footpath which presented itself. Creeping as well as he was able by the gable-ends of houses and walls, he at length reached the door which he knew to be the back entrance of Master Elliot's house. Not a light was to be seen, or a sound heard: the scene bore the silence of death itself. He stood reasoning within himself how he should act, and in which way he should best effect an entrance, when the distant ringing of a heavy bell sounded in his ears, accompanied with a sonorous and melancholy yell · he listened— again he heard it—a cold shudder thrilled through. his whole frame ; it was the DEAD CART! Without hesitating another moment, he stepped backwards, made a spring, and with a violent effort gained the summit of the wall.

He was now able to discern lights moving in the lower part of the house, and letting himself down inside the wall to his full length by his hands, his feet rested on a low out-house or lumber shed, from which he descended without much difficulty. Having gained an entrance so far, his object was now to escape detection by any of the inmates till he could by some rare opportunity steal his way into the house. He had not remained in this suspense long, when a window opened just over his head; a female appeared from it; she looked out and seemed merely stealing a breath of pure air to refreshen the pestilential atmosphere that was raging within. Arthur looked up, fixed his eye intently upon the form, it was of the same stature as Constance, yet he could not discern the features; he concluded it must be her, as she had no sister near her age: dared he sound her name? No, the risk was too great: it might ruin all. Then again he surmised how could it be Constance, seeing she was plague-stricken? But ah! *who* had told him so? —no one!—'twas his own heated imagination—it might be wrong—could it not have happened to her father, mother, brother, or—and he bit the words between his lips—to his rival? Would that it were so! As he was communing within himself, the female form withdrew inwards, raised an arm to the window to lower it, when Arthur, knowing it to be his only remedy, coughed aloud, once or twice. The window immediately but slowly opened, the person lifting it looked over the sill down into the area below, but owing to the darkness of the night nothing was discernable. A gentle voice called out, "Is that you, Lawrence?" That sound determined all—for Arthur knew then that it was Constance; but he answered not. Once more lowering the window, Constance withdrew, and all was silent as before.

Arthur Latymer, once satisfied he was on the right scent, was not the man to let his game escape him for the want of pursuit. He therefore lost no time in gaining the window-sill, which to him was no easy matter. Having climbed to the roof of the outhouse by which he had descended, he clambered to the window with great difficulty, by placing his toes in crevices of the wall, and clinging to the jutting stone-work with his hand. He had by these means raised himself to a level with the window, and could now observe what was going on within. Constance was kneeling before a fire, ardently watching a small vessel, the contents of which she kept stirring; this was one of her father's strong-herb decoctions, which was to be given to her mother, as the last dose previous to the doctor's arrival. One hand supported her cheek, and she seemed in a deep study; Arthur could not exactly divine whether himself, or her plague-stricken relative, whoever it might be, was the object of such contemplation, but flattering himself that he was not altogether out of her memory at that moment, he raised up the window with his right hand as he balanced himself in his dangerous position with his left. Swinging himself forward, he descended into the room before Constance could look up to discover who the intruder was, whom, as she beheld, she started from her kneeling position, and a shriek was on her lips, when Arthur, darting forward, caught her in his arms, and allayed all her fears by discovering himself.

"Do you not know me, Constance?" he exclaimed, straining her in his embrace, as she struggled to free herself from his grasp—"have you so soon forgotten our appointment?"

"Oh, Arthur—at such a time as this—know you not—"

"I know nothing," replied Arthur, catching her up before she had hardly uttered her sentence. "I know nothing beyond the plague being in your house; I know not who is infected; at first I feared it was yourself."

"Would that it were so, rather than this should have happened," exclaimed Constance, in a tone of deep anguish. "You must not stay, indeed you must not, Arthur!" How did you enter the house?

Vide page 26.

"How I obtained admittance, Constance, is a matter of no moment; suffice it to say that it was the hour of our appointment, I knew you were in the house, and while there was a window or door, ever so securely bolted or barred, I would have made my way, though a pestilence was raging in tenfold fury within its walls. No, Constance, nothing could separate us, when I had sworn to meet you—but we lose time, I have come to save you; you must leave this house, lest you become a prey to the fangs of this horrible disease!"

"Leave this house!" replied Constance in a tone of mingled surprise and indignation, "why, Arthur, you must be raving, sure ; leave my mother in such a time as this. O no, no; you mistake me, sir : I would not leave her bed-side, her death-bed, for aught I can tell, though the riches of nations were strewed at my feet, and my staying would be certain destruction by the plague itself! Leave her!—elope, now! O Arthur, Arthur, you know me not yet, to judge so lightly of my affections to a mother!" and overcome with this struggle between her pride as a daughter, and her constancy as a mistress, Constance sunk into a chair, and covering her face with her hands, gave vent to her emotion in a flood of tears.

Arthur Latymer had now a difficult part to play ; he found he had touched upon a too tender string, and he now tried to soothe her anguish, by expressing his regret at her mother's illness, yet at the same time urging to her the necessity of flight to secure her safety from the disease, and to crown his happiness as a lover.

"Did you not promise me, Constance ?" he argued in a reproachful tone —"nay, solemnly swore to be mine this night, to fly with me from cruel and unrelenting friends, to live in luxury and happiness with him who adores you. You did, and well you remember it, Constance, though I can see by

4.

that tear, an I your avoiding my glance, that you mean to deceive me—perhaps for some more favoured lover—the serving loon of your father, forsooth—say Constance, is it so?"

"Oh! Arthur!" replied Constance in accents of bitterest woe—"is it not enough for me to submit to daily, nay hourly, reproaches, and ill-treatment for your sake—to have at the present moment to lament the dangerous illness of a beloved parent, and having the double capacity of nurse and daughter to fulfil, but I must be taunted with deceit and unfaithfulness after all, and by you."

"Nay, dearest, take me not so severely to task; I did but jest, in truth I did not—I could not, dared not doubt the sincerity of your affection, for are you not mine by every dear tie? And what prevents us from making our bliss complete—surely not the sickness of your mother!—your presence cannot save her life, and may endanger your own! and think you I can stand tamely by and see you drop gradually into the tomb without stretching forth a hand to retard your progress? No, Constance, believe me I am not so common-place a lover. A few hours, and your mother will add to the number of victims that have fallen beneath the ravages of this monster of death! So come, my dearest; my own Constance, let us at once leave this scene of danger, for a dwelling-place of liberty and love." And seizing her in his arms he was about to carry her from the room, when Constance, by a violent effort, stayed herself by catching hold of some drapery which hung suspended from the wall.

"Arthur! for Heaven's sake leave me!" she exclaimed; "you will alarm the house; and should my mother learn of your presence here, it might finish the blow at once. Another time—a few days—and I solemnly promise to be yours! Arthur, for Heaven's sake release me! I hear some one approaching! oh save me from this shame of detection, I pray! Nay, then, I will be free—I—I will not be dragged from my home thus!" Here, with one sudden effort, and by a desperate struggle, she not only loosened the grasp of Arthur's arms from her waist, but pushed him with such force from her, that he staggered back a few paces, and fell backwards upon the floor, carrying down in his descent several articles of furniture, the echo and din of which resounded loudly through the house, which had previously bornd the stillness of the grave.

Arthur being aware from the tumult occasioned by his fall that some one was likely to approach the apartment to investigate the affair, desperately resolved to lose not a moment, but to bear off Constance at all risks; so once more approaching her, he whispered a few tender appeals in her ear, but his manner was less gentle than formerly, for, throwing open the window by which he had entered the room, he lifted her in his arms, at the same time stifling a suppressed shriek, by pressing her face towards his own, and darted on to the casement of the window seat, ready to bound forth with his prize. He paused for a moment to place the now nearly-fainting girl in such a position as might be safest for her in his leap to the ground; and Constance, taking advantage of the pause, grasped the long hanging curtains which hung down at both sides of the window, and giving one loud, long, and supplicating cry for help, struggled violently with Arthur on the brink of the casement.

The window at which they stood was upwards of twelve feet from the paved area beneath, which was a most herculean leap for any one so burdened as Arthur was at this moment, and which most likely would be attended with danger to both. Constance saw the danger to which the infuriated passion of her lover had brought her; and her struggles were rendered doubly desperate by a desire of self-preservation, and an indignant feeling against being forcibly carried from her home, at such a trying moment.

Voices and footsteps were plainly to be heard from the bottom of the house, and a loud clattering directly afterwards announced that some one was hastily ascending the stairs, to answer the incessant cries Constance was making for help.

"Constance," exclaimed Arthur, hastily; " I ask you once more ; will you come with me willingly, or must I jump, and thus endanger both our lives ? One word, or I leap !"

The only answer Arthur received to this appeal was a louder and more piercing shriek from Constance for help, and a tighter grasp at the window curtains to save herself. Her lover made no reply, but tightly encircling her waist to compel her to loose her hold, he was about to make a bound into the yard beneath, when a tremendous blow on the head caused him to reel backwards, and he fell into the room stunned by the blow, whilst Constance, rescued from his gripe, fell swooning into the arms of Lawrence Wood.

Lawrence would have slain his rival on the spot, had not Constance [in tears prevailed upon him to keep peace ; but nothing would pacify him till Arthur Latymer was separated from her ; so bidding Constance a hasty adieu, which was unheeded by her, Arthur followed Lawrence out of the house without either speaking a word.

Though boiling with rage, Lawrence had kept silence for fear of disturbing his master, for as Doctor Calder had arrived a few minutes before, they were busily employed waiting upon Mrs. Elliot in her chamber, the door of which they had to pass.

Having gained the street, Arthur Latymer was about to depart, but Lawrence caught his flowing robe, and demanded him to turn. " We have a long account to settle ; and the sooner it is squared the better," exclaimed Lawrence, giving full vent to the passion he had been so lately compressing.

" Away, varlet !" roared Latymer, " I have no words to waste with thee ! Seek some fellow scullion to wage war with ;—I quarrel not with menials !" Saying this he turned on his heel, and would have left the spot, if Lawrence had not forced him to stay by seizing him by the throat, and dealing him a violent blow on the head with his cudgel. They struggled together for a few minutes, when Arthur Latymer, managing to shake his antagonist from him, drew his sword and was on the point of running it through the prostrate form of Lawrence, when Scrubb suddenly appeared, and bringing his cudgel to bear on the sword with great force, shivered it to atoms ! Arthur, perceiving a second foe in the field, and himself unarmed, fled ;—and Scrubb, lifting Lawrence in his arms, bore him into the house.

CHAPTER IV.

HAVING once more brought Lawrence Wood before the reader in the character of a friend-in-need to Constance, we must say a few words respecting his absence from his master's house on his visit to Dr. Calder's.

Upon leaving the house of his master, he proceeded at a brisk pace along Cheapside, towards the residence of the man of physic in Watling-street. It was a dark gloomy night, and one well suited to the errand he was engaged upon : the very streets looked smitten, as the houses appeared in long high black rows, with here and there a light to be seen flitting to and fro from some of the adjacent windows, bespeaking, no doubt, the kind attendance of some courageous relative to a suffering victim to the plague ; perhaps some one one performing the last kind offices, preparatory to delivering the body of a beloved husband, father, wife, brother, sister, or *lover* (and Law-

rence heaved a deep sigh) to the revolting and unnatural custody of the dead
cart! Thus ruminating within himself, his contemplations took a view of
affairs at the house he had just left. His good old mistress had been singled
out to serve under the black banner of contagion, and it grieved him sorely,
for she had ever been a kind friend to him, and he having entered the service
of Master Elliot when young and an orphan, her kindness had filled up the
want of a mother to him, and if she should fall a prey to the disease, her
loss would be sorely felt and deeply lamented by him. But then he dreaded
lest the infection should spread in the family, and attack his good old master
who had reared him up from a boy; or what a pang it would occasion them
if it bereaved them of their only son, now approaching to manhood—that
would prove a loss indeed. By some unaccountable circumstance, that will
frequently happen when dwelling on the calamities of those dear to the
memory, the thought of Constance being in danger was the last to enter the
mind of the moody youth. There had been a time when she would have
been the first, perhaps the only, object of his fears; but now, thought he to
himself, why need her welfare concern me? She is lost to me—I fear for
ever! And giving way to his feelings, he could scarcely repress a tear.
How long he would have dwelt upon this melancholy theme it is impossible
to say, had he not accidentally struck his foot against an upraised stone, thus
causing him to look about, when, discovering he had passed the doctor's by
at least some dozen houses, he quickly retraced his steps, and soon arrived
at the depot of physic.

The houses of private surgeons were not quite so handsomely decorated
with large variegated lamps before the door as they are at the present
period, so Lawrence had to grope up and down the door-posts till he could
find the handle of a rickety bell-wire; its extreme looseness rendering it
somewhat difficult to tell whether it bore any connection with the bell at all;
however, another hearty pull soon settled the query, for in a few moments
the door was opened sufficiently wide enough to allow an old crone to render
the tip of her nose and the end of her fore finger visible to Lawrence, as he
stood on the step, waiting to walk inside.

"Your business, young man—speak, and quickly, too," said the woman,
her nose and chin chattering together with the cold. "This is not an hos-
pital or infirmary. let me tell you, that you should frighten people out of
their wits, and endanger the fastenings of their bells by such tugging as you
have given us a specimen of. Speak, can't you? This is Dr. Calder's, and
if you want him he can't come, so you know your answer."

"You have guessed right, old mistress," replied Lawrence, "it is Dr.
Calder I seek, and I trust I shall not be disappointed; my business is urgent
in the extreme. I must see him."

"Oh I do not doubt all that," replied the woman in an unfeeling tone;
"it is the same with every body; they all say he must come directly, as if
there were no other doctor in all London could cure the plague but Dr.
Calder, and no other housekeeper, charwoman, or servant-of-all-work to be
roused out of her bed these shivering nights but Peg—its curst vexing and I
know it."

"Indeed, my good woman," resumed Lawrence, "a great part of the
'shivering' calamities you speak of are attributable to yourself, for if you
had civilly asked my business, and acted on my reply, you might by this
time have been snug in your bed again; so, now, just step up to your master
and tell him that his immediate presence is required at Matthew Elliot's,
the stationer of Cheapside, and that a person is now waiting to speak with
him."

This request being accompanied with a silver inducement, soon found a
ready performer in "shivering Peg," who, asking Lawrence to step inside,

bustled up stairs with the message to her master, and in a very few minutes returned and requested him to follow her.

Lawrence crept his way up a narrow staircase, and entered a room pointed out to him by the old housekeeper, where he found the man of lotions in his shirt sleeves hard at work, mixing, cordials and compounds, making pills and ointments, and other important prescriptions for his numerous patients. Without leaving off, he motioned Lawrence to be seated on a low stool near a handful of fire, in an old-fashioned grate, and then began to question him as to the purport of his errand.

"And so, young man, you have come from good Master Elliot, eh ?" he is an old friend of mine, a very old friend; I would do any thing to serve him ; I trust that none of his family are infected, but that he has only sent for my advice, to make use of as a preventive. Say, is it not so ?"

" I am sorry to say it is not," replied Lawrence ; " my message is to request your immediate attendance at my master's house, to prescribe for his wife, who has been seized with the plague."

" Ah !" exclaimed the doctor in surprise, pausing from his work, and fixing his sickly glance upon Lawrence Wood. "The wife of my old friend attacked with the plague ! I will wait upon her instantly—she must be saved ! Good Master Elliot ! I know him for the best citizen in London. But how shall I act ? Ha! let me see : here is this lotion and box of pills for old Ralph Garland, the bell-ringer of St. Paul's; and this letter for Andrew Gowles, the coffin-maker, which must be delivered before the medicines, and to-night, but I should like to be at your master's house before taking them. I have no one to send at such an hour of the night ; let me see"—

And here the learned man of drugs and herbs sat down beside Lawrence to consider what was best to be done ; for, like a true lover of his patients, he could not relish the idea of losing two chances for the sake of one, dear as Master Elliot's friendship might be.

"I. can suggest a plan, doctor," said Lawrence, breaking the silence which had prevailed for the last five minutes, " which, if it meets with your approbation, will, I think, serve all purposes. If there is nothing else required but the safe and punctual delivery of these orders, I will undertake to do that at once, whilst you can repair without delay to my master's house, where your presence is eagerly expected."

" Capital, indeed ! and so you shall," replied the doctor ; and jumping from his seat he proceeded to pack up the medicines, and write his directions upon them, which done, he handed them over to Lawrence ; giving him strict injunctions that when he arrived at Old Saint Paul's with Ralph Garland's medicines, he was to ring the bell at the South Door, opposite Paul's Chain, and it would be immediately answered.

" You may depend upon your instructions being fulfilled," said Lawrence, taking the letter and packet of medicines from the doctor, " and you will be kind enough, no doubt, to proceed to my master's house directly."

" I will be there in less than ten minutes," replied Doctor Calder ; come, I will light you down stairs, and then take my departure immediately. Lay fast hold of the side balustrade ; these old stairs are not used to visitors, I can assure you."

" So I presume," thought Lawrence, without venturing any reply, for as he followed the doctor down the old staircase, he kept on his guard, lest they should give way altogether, and thus bring him to the groud floor in a way more speedy than safe.

" There, you can open the door now, I dare say," said the doctor, as he stood upon the stairs, holding the flickering taper aloft to light Lawrence along the narrow passage which led to the street door. The door was so barred, locked, and bolted as not only to attract the young man's notice, but also to give him some trouble in opening it, seeming to him as if the professor of physic almost dreaded a siege, or forcible entry of applicants for his attention, and had adopted this method for security.

As it occupied Lawrence a few minutes in forcing back bolts, wrenching out bars, unhooking chains, and twisting the large rusty key in its ancient lock, the doctor imagined he might be purposely loitering for some trifle or fee by way of reward ; or even that he might not relish his errand to the plague-stricken bell-ringer ; surmising this, he made offer of some strong antidotes to infection.

" A piece of tobacco soaked in oil of camphor, or a sprig of Indian ginger, both excellent preventives, I can assure you," said the doctor.

" I need them not," replied Lawrence ; " I trust to a higher power than man's to keep me safe from the dangers of the plague ; as yet I have never shrunk from it, or rashly ran into its snares ; if it is to be my fate, I must submit. I thank you for your kindness, and wish you for the present good-night." So saying, he closed the door after him, and left the house.

As Lawrence progressed on his way to the coffin-maker's, which was directed as being situate in White's-alley, Cripplegate (a low, disreputable neighbourhood), the thought gleamed across his mind that it was somewhat peculiar for the doctor to be so imperative about the letter being delivered to Andrew Gowles himself ; and also in the medicine to a sick—perhaps dying—man, being considered as secondary to a letter to a coffin-maker—a message concerning the dead to be attended to before assistance to the dying ! And then a correspondence between a doctor and a coffin-maker ! There was something unnatural, at all events indelicate, about it ; for who would like to employ a medical man in league with an undertaker ? a man who would gain considerably more by your death than by the few medicines you might require to save life ; as, in cases of the plague, the medicine and attendance required was no great quantity, it being soon settled ; the balance between life and death in this disease being squared up at a short notice. These considerations took deep hold in Lawrence's mind ; he suspected no good from them : it argued no good of the doctor, and much worse of the coffin-maker, whom he determined to watch well when he saw him. For that purpose he hastened on, and soon got to the end of Wood-street ; crossing London Wall, he made his way towards Moorfields, near which quarter the coffin-maker resided, although it was usually called Cripplegate. Passing down a muddy lane, which threatened every step he took to engulf him in its miry bed, Lawrence turned down a dark passage, which he knew to be White's Alley, by a low public-house being at the corner, in which you might always hear noisy carousing and drunken revelry at all hours of the night, and being directed by Dr. Calder that Gowles's house was the third house on the right hand, he readily found it ; at the same time raising his cudgel to bestow a lusty knock on the shutters, when a loud laugh and hallooing from within caused him to refrain for a moment to listen. He stood for several minutes to try to hear what they were saying, but not being able to glean any thing further than that there were several voices, and all of them singing riotously at once, he gave over the attempt, and knocked again loudly at the door.

Footsteps were at last heard approaching the door, which was opened by a labouring-looking man, with a long pipe in his mouth, and a lantern in his hand. As he came forward to ascertain who it was that had disturbed their revelry, Lawrence plainly saw that he was intoxicated.

" Who knocks—I say—who knocks ? dy'e hear ?" growled out the besotted assistant of Gowles (for it was one of the coffin-maker's men). Upon receiving no answer from Lawrence, who was for the moment off his guard, and not paying any attention to the questions put to him, the man blustered forward, and bouncing the lantern in Lawrence's face roared out, " Can't ye speak ? Who are you ? and what do you want ?"

Without making any reply, Lawrence darted into the house, and made his way to a room at the rear of the house, where he saw a light glimmering through a crevice in the door, but just as he was about to enter it, the song or yell he had heard before broke out with redoubled vigour, and he concluded it would be best to wait outside till it was over. As he listened attentively, the following caught his ears :—

The plague may be a dread to some,
    But 'tis better than health to me ;
They call it a curse, but that's all a hum,
    As for coffins, what better could be ?

CHORUS.—So lads as you rap,
        And drink from the tap,
            Sing success to the plague !
            Death, asthma, and ague !
        Yes, the plague ! well-a-day, well-a-day !
            So rap away rap,
            At coffin and tap.
        Oh the plague ! well-a-day, well-a-day !

We've coffins in store for young or for old,
    For poor, wealthy, sad, or for gay ;
What matter to us, we finger their gold,
    And work merry by night and by day !

Chorus.

The tailor so prime may dress you up gay,
    In silks or in velvet, what not ;
But *we* dress your friends in a different way,
    And leave 'em to slumber and rot !

Chorus.

So let's hope the plague will last many a day,
    'Twill make our hearts merry and light ;
For those whom we lay in the dead-pits by day,
    We can *ease* of their coffins at night !

Chorus.

Boisterous applause followed the song, and Lawrence, who was filled with disgust and astonishment, suddenly opened the door. He absolutely recoiled at the scene before him. In the midst of a large room, the sides of which were crowded with coffins piled to the very ceiling, sat about a dozen low-looking fellows, with pipes in their mouths, and flasks and glasses before them. Their seats were coffins, and their table was a coffin set upon a bier. Seated on a pile of coffins, waving a glass in one hand, and a bottle in the other, was Andrew Gowles, acting as president or chairman of the assembly. A more hideous personage could not be imagined. He was clothed in a suit of rusty black, which made his meagre limbs look yet more lean and ghastly. His head was quite bald, and entirely divested of any artificial covering. His throat was long and scraggy, and supported a head unrivalled for ugliness. His nose had been broken in a fray some years since, and was almost compressed flat with his cheeks. His few remaining teeth were yellow and discoloured, with large apertures between them. His eyes were bright, and set in deep recesses, and now that he was more than half intoxicated, beamed with unnatural brightness. The persons by whom he was

surrounded were congenial spirits ; searchers, watchmen, buriers, apothe-
caries, and other wretches who, like himself, gloried in the pestilence, because it was a source of profit to them. *

Perceiving a stranger in the room, Gowles in a stentorian voice bawled
for "order!" which, when it was procured, he rose from his seat, and staggering towards Lawrence Wood, in a thick and intoxicated voice inquired
what brought him there. Lawrence, who was nearly suffocated by the op-
pressive stench of tobacco smoke, and the sour belching of Gowles's breath,
which he puffed upon him full in the face, was for a moment unable to reply,
but, as soon as he could recover himself, he pulled the letter from his vest,
and giving it into Gowles's own hand, after first ascertaining he was that
celebrated personage, added—" That letter from Doctor Calder will explain
all!"

" From Doctor Calder!" ejaculated Gowles, thoughtfully. " Oh, you are
welcome ;" then turning to his companions, and pointing to Lawrence, he
observed, " He's a friend, from a friend ! Let's pledge him in a brimmer."

" Ay, aye—let him drink to the plague!" replied one of the gang, and
filling a flask of wine he handed it to Lawrence.

" No, I had rather not drink," answered Lawrence ; disgusted at the brutal
frivolity of the wretches around him.

" Not drink !—not drink to the plague !" exclaimed Gowles, his countenance lighted up with a fiendish grin of surprise ; " Why, you wish your
master plenty of trade, I suppose, don't ye ?—and if *he* has plenty, why of
course *we* have plenty, too! so what can be better for all—come don't be
prudish or afeard ; your master says in his note, here, ' he *hopes* to have *plenty*
of business for us !' "

" The villain !" muttered Lawrence to himself; " my conjectures, then,
were true !" Turning to Gowles, with a disdainful look, he answered,
" You mistake me ! I am not one of Doctor Calder's servants, but am a
friend of one of his patients. He requested me to deliver that note to you
alone. I find, by your confession, it requires both secresy and accuracy : I
am glad it has reached you through my hands—he will doubtless do all in
his power to keep his word with you !"—and without waiting to make or
receive any further reply, Lawrence hastily quitted the room, and was soon
outside the house on his way to Old Saint Paul's Cathedral.

It would be useless to attempt a description of the state of Gowles's mind
at Lawrence's reply ; he had taken him for an assistant of the doctor's, and
had therefore spoken freely concerning a compact which should have been
known to no one—much less the friend of one of the Doctor's patients !
The reply of the young man, given in such a pointed way, which plainly
evinced that he understood all, completely sobered the guilty-minded coffin-
maker, who, in a paroxysm of rage and despair at his secret being discovered,
knocked out all the lights in the room, and ordered every one to leave the
place ; then rushed up stairs to the top of his house, locked himself up in a
garret, which went by the name of his bed-room, and gave vent to all the
curses and oaths that he was master of, and this was not a few, for to use the
words of a particular friend of Gowles's, in a quarrel one day, he said that he
carried in his memory a stock of oaths sufficient to make a Pope bankrupt of
his absolutions ; or, if used, would take all the souls in purgatory a thousand
years to absolve !

The compact alluded to by Gowles was one of a most infamous and dis-
gusting nature ; it was no less than burying the corpses without coffins, or
charging the relatives the same as if they were used, sometimes going so far
as to plunder public burial-grounds of not only coffins, but any ornament or

---

* See page engraving—" Scene at the Coffin-maker's," given with No. 2.

Vide page 34.

valuables that might have been buried with the deceased person, of which
the brutal undertakers had due notice from their villanous accomplices, the
surgeons; and report and popular opinion went so far as to say that a sort
of trade or compensation was carried on by both parties—surgeon and coffin-
maker—to supply each other with employment and profit; but whether
Dr. Calder and Andrew Gowles carried on a traffic of this description remains to be seen.

Having reached Old Saint Paul's, Lawrence made his way round to the
south door, opposite Paul's Chain, as Dr. Calder had directed him, and perceiving a long bell-wire which for years had swung loosely in the wind, void
of any fastening or handle, he pulled away at it lustily till he could hear it
echo and re-echo along the nave of the cathedral in hollow dismal sounds.
He repeated it a second and third time, when the door was slowly and cautiously opened by one of the vergers, who, upon hearing his business, and
being requested by Lawrence to convey the packet of medicines to the sick
man, had well nigh swooned with fear at the demand.

"Oh, not for worlds could I do your bidding, young man!" exclaimed
the verger in extreme terror and alarm. "Alas! poor Master Garland, I
fear, has little need of medicines now; he is too far gone. Good Dr. Calder
told me in confidence, the last time he visited him, that he could not last
twenty-four hours out, and that will be to-morrow noon. I suppose what he
has sent is merely a soothing draught?"

"It must be a very plenteous one, then," replied Lawrence, "for the
packet contains two or three bottles, besides ointment and pills. It is hard
the poor man should lay and want these necessaries. If you will show me
the way, I will carry them to his bedside myself. I fear not infection; and
if I fall a victim to the disease by assisting the helpless, why—I might die
doing worse, that's all. Lead on, old man; I'll follow."

5.

The old verger now hobbled nimbly along the pavement of the principal avenue of the cathedral, and passed through many intricate windings and staircases; but Lawrence heeded him not, with the exception of following the light, being chiefly occupied in surveying the noble structure, having never before visited the part he was now traversing. On reaching the sick man's chamber, the old verger hastily pushed open the door and exclaimed, "There, you will find him yourself now," and suddenly disappeared.

Lawrence groped his way into the chamber, and there beheld a sight which nearly froze him with horror. Upon a low pallet or couch lay the plague-stricken bell-ringer, apparently in the height of the disease, his groans and shrieks resounding through the apartment, while an aged woman and a little girl were piling blankets and wrappers upon him to keep him warm. Beckoning the nurse to him, Lawrence delivered the medicines to her care, with the doctor's directions to apply them as specified instantly, and he (the doctor) would be there early in the morning. The old woman made no reply, but shaking her head mournfully, placed them on a table by the bed-side. The scene was so revolting to the feelings of Lawrence, that he took his leave at once, but had to grope his way back the best way he could, meeting with several falls and bumps against pillars and steps, and upon once more reaching the street he commenced running at a swift pace, calling at the Commissioner of Health's office in Old Change to give notice of the plague being in his master's house, and from thence proceeded at once to Master Elliot's. His return home was the noise heard by Constance in her struggles with Arthur Latymer.

CHAPTER V.

WE must now return to Sir Robert Harlingham and Captain Blount, the two gamesters, whom we left on their way to Moreton's house in the Strand, arising out of the *fracas* in the Dice-room at the St. Dunstan's Head. On arriving at the house, the libertine immediately placed the key in the door to make sure that he was not deceived, and after a hard turn, and a pressure with his knee, it gave way to his efforts, and swung back with a grating sound.

"So you see I have rightly conducted you," exclaimed Blount, rather pompously; "and as I have a similar affair of my own in hand, I shall now take my leave."

"Do you leave me, Blount?" replied Sir Robert, surprised at his companion's sudden change of mind; "I was about to request you to keep a look-out, in case of a surprise."

"That is impossible," replied the captain; "Moreton, you well know, will not return to-night; he will be too anxious to win back some of his losses, and for that purpose will be a guest at the Devil* in Fleet-street. If I thought there was any real cause of danger, and you actually required my protection, why, soul and body, man, you should command every inch of my sword for ever. Death and hailstones, but you should!"

"Your protection I scorn, but your assistance I expected," answered Sir Robert reproachfully.

"Both you know, Sir Robert, are ever yours to command; but, on the present occasion, I must beg to be excused. Farewell; may your lady bird prove not too coy;" and so saying, he departed.

* A noted gambling-house.

" Base, cowardly poltroon !" muttered Sir Robert, as he looked after him. " No matter ; no interruption short of death shall drag my prize from my grasp !" so saying, he crept lightly along the passage, leaving the door ajar, to be more easy of egress, and proceeding cautiously up the stairs soon found the landing. Here he was somewhat at a loss to ascertain which room the fair one occupied, till a heavy sigh and softly-uttered moan decided for him which room to enter. Knocking smartly at the door of the room he judged the sound came from, he received no answer in reply. He knocked a second time, louder, when a female voice from within inquired, " Who's there ? Henry, is it you ?"

" It is a friend," was Sir Robert's reply, as, opening the door and stepping into the room, the lady appeared before him.

The young lady thus introduced was Estelle Poynton, and was the avowed paramour of Captain Moreton, who having fell in love with her some time back when with his regiment in the West of England, had prevailed upon her to elope with him ; a marriage at the time, he said, being impossible. They loved each other fondly, and with the exception of being an outcast from her friends, Estelle knew no grief or care ; latterly, however, Moreton's long absence from her, sometimes for days and nights together, rendered her very unhappy. She was loth to think that he slighted her, yet her heart prompted her to the belief of such a surmise. It was now two days since she had seen or heard of him.

Upon the entrance of Sir Robert Harlingham, Estelle uttered a cry of terror mingled with surprise at the sight of a stranger at such a time of the night, but she was somewhat checked from raising any alarm by the knight placing his finger on his lip, and motioning silence. In truth, he was staggered with her beauty ; he had heard much of her, but the praise had entirely underrated her attractions. At length he addressed her.

" I trust you will excuse my rude intrusion, lady, when I announce that I am a friend of Captain Moreton, and bear a message from him to you."

" A message !" exclaimed Estelle in alarm ; " will he not come himself ? Has any thing happened to him ? Oh tell me, sir, I implore you !"

" Nothing, my dear madam, of consequence, rest assured," answered the knight. " However, if you will award me the hospitality for a few minutes which my friend assured me I should receive, every thing shall be explained."

" You must excuse my terrors, sir," replied Estelle, " and accept in their stead my thanks for this kindness ; but tell me, I beseech you, every thing ; keep me no longer in suspense—'tis more than I deserve, or can bear :" and her she gave full vent to the emotions of her heart in a flood of tears.

Sir Robert was too adept a gallant not to know how to appreciate a mood so melting, or a moment so favourable as the present ; and taking Estelle by the hand he seated himself beside her on a low couch.

" Nay, now, my dear madam, this is breaking your promise," he whispered tenderly in her ear.

" I own I am wrong and foolish," she answered, " but the dreadful doubts and suspense I have endured since Moreton's absence, has almost bewildered me ; tell me, sir, in mercy, in truth, is he dead ? does he live ? will he return again to his heart-broken Estelle ;" and here again the tears choked her utterance.

" And is it thus that Moreton prizes a gem of which even a monarch might be proud ?" said Harlingham. " 'Tis strange ! and makes the reports I have heard look something like the truth ; but I was slow to judge so harshly of him."

" How ! what reports ? oh pray tell me !"

" No," answered the knight, " I would not distress you still more than you are at present."

" You cannot—'tis impossible," returned the distracted lady : " you say you are his friend—make that appear, and tell me his dangers, that I may share them, if not relieve them."

" Suppose he would not have you share them—that he prefers another's company to yours ? think you he would welcome your approach to behold him fold another in the arms which have so often clasped yourself ?" replied Sir Robert, artfully.

" Oh, Heaven ! can this be true ?" exclaimed Estelle in a tone of horror.

" Lady, you are deserted ! Moreton loves—nay, even is *wedded*—to another !"

Estelle made no answer to this overwhelming information ; she rose suddenly to her feet ; her eyes seemed transfixed as a statue ; her countenance grew ashy pale ; and uttering one long deep-drawn sigh of poignant grief, she swooned, and would have fallen, had not Harlingham caught her in his arms.

The feelings of the libertine were somewhat touched at the pang of grief he had caused to the lovely form which now reposed lifeless in his arms. He half repented that he had said so much—then laughed, and stealing from her marble lips a felon kiss, he placed her on the couch, when a draught of water being administered to her, she slowly unclosed her eyes.

The first words which the distressed Estelle uttered on recovering her senses were of Moreton. " Oh, Henry," she exclaimed, " give back the fond and faithful heart you have so basely used."

" But are there not other hearts, equally true and constant, would serve for an exchange, dearest lady ?" said Sir Robert, clasping her hand more firmly, and impressing a kiss upon it. " There are other eyes which admire you besides Moreton's ; there are other hearts which adore you as fervently, other sighs shed for your smiles, and other lips which fondly breathe your name ! Oh, lady, dear Estelle, behold one ever your admirer ; one who has long adored you in silence ; accept, then, my constant, ever-faithful heart in exchange for the one you have so basely lost."

" How, sir !" exclaimed Estelle in surprise ; " is this the language of a friend to Captain Moreton ?—you jest and mock me !"

" By Heaven and those ruby lips but I do not !" replied Harlingham, starting up, and seizing Estelle in his arms. " I swear by the light of those eyes to live and die for you ! Moreton has basely deserted you for another ; consent to be mine, and join two hearts in never-ceasing love !"

" This is base ! Unhand me, sir ! I believe you not. Oh. Moreton, Moreton, and is it thus you swore to protect me !"

" He hears you not, or hearing heeds you not. You are mine in love, be mine by choice, for Moreton will never see you more !" ejaculated Harlingham, trying to soothe the cries of Estelle.

" Monster, leave me ! you are some unprincipled libertine, and have taken advantage of Moreton's absence—nay, perhaps, purposely detained him by some vile plot—to insult me ; but I will foil you yet !"

Having extricated herself from the grasp of Sir Robert, Estelle sought safety by attempting to fly to an adjoining room ; but Sir Robert, perceiving her intention, darted after her, and overtook her on the landing-place. Finding herself detained by her pursuer, she cried loudly for help. Her cries were answered, for footsteps were heard ascending the stairs rapidly.

" Ah ! am I betrayed ?" exclaimed Sir Robert, loosening her arm, and drawing his sword : " I leave you for a time, then, to grapple with my new foe !"

Estelle made no reply, but taking advantage of the slackened grip of her detainer, escaped into the adjoining room, and before Sir Robert could prevent her, she had turned the key, and defied all further attempts at insult,

Sir Robert now turned his attention to the approaching footstep, which appeared to be close at hand: he guessed it could be no other than Moreton himself, so preparing for the worst, he dashed down the stairs, sword in hand.

The adversaries met at a sudden turn in the winding staircase. It was Captain Moreton himself, who having reached his home at that moment, and hearing Estelle's cries for help, drew his sword, and rushed up to her assistance. By the glimmering light of a small lamp, Moreton beheld Harlingham a few stairs above him.

"Villain! defend thyself!" exclaimed Moreton; and with one bound he grasped the sword arm of the knight, and plunged his rapier full at his breast, but a sudden movement of Sir Robert saved him, and clasping each other by the throat, the two combatants rolled down several stairs, tightly clutched in each other's embrace. By the fall, the lamp was extinguished and shattered to pieces. The darkness which now prevailed made the foes more desperate: with one hand tightly fixed in Moreton's throat, Harlingham was grasping his sword with the other; Moreton at the same time drawing a heavy-loaded pistol from his belt, and waiting an opportunity of discharging its contents at his adversary's head. Brief and dreadful in the extreme were the struggles and efforts for mastery between these men: they were both powerful, and their causes of resentment most poignant. At this moment, Moreton, taking advantage of a stooping position of his antagonist, discharged his pistol, but the movement having been observed by Harlingham, he immediately knocked his arm up, and passed his sword through his heart as the report of the pistol rang through the house like a thunderbolt. Hurling Moreton from him, Harlingham fled from the house with the speed of a greyhound, for he knew he had killed his victim!

The report of the pistol aroused the inmates of the house; Estelle, fearing some mischief had happened, also flew to the spot. Upon lights being procured, she started on beholding at her feet a body weltering in blood. The folds of his cloak had fallen over Captain Moreton's face as he fell, and Estelle, full of horrible suspicions, raised it, and beholding her lover's countenance, ghastly and contorted in death, gave one long, loud, heart-broken shriek, and fell senseless upon the floor!

* * * * * * * * * *

A few days wrought the consummation of this tragedy. Estelle but recovered one fit to enter another; she gradually grew delirious, raving for Moreton, and dealing curses on the head of his murderer! At the expiration of the third day she sunk into a swoon from which she only recovered to join her lover in death.

Reader; we draw the curtain over the lamented fate of the gamester and his mistress! Suffice it to say the villain Harlingham fled the country, and was never seen on its shores again.

CHAPTER VI.

HAVING briefly alluded, in a previous chapter, to a sort of compact or "private understanding" between Dr. Calder and Gowles the coffin-maker, we must now clear up the affair by representing it in its true light. During the dreadful ravages of the plague, at the period to which this tale refers, unprincipled men were not wanting who would, for the sake of what few valuables their wretched patients were possessed of, either so far neglect them, or put them out of the way at once for the sake of the expenses

The undertakers, or coffin-makers, also, were base enough to become the tools of these villanous surgeons, offer to bury the parties, claim the expenses at the hands of the parish, and then regain the wretched shell they had sold by plunder at night! Connected with these wretches were a class of women denominated "plague-nurses," who, under pretence of nursing and tending their victims, either robbed them to a great extent, or took the first opportunity of putting them out of the way altogether, which was an easy task in a disease like the plague, where the least chill was sufficient to give a fatal termination to the disease. It was in a compact of this nature that Dr. Calder, Andrew Gowles, and Mother Hagget (a plague-nurse of great notoriety), were concerned. But it was only to certain patients that the doctor could introduce his creatures; for instance, the case of Mistress Elliot, her husband being a man of too great discernment to be imposed upon; and, besides this, a sort of real friendship existed between them, which was the cause of Mother Hagget not having been introduced to the family.

Ralph Garland, the bell-ringer of Old Saint Paul's, was still raging under the disease in all its terrors, when Mother Hagget received a communication to attend Dr. Calder at the sick man's bedside, immediately. The doctor was too good a customer to be slighted, so tossing up the remains of a tankard of canary, which she always indulged in thrice a day to keep away infection, the wretched crone set off to obey the mandate.

On arriving at the cathedral, she was speedily ushered to the bell-ringer's apartment, for the attendants who had been waiting on him were glad to see a nurse arrive to ease them of their labours. She there found the doctor: he was sitting on the bed, holding the sick man's wrist in one hand, and his watch in the other, with which he was attentively counting the rate of his patient's pulsation. After a few moment's contemplation, he replaced it in his fob, shook his head, and ordered all present to withdraw, except Mother Hagget, whom he beckoned to his side.

"Hagget," began the doctor, "I have sent for you to attend this poor man; he has been under my care these three days, but I find he requires better and more skilful attention than those about him can bestow."

This sentence was delivered in a tender, feeling manner, and with a sorrowful air. As the doctor still observed two or three vergers, and the woman who had been attending on the sick man, loitering about the door of the apartment, he judged they might be listening; but, once convinced of their absence, he caught Mother Hagget by the arm, and drawing her close to him whispered in her ear, "Hagget, this is an important affair: he," pointing to the sick man, "is in a raging fever; the least chill will do for him—a blanket removed, or a cup of cold water, and he would be a dead man in an hour; you understand me?"

"I do," muttered the hag.

"He has a hidden treasure somewhere; it must be considerable, as he had three hundred pounds left him about two months ago by an old uncle; it is secreted in some of the vaults, or in the belfry, I suppose; you must find that out at all risks; it will be a handsome thing, I can tell you, for both of us: I will get it conveyed away, and the people about him will naturally believe the secret died with him: for I do not *think*," resumed the doctor aloud, as he observed the parties again approaching, "he will recover, under all circumstances. You will remember what I have said, Mrs. Hagget," he continued, as he stood with the door open, ready to depart, "not the least chill or air; administer the ointment I have left once every two hours; I will call early in the morning to see how the old man is—good-night."

"Good night, Mr. Calder," replied Hagget, as the doctor closed the door after him.

Upon being again left to herself, the nurse stepped softly to the bed to observe the patient more closely. He was in a deep slumber—or, rather, a dead stupor—yet sweating at every pore.

"Ah!" she exclaimed, "this perspiration won't do, Mr. Calder; if he goes on like this, he will live to spend his treasure himself—let me see; yes, this rug must come off, and I must uncover his feet—there ," and, coolly suiting the action to the word by pulling a thick rug from the bed, and removing the clothes from the feet of her patient, that he might gradually chill upwards, she took a seat by the fire, and after making herself a choice mess of spiced wine and sack-posset, with some corn beef and pastry, she sat down to contemplate the affair.

"So, Dr. Calder intends me to have *all* the labour, and only *half* the treasure," she began, muttering to herself. "Well, let me consider this matter: can't I manage to get it all myself, and tell the doctor he never disclosed where it was concealed? but then how shall I remove it? he may suspect, and find all out—no; it will be the best way as he says: this, and the little I have scraped together—thanks to frightened relations leaving their homes—will make me comfortable for the rest of my days. This will be a job for Gowles, too. I wish," continued the hag, after a pause, "Calder had sent for me at Elliot's; I might have made a good thing of it. I know old Elliot has money in the house; and I would have had them all stiff in a fortnight but what I would have found it—Miss Prettyface and all, though she does love a fine gentleman, and thinks no one knows it: never mind, they may all have a ride in our dead-cart yet! the plague ain't half over, and I trust will not be for six months to come."

Here she was suddenly roused from her reverie by the waking of her patient, and rising from her chair she shuffled to the bedside.

"Well, what ails you now?" she roared out in an uncouth voice.

"Who are you?" inquired the sick man, rising up in his bed: "where's the doctor? where are my friends?—ah! they have all left me, and sent you to kill me! I know it; I know it!"

"Know what?" said Hagget.

"That you're a devil! I hate your crew! I suppose they were all afraid of me. Ah! let 'em go; let 'em go!" and sinking back on his pillow, Ralph Garland seemed quite overcome by the exertion it had caused him.

"Well, this is very fine thanks, any how!" replied Hagget, "for coming here in the middle of the night to wait upon you. I suppose, after all, I shall get nothing for my pains but what the doctor chooses to give me."

"Ah! that's the cry with all; give, give—pay, pay! I have no one to give me even a glass of physic without I pay them for it."

The wretched man covered his face with his hands, and shook his head backwards and forwards for some minutes, uttering at the same time a low, melancholy moan. At length he started up in a phrenzy of despair.

"Woman! I am rich! I have gold—plenty of it! I will pay you, and well too, if you will but save me. I cannot, must not, will not die yet! I am not prepared to die! To die, and leave all? Oh, oh, I cannot think of that! Hush! do you hear any thing? They are forcing my chest! Ah! villains! but I will be amongst them?"

The frantic man would have risen from his bed, if Mother Hagget had not suddenly pushed him down again. She knew this was the time to sound him for her purpose, and she was determined to make the experiment.

"What chest, Mr. Garland? I see no one here, neither do I hear any noise. It is your fancy," replied the hag in a soothing tone.

"Warmth! heat! I freeze?" cried out the invalid, who was shivering with cold from the effects of his nurse's kindness. "Oh, save my life, and I will give you gold—handfuls, handfuls—for I have got it!"

"He only raves," thought Mother Hagget. "I had better dose him into a slumber; this fit will make him dream of his treasure, and I will then whisper in his ear, and he will no doubt answer me. He will not be the first dying man from whom I have gained a secret that way: once known, he dies! This shivering fit has fixed his fate already!"

She now proceeded to make him a hot mixture of mallow leaves and honey, well spiced and mixed up with rosemary: this dose she speedily administered to him, well knowing that in a few minutes he would freely perspire, and be in a sound sleep, in which condition the slightest chill of the blood would make him a corpse in little more than an hour. His friends might say or think what they liked; the plague was too convenient a disease to leave room for calculations of this sort. Having replaced the covering, she watched beside her victim till he fell into a sound sleep.

As soon as Mother Hagget considered her patient under the full influence of the sleeping potion, she searched carefully round the room, but no signs of chest, box, bag, or key could she perceive. She also calculated that the sick man would probably be dead before dawn, and that if the secret was to be wormed out of him, it must be done at once, or she would have no time. Accordingly, she gently raised the head of the dying man (for he was now dying fast—a cold clammy sweat having made its appearance on his brow and hands), and seating herself beside him, whispered in his ear—"Take care of your gold, Master Garland! There are thieves! thieves!"

A convulsive start and clenching of the fists was the only response.

Again approaching his ear she called out "Your treasure; where is your treasure?"

"Ah! 'tis mine; touch it not!" murmured the old man in his stupor.

"Know you where it is? have you left it secure?" inquired the nurse, still whispering in his ear.

"Yes, yes! the stone vault is a good place: see, that is the place! beneath that marble slab! No one knows of it but myself. Ah! ah!"

As he murmured the above sentence, a faint laugh played over his livid features.

"Beneath a marble slab in the stone vault!" said the nurse to herself. "Come, that is a beginning?" then resuming her questions to her patient, she exclaimed, "Have you the key, Ralph? Here is gold, more gold; let us fill it!"

"Ah!" shouted Garland, bolting upright in bed, his eyes still closed in sleep, but his countenance horribly distorted with rage and fright; "'tis hid, 'tis hid! You cannot find my key. Go, go; it hangs on the nail near the grating of the vault in my bedroom! Step softly, softly!"

Casting her eyes up to the roof, Mother Hagget perceived a small round grating, which threw a light from the passage across the aisle to the stone vault. Upon raising the lamp, also, she perceived a key hanging on a nail, artfully entwined within the small bars of the grating, which if not pointed out would never be discovered. By placing the stool upon a table, she was enabled to touch the key, and after a little exertion she succeeded in securing it. Having now obtained the wished-for talisman, and acquainted with the vault in which the treasure was secreted, she had nothing more to fear by her patient's death, and as it was now waxing hard towards morning, she considered it would be expedient to get him out of the way at once, as he was sleeping, or rather stupified from the effects of the powerful draught she had administered to him.

Cautiously approaching the bed, she gazed for a few moments upon the convulsed sufferer before her, who was now writhing in agony. Suddenly he uttered a stifled cry, violently gnashed his teeth, clenched his hands, and partly rising would have leaped from the bed, had not his attentive nurse

Vide page 42.

sent him back again by a violent blow on the chest.   This startled him ; his eyes opened, and glared wildly at her ; he would have spoke, but utterance failed him ; he sent forth a dismal howl of despair and pain, as he dashed his head about with great violence.   Taking advantage of his delirium, she seized a small mattrass from the bed, and placing it upon the wretched man's face, threw the whole weight of her body with it.   The struggling and plunging from beneath was now violent in the extreme : Ralph, though in the height of a delirious fever, had gained new strength with it for the time, and the workings of his body, and the up-heavings of his chest were so powerful, that Hagget, who was a very strong woman, could with difficulty maintain her position.   She crawled, however, upon the bed, and pressing with all her might upon the rug which covered his face, kept him down: The struggles of the dying man gradually grew less frequent and weaker, till at last they subsided ; but it was not till the body beneath her had ceased to move for some time, that the hag would shift her position, and when she did it was but to gaze on her victim.   A fiend-like laugh played upon her coun- tenance, for she was satisfied.   Rising from the bed, she displayed the corpse of old Ralph Garland stamped with all the frightful horrors of a violent death ; his eyes having nearly burst from their sockets, his face purple from the effects of strangulation, and his teeth had bitten through his lower lip ! Hagget herself was horrified, for throwing the rug over the body, and catch- ing up the lamp, she departed to seek the hidden treasure.

Accordingly, she made her way up a flight of stone steps which led to the arched passage, opening to the principal naive of the cathedral.   Creeping across the pavement, and secreting her lamp as well as she was able from the wind which whistled in sharp gusts through the magnificent building, she descended a flight of iron steps below the chapel, which led to the stone

6.

vault. This vault or cavern was the receptacle of deceased members of honourable families, and was a select place of burial, being more airy, and less
liable to damps ; so destructive to marble tablets and costly escutcheons.
There was but one marble slab horizontally laid down, and Hagget therefore
concluded it must be the one which covered the secret she was in search of.

Placing her lamp on a jutting piece of stone-work in the vault, she proceeded to try her strength with the mason-work, but it proved immovable
to all her efforts. She next obtained the assistance of a large iron-spiked
railing, which had previously been used as a part of the old gate of the vault.
By dint of great exertion and much perseverance, she succeeded in forcing
the head of the spike under the slab : this encouraged her to renew her
efforts, and bringing her whole strength to bear upon the lever, she made a
desperate attempt to raise the stone with it ; but at this critical juncture, and
when she fancied a slight movement was visible on the slab, the iron lever
snapped in two like a twig, and one end flying up above her head, descended
with great force, ringing with a loud crash on the stones beneath, and shivering the lamp to atoms. This failure aroused her fears to the utmost, lest the
noise should bring some one to the spot, and discover her. Prompted by
this consideration, she groped her way out of the cell, but all attempts to
find the iron stairs proved vain. After wandering up and down the low-
arched passages for some time, muttering oaths and curses at her defeat, she
suddenly perceived a faint ray of light breaking through the niche of a loop-
hole, and darting towards it she saw that it was the dim glimmer of morning. This made her the more anxious to regain the bell-ringer's chamber,
well knowing that the cathedral attendants would be stirring at daybreak, and
also that Dr. Calder had promised to call on his patient early in the morning,
The glimpse of light falling upon a small door, without waiting to consider
where it might lead to, she pushed it open, and found that it led to the
middle aisle of the cathedral : along this she hurried, but was obliged, occasionally, to secrete herself behind the pillars, to avoid discovery by several
vergers who were going to early matins, and who passed close beside her.
As soon as they were out of sight, she darted from her hiding-place, and
was once more at the bedside of her victim.

Shortly after the business of the day was stirring, Dr. Calder paid a visit
to his patient in Old Saint Paul's. He had been suffering between doubt and
fear as to the result of his instructions to Mother Hagget. He knew she
was a cunning woman, and could manage these affairs excellently well, and
he doubted not that all must be over with the old bell-ringer, if the nurse
had but obeyed his directions : but Dr. Calder, black-hearted as he was,
dreamt not of the way in which his wretched patient had met his end.

Upon his arrival at the cathedral, the old verger who had been in the habit
of attending upon Ralph Garland prior to the arrival of the plague-nurse,
informed him, with a sorrowful air, that their friend and brother was no
more.

"Ah, poor soul !" replied the doctor, "I guessed as much : I knew last
night that a miracle alone could save him—(from the hands of Mother
Hagget" he muttered to himself). "The plague is making dreadful ravages
with both young and old ; we know not how soon our own turn may come.
However, as I am here, I will pay Master Garland one more visit, to see how
affairs may be settled with respect to his funeral."

Hastily dropping the conversation, the doctor made his way to the dead
man's apartment. Finding the door open, he stepped softly in, and was
somewhat surprised when, on looking round the room, he discovered, seated
in a large arm chair before the fire, with a short pipe just falling from her
mouth, Mother Hagget. A large tankard of sack warming by the fire-side
plainly told how she had been employed. The bed had been pushed out of

the way in a dark corner, and a rug covered the corpse which lay stretched upon it. Advancing to the side of the nurse, he tapped her roughly on the shoulder, when she started suddenly.

"Who wants the nurse now?" she exclaimed, in her half-dozy meditation; but perceiving the doctor, she calmly reseated herself, and stooping down, relighted her pipe.

"So poor old Garland has left this world, nurse?" said the doctor; cautiously looking round to be sure no one heard him.

"Oh yes," replied the nurse, puffing away at the pipe, "but it was a harder job than you thought of, though, Mr. Doctor, I can tell you."

"How so?" inquired the doctor eagerly.

"Why, the old fool did nothing but rave about his treasure—he thought of nothing else, cared for nothing; I did all I could to prepare him for death, but it was of no use."

"Then how did you manage with him, Hagget?" quickly inquired the doctor: "no rough usage—no tell-tale marks, I trust?"

"D'ye think I'm a fool or a child, to be catechised?—there's the body," she replied, pointing to the bed with her pipe: "if you are not afraid, go and look at him. You'll find him very much altered, I think."

Acting upon her advice, the doctor went to the bed, and raising the rug which covered the corpse, uttered a cry of horror, and hastily retreated.

"Does he shock you, doctor?" said the nurse jeeringly.

"Wretch! what have you done?" exclaimed the doctor in an angry tone. "This is the effect of a violent death by poison or by strangulation."

"Neither," replied the nurse sullenly. "He is dead—as dead as you would wish him to be, Doctor Calder: ask me no further questions, nor make any more fuss about the matter. I suppose you will expect your share of the treasure: if there is any risk, I have run it."

"'Tis a serious affair, and requires much secrecy and judgment in carrying it through," replied Dr. Calder. I would have managed it differently; but however, as it is, a golden fee to our friend Gowles and the city searchers will make their examination very slight. But the treasure, Hagget, the treasure: have you discovered it?"

"I have not," she answered; "but I know where it is hidden, and now old Ralph is dead the sooner we make ourselves masters of it the better: 'twill be more profitable than standing here lecturing over a corpse!"

"Well, well, have it so. I will merely finish what I am about, and then accompany you," replied the doctor, who was engaged in tying up the jaws, and otherwise composing the features of the dead man, which having done he prepared to follow the nurse, who bearing a small lamp led the way from the apartment with much caution and secrecy.

Mother Hagget merely retraced the steps she had taken a short time before, and soon led her companion to the dark recesses of the stone vault, where she halted before the marble tomb.

"There," she exclaimed, pointing to the stone, "there lies hid the treasure we seek, but I fear it will be a troublesome job to secure it."

"It appears difficult, indeed," replied the doctor, "but I think with a little perseverance we may secure it."

The treasure sought for by the doctor and his worthless companion was the fruits of many years' savings hoarded by old Ralph, and had been deposited by him for safety within the narrow confines of a marble tomb. To force this tomb open, therefore, was the first step to be taken by the doctor. It was a square masonic structure: the inscription had been defaced by time—the only words visible being "Sacred to the Memory." Having surveyed the tomb all round, the doctor concluded that the best way would be to force the front stone out of its place: to effect this, he seized a crowbar, and tried by main strength to wrest the stone from its cemented bed, while Mother Hagget stood by his side, holding the lamp, which shed but a dim, glimmering light. After many ineffectual attempts to force open the tomb, Doctor Calder resolved upon raising one of the slabs which formed the pavement at its base, and by the aid of Mother Hagget he accomplished this feat without much trouble ; but judge of their surprise, when, upon removing the slab, they discovered the chest immediately beneath it. By strenuous efforts they raised it from its hiding-place, and had just rested it upon the pavement, when footsteps were heard approaching the vault. Instantly their lamp was extinguished, and they both took shelter behind a tomb, which served them for a screen, yet discovered their intruders to them, who were evidently on the same errand as themselves, for they started at beholding the chest, and one of them exclaimed " We are betrayed !"

The intruders upon the labours of Dr. Calder and his companion were no other than two of the vergers of the cathedral ; one who had acted as porter and steward, and who had been doorkeeper upon all occasions of visiting to Ralph Garland ; the other was a servant of the dean's, and filled the twofold office of house-steward and butler at the Deanery, and occasionally verger and assistant sexton and bell-ringer at the cathedral. These men had for a long time previous to Old Garland's illness watched him frequently pay stolen visits to the stone vault ; they had dogged him, and observed him secrete what they considered must be gold or silver in this chest, and then replace the slab. However, no opportunity had presented itself by which they had been enabled to make an attack, as Ralph had always been in the habit of keeping the keys of the vault ; no one, therefore, could obtain access to it, unless by his knowledge or permission. His death having now terminated all these obstacles, they had determined upon possessing themselves of the treasure he had been so long hoarding up, and for this purpose had paid a visit to the vault at this critical moment.

" Who can have been here ?" exclaimed one of them, glancing round the vault.

" Indeed, I know not," replied his companion, " but I can pretty well guess. In truth, I do not half like that doctor who visited old Garland, and the woman who came yesterday ; she was a perfect fiend to look upon. I suspect they have had a knowledge of this treasure, and have been trying to secure it, but they have doubtless been disturbed in the attempt, and have left it till a future time to carry it off."

" I think you are right, friend," answered the other, " and I agree with you in thinking that poor Garland's treasure has been his death. However, let us disappoint them, and serve ourselves at the same time."

" It's our only remedy," replied the verger. " Let us once have this securely hidden, I will denounce the doctor by my suspicions, and have the matter thoroughly investigated. I should take a pleasure in seeing that hag roast—but come, we lose time, let's remove it ; here, grasp this end tight ; we must carry it between us, though it does not seem very heavy."

Doctor Calder and Mother Hagget, who had been silent listeners to all this conversation behind the tombstone, were not able to exchange words with each other, but the looks they bartered were equally understood by both parties. The doctor was dumb-stricken to hear himself suspected and actually threatened ; the treasure he had so doted upon was also about to be wrenched for ever from his grasp ; wealth which would perhaps place him in a state of future independence ; his fame and fair character about to be impeached by a damning charge, which bore such strong proofs as left no doubt of a conviction ; these reflections harrowed up his very soul to the rage of a demon, as he had heard his name handled by the two vergers, who, like himself, had come to gain felonious possession of the treasure. He had but one step to take to save his name, his reputation, and his life, and upon 'so great a risk he was resolved to run all hazards, and make one startling effort to save himself.

The two plunderers had now raised the chest between them, while a small lamp which they had brought was placed upon the top.

" Proceed carefully, brother," said the porter to his fellow verger ; " let us but get clear of this stone vault, and gain the secret passage, and I care not then if the doctor himself and his witch of a nurse come in pursuit of us—take care, there is a step there ; bend your head as you turn round."

At this instant the two men bearing away with them the bell-ringer's mysterious chest were passing round the corner of the tomb behind which stood sheltered the doctor and the nurse. Their heads were both turned away from the two secreted guilty accomplices, and as the foremost of the two vergers was about to ascend the iron staircase to leave the vault, Doctor Calder sprang forward, and grasping the iron crowbar in his hand which he had been using to force the tomb, he whirled it round his head, and brought it down with a powerful swing upon the head of the unsuspecting verger. Mother Hagget, who had watched his motions, now instantly rushed upon their remaining victim, and grasping him tightly by the throat, plunged a short knife into his breast repeatedly till he fell.

This was but the work of a few seconds. The two men now lay dead and bleeding at their feet, and the doctor losing none of his self-possession laid hold of the shoulders of one of the men, and requested Mother Hagget to raise him by the heels.

" We have no remedy left," he exclaimed, " but to bury them in the grave they have made for themselves :" so saying, they threw the bodies into the aperture where the chest had been deposited, and covered them over with the slab. Mother Hagget removed the blood stains from the tomb by besmearing it with mire from the floor of the vault, and having thus disposed of the bodies, they wrenched open the chest to calculate the amount of their gains, but what was their inexpressible surprise and disappointment, when groping amidst its contents they found nothing but a few remnants of tattered garments and old nails, which the miserly bell-ringer had thus hoarded up ? Uttering a cry of rage and horror, he rushed from the vault, and Mother Hagget was not slow in following him.

CHAPTER VII.

THE house of Matthew Elliot, which had been for many weeks a scene of sickness, despair, and lamentation, was now beginning to assume its original and serene appearance, for Mistress Elliot had so far recovered all effects of the plague as to be pronounced free from danger, and no further dread of infection- was feared for the present. It was a goodly sight to behold the family once more collected together round the homely fireside ; and on this occasion a fervent and humble offering of thanks was presented to the Most High for his interference and mercy.

On the following day the stationer's warehouse was all bustle and business —the dreaded cross was removed from the door by the servants of the Commissioners of the Board of Health, the house was pronounced free from the plague, and Master Elliot himself regularly besieged by neighbours and friends presenting themselves to him to pay their respects to him, and congratulate him upon the safe recovery of his wife, and the providential escape of the other branches of his family.

After the first two days had passed over, and things had fallen once more into their ordinary routine, and visitor's congratulations had ceased, the news of a whole family being preserved from the plague, though closely confined in the same house with a person who was stricken by it, gained such circulation that many parties began to think differently, as it had been held in great repugnance by the citizens through weak-mindedness and foolish fears, and many families who were quite free from the plague so far gave way as to resolve to close their houses entirely, until the plague should have died away, little thinking at that time how long it would remain with them.

It was on a Monday morning, the fifth day of Master Elliot's house being open, that an old and esteemed friend called upon him to congratulate and condole with him on the happy termination of his wife's sickness. This was no other than Mr. Briefwell, the lawyer, upon whom Master Elliot and his family had called the day of the boat-race, but who, they were then informed, had removed his family to the country. His name and presence were no sooner made known to the worthy stationer, than he left his counting-house, and ran to meet him. The salutations and friendly greetings of these worthy men were genuine and heartfelt in every degree, for they had been companions from their boyhood upwards, and had always entertained for each other the strongest and most unfeigned regard.

Leading the way to the inner room, Master Elliot presented his friend to his wife, who was also much rejoiced at once more beholding him. After a short conversation with his old friend, Master Elliot begged leave to be excused for a short time on pressing business, and as he was about leaving the room Constance entered it, and the worthy stationer took advantage of this by introducing her to his friend as a substitute during his absence.

Constance warmly returned the greeting of Mr. Briefwell, for he was one with whom cold restraint was unnecessary.

"And what do you think of your father's project of six months' solitude in the country? for such he informs me are his intentions, and to set about them shortly, too, with his whole family."

"I do not think there is any occasion for such seclusion," replied Constance, rather peevishly. "At least, if my father will have his whim, let it be voluntary. I for one would rather remain in town."

"Ha, ha, ha!" laughed the jocular old lawyer; "I see what it is—I solve the mystery and the objection at once—some lover, eh? Ha, ha, ha! what a dreadful thing this love must be, that a person would sooner remain in this universal grave, this infected city, to be enabled to enjoy the company of a lover, rather than seek safety in seclusion. Oh my dear Mrs. Elliot, how happy I am that I am past the age of the tender passion, in such troublesome times."

Constance made no reply to this attack upon her weakness, but busying herself with some trifling employment inwardly vented her disappointment and vexation at Master Briefwell's taunt—and on such a subject, too, before her mother, who was so inveterate against Arthur Latymer.

"Ah, my dear friend," exclaimed Mrs. Elliot to the assertion which had fallen from the lips of Briefwell, "I am sorry to say that the very subject you have spoken of is the only sorrow I know. Constance has a lover, and one whom I am sure no one would admit as a suitor for a daughter's hand, who studied her welfare."

"No one has ever raised an evil report about him, I am sure, mother," replied Constance sharply.

"Neither, my child, has any one of known respectability ever made any declaration in his favour," answered the mother. Then turning her conversation more pointedly to Briefwell, she resumed; "He is not only a stranger to us all, but a mysterious stranger; all we can hear of him is, that his name is Arthur Latymer, but where he resides, by what business he gets his living, or who are his friends, no one can tell—no, not even Constance herself—I challenge her to the task."

"You know I have repeatedly said I never asked him for such information, mother," replied Constance, nearly bursting into tears with vexation.

"Had he been sincere in his attentions to you, Constance, he would not have wanted asking for such necessary information," returned Mrs. Elliot. "But I fear he is no good—in fact, we shall count him such until he shall make known more of his circumstances."

"But Master Elliot, what says he to the young man?" inquired Briefwell.

"Alas!" replied Mrs. Elliot, "my husband knows but little about it; in fact he considers it at an end some time ago, as he flatly denied the young man admittance to the house on his first uninvited visit."

"It is certainly not in his favour to be so secret, I must admit," rejoined Briefwell. "I trust he is not one of those fashionable gallants who are such pests to society, and such a disgrace to our Court; I know much of them, from my business with the Solicitor General, and I also know that the peace of more families than one has been destroyed by their licentious and dissolute conduct."

"Constance possesses a miniature," replied Mrs. Elliot, "which, if she likes, she can show you. I fear he is not respectable, or his conduct would be more candid. The miniature, Constance; fetch it, and show it to Mr. Briefwell."

"It is here," exclaimed Constance, and drawing a small golden locket from her bosom, she handed it to Briefwell; at the same time averting her face from his glance, for tears were standing in her eyes, which wanted but a sigh to send them gushing forth.

"By Heaven, I guessed aright!" exclaimed Briefwell, as, pressing upon a spring, the locket flew open, and disclosed to his view the features of Arthur Latymer.

"You know him, then," cried Constance, stepping towards him, her bosom racked by doubt and fear lest he should disclose some unwelcome news.

"I do," replied Master Briefwell.

"His name!" inquired Mrs. Elliot. "Is it Arthur Latymer?"

"No," answered Briefwell.

"Oh, then, in mercy tell me, I implore you, and relieve me from the anguish which now racks my heart," exclaimed Constance, in accents of the most poignant grief.

"And is this a faithful resemblance of the person we have been mentioning?" asked Briefwell of the troubled maiden.

"'Tis his very self," replied Constance.

"Then this is the portrait of George Villiers, Duke of Buckingham, the favourite cavalier of the king, and the boon companion of the villainous Rochester."

"Merciful Heaven! can this be true?" exclaimed Constance, and giving vent to her grief she sank into a chair, and shed a flood of tears.

"My suspicions are verified," said Mrs. Elliot. "I always reckoned him some butterfly lover with an assumed name."

"He could not be a more unprincipled one," replied Briefwell. "Possessing features and form of a handsome appearance, his addresses are generally favourably received by the various women he pays court to, for they are as numerous as the moons in a year. He has mistresses for every day in the week, and seldom carries on an acquaintance with any of them beyond a few weeks."

"Base, perfidious man !" sobbed Constance.

"I am well pleased with this discovery, friend Briefwell," said Mrs. Elliot. "I suppose, Constance, your hopes of becoming a duchess are not strong enough to allow you to favour this dissembler's visits to you any more ?"

"I will never see him again," replied Constance, smothering her tears.

"That is a brave resolution, if strictly kept," exclaimed Briefwell. "Depend upon it, dear Constance, he means you nothing honourable, or he would not thus have deceived you. To my certain knowledge there are four women of fashion at this present time his avowed mistresses. Why, his conquests in love surpass even those of the king himself. See him no more, Constance."

"I have determined, and I will keep my vow," replied Constance.

"That is a noble resolution," replied her mother. "Oh, Constance, you have removed a weight of stone from my heart," she resumed, tenderly embracing her.

"For the present farewell," said Briefwell, as he was preparing to take his leave.

"Stay, I will rejoin my husband with you," replied Mrs. Elliot; then whispering to him in an under tone, she said, "At present he must know nothing of this disclosure. I trust there will be no further occasion for concealment, but that she will at once and for ever banish his memory from her heart."

"I trust so, and shall keep your counsel," answered Briefwell; and after taking an affectionate leave of Constance, he left the room, accompanied by Mrs. Elliot.

Left to herself, Constance sank into a chair, and taking the miniature of her faithless lover in her hand, she gazed upon it with a sorrowful, heart-broken look, but suddenly she was overcome by her grief, for burying her face in her hands, she sought fresh relief in tears.

Lawrence Wood, who had watched the departure of Master Briefwell and Mrs. Elliot from the room, had tapped slightly at the door for some time, but not receiving any answer, and knowing Constance to be within, he gently opened the door, and entered the apartment. Here he beheld her weeping, with the miniature in her lap, and going softly up to her, unperceived, he took it up, and could hardly restrain a curse when he found it to be the portrait of Arthur Latymer.

As he stood gazing on the likeness, his presence was noticed by Constance, who endeavoured to snatch it from him, but failing in this, she begged of him to return it, and then respectfully reproached him for his intrusion into her presence.

"Constance, hear me before you judge," he replied. "I knocked for admittance, and receiving no answer I entered. Had it been the original of that bauble there," he added, pointing to the portrait, "he would have been welcome, I doubt not."

"You would not say so, Lawrence, if you knew who the original really was," answered Constance.

"How can I doubt? is it not Arthur Latymer, your favoured, mysterious lover?" asked Lawrence.

"And that Arthur Latymer is no other than the famous Duke of Buckingham! Now, what do you say to his being welcome?"

"The Duke of Buckingham!" exclaimed Lawrence, in surprise and amazement.

"He is no other," returned Constance, closing the miniature in its case, and dashing it into the fire. "And as the Duke of Buckingham, he can be no company for a tradesman's daughter. Added to this, he has basely

Vide page 51.

deceived me, and were he King Charles himself I would be no longer fooled by him." Having given breath to her offended pride, which had been pent up within her breast ever since the disclosure of her lover's duplicity, Constance paced the room in vexation and anger. Lawrence was completely staggered with the disclosure that had been made to him; but having witnessed Constance's treatment of the miniature, he judged that the original was in no great favour at this moment, so he took courage and addressed her on the subject.

"And whom may we thank for this information, Constance?" he inquired.

"It was Mr. Briefwell, who having called to see my father, was shewn the portrait, and at once recognised the likeness. He is in the habit of seeing the duke, daily," replied Constance.

"It seems probable; but too good, I fear, to be true," thought Lawrence; then addressing Constance, he observed, "But can you so easily dispose of him, now; consider, Constance, he is a great man, a duke, and a match with him *must* prove a happy one, for 'twould make you—a duchess!"

"And think you, Lawrence, I prize happiness in greatness? No! as Arthur Latymer I could have loved him; aye, though he were a beggar. But now I despise him for his trickery! A duchess, indeed! Oh, no; his intentions inclined not that way—the great Duke of Buckingham, the rival libertine of our unprincipled monarch, has too many powerful attractions at Court to look down upon a poor citizen's daughter for a partner! But he is banished for ever from my memory; I now despise him as much as I might have loved him."

Constance here turned aside, hiding her face with her hands, but not so

7.

successfully as to prevent Lawrence catching a glimpse of a few tears which trickled down her snowy cheeks.

"But if the haughty Duke of Buckingham would not condescend to wed with a citizen's daughter," observed Lawrence, taking Constance gently by the hand, "there are others whose hearts are more fervent and sincere in their love, though their name is of not quite so high a sounding. So banish not all for one, Constance. You must not take a vow of eternal celibacy, remember."

"Ah! Lawrence!" she answered, trying to appear composed in the midst of her tears; "I have no heart to give, now. 'Tis, I fear, lost upon a worthless speculation."

"Say not so, Constance," he replied; "we have too long been familiar with each other's dispositions to require such formalities as strangers have in their acquaintance. Promise me but your hand, and as I live I will swear to win your heart: I would die, at least, to deserve it. Look upon this intruder as one who would seek you for a jewel he might possess, and when he had obtained it, would leave you to solitude, misery, and shame. Oh, Constance, reject not the sincere for the unsincere. True, I cannot boast of the title of a duke, but I can glory in the character of an honest man, and one whose heart ne'er knew care, till pierced by the bright love glittering from those eyes!"

Taking her hand within his own, he knelt before her, and conjured to her memory the many fond meetings they had experienced : the constant pledges of affection she had vowed to keep; and pourtrayed in glowing terms the happiness it would give her parents to see them united.

"Lawrence, I know I have deeply wounded your honest heart," replied Constance; "and the bitter pangs of disappointment which now wring my own is a fit retribution for it. I have been deceived by him I fondly loved; but as I hope to live, I could not love that man again, though the wealth of kingdoms were beneath my feet. If with the chance of reclaiming my lost heart, you'll take my hand,—for once, for ever, I now give it you!"

"Thanks! dearest Constance, for that gift!" exclaimed the passionate lover, in ecstacies with his mistress's kindness; and pressing her hand to his lips he responded, "And never shall this gift be forgotten while I've life!—and may death be my reward if I slight it!"

Constance and Lawrence Wood were thus, once again, avowed lovers. How fondly beat the heart of the delighted youth to find himself once more in possession of the object of his adoration; and the maiden herself was no less pleased, for, stung to the quick by the deception which the duke had practised towards her, and disgusted by the recital which Briefwell had given her of his numerous amours, and the variety of his acknowledged mistresses, she felt all that pride and triumph so dear to the breast of an injured woman, when she fancies she is revenging the wrongs she has received from a faithless lover, by accepting another in his stead.

A fond and uniting embrace sealed the protestations so newly made by the lovers; Constance having agreed to keep out of the way, and leave the management of the duke's (for we shall call him Arthur Latymer, no longer) reception to Lawrence, whenever he might arrive. In those few moments the anguish of months was banished for ever!—in that solemn pledge made by Constance all the injuries and pangs she had caused the heart of Lawrence to writhe under, were forgotten! And joy—pure unalloyed joy—was found to exist in the fond and mutual kiss paid to the god of love as a trophy of sincerity, by these re-united lovers; for the heart of Lawrence Wood bounded with as much delight, when placing his arm round the taper waist of his mistress, in leading her from the room, as did the heart of Caesar when he gained his first wreath of Roman glory!

CHAPTER VIII.

THE Fleece Tavern in the Old Jewry was, in the reign of Charles the Second, one of the principal taverns in the city of London. It was the constant resort of merchants, bankers, first-rate tradesmen, and not unfrequently courtiers and statesmen, and was much used by clerks and city gallants in the evening. On the day that Master Elliot's house was thrown open, and declared free from the plague, an holiday was given to the whole of his establishment, and Scrubb—the poor, neglected, plague-dreading Scrubb—was not slow in availing himself of the opportunity thus afforded him to pay a visit to his dear Pauline, who, as it has been before mentioned, held a sort of confidential situation under the cook of the establishment; always coming in, however, for an equal share of what was turned into money by Dame Sirloin, her commander-in-chief. Perhaps, also, it would be as well to mention that if it had been possible for Scrubb to have been punctual in his visits to his mistress, many of the sly pickings which took place occasionally would very likely have fallen to his share, instead of finding their way into the hands of strangers.

Scrubb was in glorious spirits, for he had glorious news to tell Pauline: besides, he was enabled to inform her now, by ocular demonstration, that through the excellent and powerful qualities of his famous " Royal-antiplague-infection-exterminating-health preserving-Narcotic," and the efficacy of the " Never-failing, slightly-drawing, hardly-paining, royal London Coronation breast salve;" which he had three times a day with coarse flannel on his breast-bone, his knee-caps, his elbow joints, and his shoulder-blades, till those par s of his body were fretted and inflamed into a violent rash. These precious antidotes he had brought with him, and he intended trying his persuasive powers to the utmost in the hope of prevailing upon his Pauline to adopt them immediately.

By means of a back passage which led from the Old Jewry into Grocer's Hall court, Scrubb attained the kitchen door, and pausing to look through a cracked window before he went in, he took a tolerable survey of the whole kitchen. Seated in a large arm-chair, before a blazing fire, sat Dame Sirloin, sweating and blowing like a baited bull, wiping the perspiration off her face much in the same style as a modern servant-maid would mop a doorway, whilst poor little Pauline was slaving away, doing all the work (which all deputies ought to do, and get the least pay): she was now stirring the contents of an immense copper pan, which was steaming on the fire; then she had to run across the kitchen, and attend to some mince meat which was slowly basting on a little oven; then the plucking of four large fowls which had to be boiled, served up, and eaten by four o'clock (and this was past two) —to keep the pig turning which was roasting at the fire; to turn out the hot cinders from making war upon the fat in the dish beneath; to make three jellies, two pigeon tarts, and mix a syllabub. These various occupations kept the little maid upon a continual trot, and almost, in the heat of the confusion, drove all thoughts of Scrubb out of her head.

Not deeming it prudent to enter the territory of Dame Sirloin at the present momentous crisis, Scrubb gently opened the window, which caused Pauline to look up, and giving one loud scream for joy, she let drop the fowl she had prepared for dressing, flew to the door, and in the next instant was swinging round Scrubb's neck with both arms, and kissing him from his forehead to his chin, forgetting all her troubles in the joy of meeting him again.

Scrubb was not backward in repaying the favours so plentifully bestowed upon him by Pauline, and after the first congratulations were over, he commenced a faithful account to her how he had doctored himself throughout the whole period, and recommended her to adopt the same precautions without delay.

"Stay, dear Scrubb," said Pauline, interrupting him; "with this little key we can let ourselves into my own room, and we can there talk without being disturbed. Come, this way, Scrubb;" and leading the way down a short flight of steps, he followed her till they came to a low stone kitchen, which Pauline informed him was her own "private apartment."

"Well, and a very nice apartment it is, too," replied Scrubb, glancing round: "there's plenty of room for a table and a few chairs, and a small chest of drawers, and with the aid of all these things a loving couple like ourselves might live very comfortably: don't you think so, Pauline?"

"Shame upon you, Scrubb, to talk about such matters now! I am quite shocked!" replied the maid, rather timidly. "But I won't be angry with you now, Scrubb, for I am so glad to see you—you cannot think how glad I am!"

"Ah, my dear Pauline!" replied Scrubb, pulling a long face, "you would never have seen me alive again, if it had not been for the great care I have taken of myself, coupled with the very skilful medicines I have been fortunate enough to obtain. I would recommend you to take some of them, too, Pauline, and for that purpose I have brought them with me."

"Oh, have you?" observed the maiden, laughing, "let me look at them, Scrubb."

"The first is a famous narcotic, which I purchased of a flying apothecary in Brydge-street, on the first of April for a dollar and a half. 'Tis a precious mixture!"

"What? nauseous, you mean," suggested Pauline.

"No; I mean precious; rare, valuable, inestimable, untastable, unsayable, precious!"

"And pray what is this, Scrubb?" asked the inquisitive young cook, trying to open the box of "anti-infection salve."

"Why, that is a still more valuable remedy than the other," replied her lover; "it must be tried to be known; you must try it, Pauline; I have brought it with me on purpose. You must rub it into the flesh with your right hand, moistened with eagle's blood, every third hour—mind, every *third* hour: it must be an odd time of day, or the charm is lost. First, on your breast, eight times each way; then on your knee-caps; seven times on the right knee, and five times on the left knee—mind, seven and five, for that makes twelve, and twelve is a lucky number in physic. Next, you must rub each of your elbow joints three times; and, lastly, between your shoulder blades across and across eight times; and this must be done every third hour. Would you like to try it, Pauline?"

"Not I indeed! Why, Scrubb, you have been quite spoiled through being cooped up in your master's house six weeks. Throw the rubbish into the fire."

"Forgive me, Pauline, if I have offended you," replied Scrubb, "but I was only speaking in praise of the 'royal anti-infection salve,' nothing more. But the 'narcotic decoction' will suit you best, with a pill four times a day, and a gargle of vinegar to wash the mouth after every meal."

Here, pulling from his pocket a small box of pills, he offered them to Pauline.

"I want no such trash," exclaimed the maiden; "and I rather think you would look a little better if you took less doctor-drink, and a trifle more of wholesome food; so come, sit down, I dare say I can find a snack of some sort for you," and pushing him into a chair, she hastily threw a white napkin over the table, and going to a side cupboard, brought forth the remains of a choice dish of mince-meat, two eel-pies, a large piece of corn beef, a quince pie, and part of a calf's head, with a variety of cold jellies, syllabubs, sauces, preserved jams, strawberries and cream ; and the whole course was wound up by a dish of tripe and fried onions. This choice variety was the fragments of a large dinner which had been provided at the tavern the day before, and given by the Merchant Tailors' Company to their different officers for the forthcoming year. Scrubb, who had been terribly pinched ever since he begun to perform quarantine in his master's house, fell to without another word ; and not even the charms of Pauline herself could allure him from such a luxuriant repast.

"I hope you will find it to your liking," said Pauline, as she stood watching him conveying the food to its hiding-place in ladlefuls ; I thought that out of such a variety you might find something you would like. Now make a good meal, and I have part of a bottle of Burgundy, and a posset of sack here, which will do as a finish : by-the-bye, you must first taste this bottle of ale which I have kept for you ; I think you will say it is charming ;" and as she spoke she handed a tankard foaming with the ale to her lover, whose only answer to her remarks was by nods of the head and winking of the eyes, and reaching out his hand poured the contents of the tankard down his throat, and then resumed his eating as ravenously as before.

Pauline herself could not help watching him, for in less than ten minutes he had cleared the contents of two dishes, when making a sort of a halt, he mumbled out, his mouth crammed with food, "that he should like to taste the sack and the Burgundy, to try which he liked best."

This request being duly acquiesced in by the fair Pauline, she poured out two small-sized tankards of each, and placed them before him. These immediately shared the fate of the others, and after he had gorged away in a most voracious manner for nearly an hour, he began to comment upon every dish which had been set before him, and as he threw down his knife and fork, he asked Pauline, in a bloated, half-choked voice, "if there was any cold soup in the house."

"There is not," was the reply.

"Well, then, as that is the case," said Scrubb, puffing and blowing from the effects of the gorge he had been indulging in, "I must needs put up with a sop of this brown bread in sack ;" so saying, he steeped the bread, and went on eating it, taking an occasional sip at the Burgundy by way of a rest. The quantity he had eaten and drank began, in a measure, to animate him, for his eyes began to sparkle, and a smile actually played upon his countenance ; a thing never witnessed by any one who knew him since the day of his leaving off his infant dress for that of a more manly attire. Taking Pauline by the waist, he drew her towards him, and slyly stealing a kiss exclaimed,

"I am so glad my master has opened his house, Pauline."

"Are you, indeed ?" replied the maiden ; "well, so am I. But what makes you glad of it, Scrubb ?"

"What makes me glad of it ?" he answered, "why, two—I may say three—very strong, powerful reasons."

"Oh, tell me, what are they ?" inquired Pauline, very anxiously.

"I will," he replied. "The first is—though stop, I should like a drop of sack before I begin ; that will help me to remember it."

Pauline reached the tankard to pour him some out, but Scrubb, impatient for the draught, seized the bottle, and applying it to his lips never took it from thence till he had drained its very dregs, and breathing forth a long loud "Ba-a-h !" he hurled the empty flask to the other end of the apartment.

" Now my dear Scrubb you must tell me these reasons," rejoined Pauline, half glad in her own mind that the sack was all gone, as there would be no more interruption from that quarter.

" I will, I will," answered Scrubb, his voice getting rather thick, and his head a little confused: " the first ; let me see, the first is—ah! yes, that's the first ; the first is—I see you, my dear Pauline ; and when I see you, I don't care who I don't see, or who dont see us. The second, that's the next reason—yes, second is the next, the second is, that I never come to see you without your giving me plenty to eat ; plenty of the best, too !"

" And don't I give you some of the best to drink, besides, Scrubb ?" asked Pauline.

" You do ! yes, you do ! This is the best sack I ever tasted ; I suppose that is accounted for by my never having tasted any before : eh, Pauline, is'nt that the reason ?"

" I should guess so ; but this other, the third reason, what is that ?" inquired Pauline, rather desirous to learn what it was.

" The third ! O yes, I remember : why, Pauline, I was saying that—let me see ; I've told you one and two ; the third is, that I never see you without thinking what a nice little figure you would look behind a tripe-shop table ! I have a great fancy for the (hiccup) butchering line !"

" Then you would make me your servant, I suppose ?" said Pauline, artfully.

" Servant, did you say, Pau—(hiccup) Pauline ?" stammered out Scrubb, evidently much intoxicated, and growing furious with the effects of it : " No ; you should be like a queen—a queen of (hiccup) sheep's heads and cow's feet. A servant, indeed ! Mistress Pauline Scrubb a servant !— Ha ! ha ! ha ! Why, I would keep a dozen for you, my angel ! They should wa—(hiccup) wait on you while you ate, while you slept, while you walked abroad, and while you sold tripe by the pound, yard, or belly-piece ! And I, when I was my own master and nobody's man, I would take my favourite mixture of calomel and opium, the finest thing ever made up for the (hiccup) for the miserables ever was known, and wash it all down with stuff like this !"

And seizing on the Burgundy flask, he applied it to his lips, and took a long and hearty drink.

" Now don't drink any more, dear, kind, little Scrubb," said Pauline to her lover very tenderly. " I am sure you have had enough."

" Enough, Pauline !" roared out the offended swain at this hint of mistresses to be temperate. " Why, do you think I would drink more than enough to make me (hiccup) comfortable ? I won't be allowanced, Pauline ; recollect that, now ; that's a lesson for you against you are Mistress Scrubb. I cant't bear restriction in the victualling department ; and this is such beautiful drink that I should like to (hiccup) swim in it, I should."

Seizing hold of the bottle, he again took another draught, and began to sing very loudly, battering the table with his fists by way of chorus.

" Here's a health to jolly Cromwell !"

ran the first line of his song, which he suddenly broke off by seeing his mistress lay violent hands on the bottle, and bear it away to a small cupboard in the corner of the room, upon observing which he staggered forwards.

" Now, Scrubb, you must not have any more," said Pauline, evidently getting alarmed for the consequences. " I will bring you a whole bottle to-morrow."

" I say I will," bawled Scrubb, struggling with her to force open the door of the cupboard. " Do you think I don't know when I've had (hiccup)

enough ? I'm not getting drunk ; so open the door, I say, or I'll pull th
whole down together !"

" Now, Scrubb, my dear Scrubb, pray be quiet," said Pauline.

" Give me the bottle, then," he replied. " I'll drink as much as I like,
and then I'll (hiccup) call for more," roared the infuriated youth to the
friendly appeal of his mistress.

" To-morrow ; you shall have plenty to-morrow," she answered, trying to
lead him away.

" To-morrow's not to-day," growled Scrubb; and laying hold of the
handle of the door he tried to force it open, which Pauline resisted with all
her force. " Leave go, Pauline ; leave go, I say ; I will (hiccup) have one
more taste."

" Not a drop !" was her reply.

" What ! do you refuse, and try to govern me ?" exclaimed Scrubb, rather
enraged at her interposition. " Then here goes !" and with an herculean
effort he tugged and wrenched at the door of the cupboard, as Pauline did
all in her power to prevent him, by pushing against it with both her hands,
till, finding her power of resistance gradually getting weaker and weaker,
beneath a superior strength, she was obliged to desist, when Scrubb, pulling
it towards him with great violence, brought the whole cupboard of glasses,
shelves, bottles, pickle-jars, preserves, platters, jugs, bowls, and jelly-pots
down upon him, which, overturning him in their descent, the whole came to
the floor with a tremendous crash, accompanied by a loud scream from Pauline, who ran about the room wringing her hands in despair.

Scrubb lay for some moments as if stunned by the fall, but he was soon
struggling and kicking beneath the load of pots, pans, and jars, by which he
was nearly smothered, to gain a release ; which, after much trouble, he
effected, just at the moment that Dame Sirloin entered the room.

" Hey-day ! marry, come up !" exclaimed the old lady, as she lifted up her
hands in amazement at beholding such a litter of articles on the floor, and a
man sprawling on his back in the midst of them. Pauline, knowing the
result of such an uproar, had seated herself in a chair, and was busily employed drying up her tears with her clean white apron, as fast as they flowed
—perhaps faster.

" Well, mother Lucifer ! and who called you up, you plague-stricken old
hag ?" inquired Scrubb, rather rudely, of the lady of the cooks. " If we
had wanted you we could have called you ! and you would have been more
welcome if you had brought another flask of that fine sack of yours !"

" Oh ! dear ! oh, dear ! oh, dear !" sobbed Pauline from beneath her
apron ; and after this brief epistle she bellowed forth her tears, louder and
faster than ever !

" What means all this !—Pauline, speak ! Who is this rascal ?" demanded
the kitchen abbess of her maid, in an authoritative tone. " And pray how
comes he here ?"

" Oh, he is an honest young man, madam : depend upon it, he is ;" replied Pauline, still sobbing with grief.

" Ah ! but I doubt it !" answered dame Sirloin.

" I thank you for that (hiccup) for that compliment," stammered Scrubb,
and staggering towards her, he seized her in his arms and threatened to hurl
her down the stairs that stood before them, if she dared to say another word.

" John ! Thomas ! Anne ! Peggy ! murder ! thieves ! help !" was the only
reply made by his adversary ; who had taken such a fast hold of the balustrades, that she prevented him from putting his threat into execution.

Pauline ran to her mistress's aid, but it was in vain, for Scrubb was
straining every nerve to force the old woman from her grasp, and hurl her
headlong amidst the crew who were galloping up stairs to her rescue ; while

dame Sirloin herself, anticipating his thoughts, made good her hold on the balustrades by griping a handful of hair from his head, as an extra support for her.

Several stout men and two women now arrived to the dame's assistance, and seeing the rather dangerous position in which she was placed, proceeded at once to liberate her from the fangs of her enraged antagonist. This was a work of some trouble; for having released their captive, they had now to conquer the capturer. Scrubb defeated all their attemps for some time; till at length, overpowered by numbers, he was secured; and three pair of arms tightly held him in surveillance.

"Bring the villain down stairs!" commanded dame Sirloin to her victorious vassals; and seizing hold of Pauline by the wrist, she pushed her down before her, adding, by way of encouragement to her, a few words of advice, such as—"Well, hussy; when next you take your sweetheart into your chamber; I'd advise you to be a little quieter! He'll make a tender rib for you, no doubt! The wine seems to have flown about merrily—by my virginity, but its fine doings—fine doings! But I'll soon settle all this bobbery; your darling shall pass the night in the City Compter, instead of in his lady-love's arms! Bring the sneaking varlet along! I'll teach him to come here nosing for broken victuals and untapped wine-flasks; the hound! the cur! the wretch! the beggar! the thief!" Venting these epithets and remarks, as she pushed Pauline on before her, she led the way into the front hall of the tavern, and there brought the whole party to a general halt.

"Call the city watch! seize and bind that loitering vagabond, and let's see what he has stolen," exclaimed dame Sirloin, upon drawing up her party to a general muster; and three of the men-servants proceeded to put in force the commands of the head cook of the establishment. But Scrubb thought otherwise, for exerting all his energy in his own defence, he laid about him in real good earnest, for the attack upon him had quite sobered him. Seizing upon an oaken staff which was standing in a corner, he played such a lively tune on the heads of his foes, that in a few minutes two out of the three were laying upon their backs, and the other more inclined to give up the combat than sustain it.

In an adjoining room were assembled a party of gallants, busily engaged playing at dice, but hearing the noise of the fray, they had come out to witness it, and see fair play done to all parties. They seemed quite delighted with Scrubb's prowess, and cheered him on to the attack, till his third adversary, from the *striking* example before him, gave in, and declined any further connexion with him.

"By Saint Paul, but he's a brave lad!" exclaimed one of the gallants. "Pray, mother hell-cat," he resumed, addressing himself to dame Sirloin, "what's the cause of all this?"

"Oh a matter of nothing at all," she replied, "only that the skulking vagabond, that you please to call a brave fellow, there, has smashed a lot of glass, china, and pots and pans; to say nothing of my jellies and gooseberry jam; brave as he is, I doubt whither you'll liberate him by paying for the damage done; and he shall to jail for a rogue and a thief as he is!" she exclaimed with some vehemence.

"I'm neither rogue nor thief, mother Fireblow," replied Scrubb, stung to the quick by such an accusation. "I am an honest man's servant, and I do my duty honestly to him; and my master, Matthew Elliot, the stationer of Cheapside, will be answerable for my character, I'll be sworn!"

"Master Elliot, did you say?" inquired the same gallant, who had previously spoken in his favour; "do you mean him who has lately had the plague in his house, and who has a pretty daughter named Constance—is he your master?"

Vide page 59.

" The same man," answered Scrubb; "and a better master never trod London stones, as he is, too !"

" Then I will be your friend in this matter, my good fellow," replied the gallant. " I know your master well, and too much respect him to allow one of his servants to be placed in jeopardy. Here, old fire and brimstone," said he, addressing himself to dame Sirloin, " I guess that will satisfy all demands upon this young man, and leave a gold piece or two to buy salve for the heads of those he has so well drubbed ;" and as he spoke he threw a purse into her hand. " So, youngster, step in this room, and let's have a glass to your master's good health !"

Scrubb, who was astounded at this conduct, looked on in silence, unable to make any reply ; and Mother Fireblow, as he had called her, just gave one glance at the contents of the purse, and being satisfied that it was genuine coin, made a low curtsey to the gallants, and hobbled off ; followed, however, by her troop of emissaries for their share of the prize money.

Poor Pauline had been left unnoticed and neglected by them all, until the young gallant who had been so generous advanced towards her, and asking her troubles, for she was sobbing with grief, tried to assauge her tears by several kisses which he forced upon her.

This caused the interference of Scrubb, who having explained in what way Pauline was peculiarly interested in his welfare, was allowed to repeat the dose, and lead her from the spot; having faithfully promised to join his friendly gallants in the adjoining room, in a few moments.

Proceeding with Pauline to her apartment, Scrubb tried to pacify her by his protestations of constancy, and vowed that she should be his wife, when-

8.

ever the plague ceased.   Placing full reliance in his pledges, Pauline allowed him to depart, and he left her with an aching heart to keep his word with the gallants.

CHAPTER IX.

THE three gallants who had been attracted from their amusements by the fracas raised by Scrubb and his captors, were no other than the Duke of Buckingham, his friend Vincent Palmer, and the swaggering bully, Captain Blount.   The duke was overjoyed to ascertain that Scrubb was a servant of Master Elliot's, and immediately proceeded to concoct a plan with his dissolute companions how they might turn the circumstance to their advantage, by obtaining an entrance in the stationer's house, and consequently an interview with Constance.

"The fellow seems a simpleton," said Vincent Palmer to the duke; "I should think a well-filled purse would win him over to your purpose.   That point gained, a rope ladder at the girl's window, on a dark night, would effect the remainder."

"Now I should suggest a more open-handed, soldier-like piece of business altogether," exclaimed Captain Blount, in a haughty, swaggering tone: "Were it my case, and I was in love with the girl, and wished to carry her off, I would accomplish it at all risks.   I would proceed to the house and demand her of her parents, and if they refused me, why, gunpowder and cannon-balls!   I'd slice them all into mince-meat, and fall covered with wounds and deluged with blood in the arms of my adorable."

"Ha! ha! ha! good again, Blount;" replied the duke, laughing heartily. "How easy it is to scoff at the cannon's roar when you are beyond its reach; or to recommend cutting and slaying, when safely ensconced behind a wine flagon.   Both of you may have offered me good advice, but there is a portion of force mixed up with it, that pleases me not.   Stratagem is ever my favourite remedy; it is by stratagem more than by any other means that that crack-brained fellow Rochester has gained such an ascendancy at Court. My plan is simply this; and if you think proper each of you to lend me your aid, why I shall esteem it as a high favour to the day of my death, or if you should both happen to die before me, I will subscribe a dollar to erect a leaden monument to your memories, and send my three men-servants in full dress to march in procession at your funeral, and mourn for you threefold for myself.   My measures for attacking the fort are these; to speak in a warlike point of view, I should first undermine it, and then, springing a mine, force an entrance, and carry the breach in the confusion."

"Ha! ha! ha!" laughed Vincent Palmer; "and bear off the prize while the besieged and besiegers were fighting for it."

"Exactly so," answered the duke.

"Clandestine, by Mars!" ejaculated Blount, draining his goblet of Burgundy to the dregs.

"To the point, friends; to the point," resumed the duke; "As parsons, doctors, undertakers, nurses, and maniac preachers are now more numerous than tolerable, I mean to emerge forth as the Prophet of the Age; become Lilly himself, who I know is now comfortably settled in Normandy, and is in no great haste to return here, since matters have so greatly altered at Court.   With the gaping, superstitious few who have never seen him, I shall pass off as the miracle himself. Such a one is this serving-loon of Elliot's ; and I am very sure that the whole family themselves have never seen or visited him, as the stationer is quite another way of thinking."

" A most excellent plan, indeed," replied Vincent ; " but how will you deceive this fellow, who has already seen you ?"

" Cut off his throat," growled Captain Blount.

" Easily enough, as you shall hear," answered Buckingham ; " See, here he comes."

As he spoke, Scrubb pushed the door a little way open, and stood bowing and scraping at the entrance of the room, seemingly afraid to enter.

" Come in, young man ;" said Buckingham. " Shut the door, and take a seat in this chair, by the fire ; I have much to say to you."

Scrubb did as he was desired ; though not without eyeing the wine and the sack, as it stood upon the table before him, and longed in his heart to be tasting some of them.

" So you are a servant to that worthy man, Matthew Elliot the stationer, are you ?" questioned Buckingham.

" I am sir," replied Scrubb, modestly.

" How long have you been in his service, pray ?"

" Ever since I was a boy ; I don't even remember entering it," answered Scrubb.

" Oh, then, of course you are on intimate terms with all the family, I guess," suggested Buckingham, inquisitively.

" Why, pretty well, I may say, I am," was the answer given by Scrubb, getting rather confused at such cross-questioning.

" Ah ! so I should guess ; and being a lively, comely youth, no doubt you have made some approaches to the fair Constance herself, ere now ?"

" To Constance herself !" muttered Scrubb in surprise ; " why the idea never entered my head. Me, a poor working lad, have anything to say to young mistress Constance ! besides, if I had it would be of no use, for she has two lovers, I believe, already. Lawrence Wood, our apprentice, I'll answer for it, loves her as his own life ; but there are strange sayings going about, that some fine gentleman in disguise is in love with her, and tries to see her very often. I know nothing certain myself about it; no more than yourselves."

" No, no, certainly not," answered the duke. " The main purport of my calling you here was to prove the respect I bore to your worthy master, by rescuing and entertaining his servant. So, come ; drink to his health in this brimming goblet ; and handing a foaming goblet of wine to Scrubb he made him repeat the health to his master, which was responded to by all.

" And I, under present circumstances," rejoined Vincent Palmer, " having had the honour of being in the fair Constance's company, on a festival day in Saint Paul's, last month, can do no less than reply to that toast, by pledging her in a bumper ! Come, friends, no less ; 'tis a cheap offering to the shrine of beauty. Here's long life, health, and happiness to the most brilliant gem of the City of London, the fair and beauteous Constance !"

The advertised honours were paid to this toast in due form ; and every one of them sat down, charged with an extra pint of Burgundy.

" Having now carried it so far," exclaimed Buckingham, there is but one thing more to allude to, before we part ; and that is—in another pint bumper, though, no less—that she may be allied in love to the man of her heart's choice !"

" Provided he be a soldier," growled Blount.

" Bah !" exclaimed the duke, " you're drunk ! To the choice of Constance ! May the man of her heart win her and possess her !"

Draining off another pint this toast was also drunk, and by this time

Scrubb had very nearly settled down to the easy, unconsciable state he was in previous to the affray with dame Sirloin: he had slid down in his chair, and, ramming his hands in his pockets, kept repeating for some minutes the subject of the last pledges, to whose celebrity he had been drinking.

"May the man of her heart live happy, as the brilliantest gem of the City of London! Bravo! yes, that was it."

Then, after musing a little while to himself, during which period he was narrowly watched by his three entertainers, he suddenly broke forth into an astonishing flow of speech.

"Constance! the brilliantest—happy man of her heart—yes, gentlemen, there was a time when I fancied I was; but that was before I ever knew Pauline; for Constance has at times bestowed some very sweet smiles upon me. But who knows; she may have a worse one than poor Scrubb; and I don't care who I have, so as I live to be rich enough to set up a tripe-shop."

"And pray, Scrubb," inquired the Duke of Buckingham, "should you like to know for certain whether you will ever have a tripe-shop, be rich, be happy, and be wedded to this maid of your heart—your Pauline? In truth, should you like to have the future path of your life laid open to your view, and all your happy days brought before you at a glance?"

"More than any thing else I should like that," answered Scrubb, "because then I should know whether I was to die with the plague, or what else, and when or where, that I might be at rest as to what disease to purchase medicines for; whether it be the ague, the dropsy, the yellow fever, king's evil, or broken heart, for I am in misery to know."

"Then I can give you an opportunity, if you like to avail yourself of it, and you shall receive this information from the lips of the greatest prophet of the land, the mighty Sir William Lilly himself, who is an intimate friend of mine, and would do any thing to oblige me," replied the duke, trying to raise his imaginary hopes and fears to the highest pitch.

"What! the great—real Sir William Lilly himself!

"The same man."

"And do you know him?"

"Infinitely well."

"And would he condescend to tell me, a poor servant, my fortune?" inquired Scrubb in a paroxysm of delight, too great to be firmly believed in at first.

"If I were to ask him he would immediately comply," said the duke.

"And will you really ask him to tell me my fortune!" inquired Scrubb, completely staggered by the anticipation of such a great honour.

"I will."

"Then I hope you will be the happy man, with the brilliant heart, to wed the brightest gem of the city of London, Constance; for I think you are all three in love with her, you speak so highly of her."

"But how will you manage to see Sir William?" said the duke, doubtingly. "That is a question I had nearly forgotten. He is a proscribed man for his conduct in the time of Cromwell's life; he leaves London for France in two days, and if you do not see him before that time, you may never have the opportunity again."

"Tell me where he lives, and I would go to his house in the night time," suggested Scrubb.

"Alas! that would be impossible. He would not for a thousand guineas let any one know where he resides in London. Could you not contrive to let him come to your master's house and see you? He would come in disguise, and if you could persuade Constance to have her fortune told, too, it would be a capital chance for her, for there is not his equal in Europe—nay, in the whole world!"

"Capital!" answered Scrubb, "and so it would; but I must not let my master or Lawrence know it, or I should be kicked out of the house."

"That may be avoided by letting no one know but Constance," replied Buckingham. "Tell her who it is, and that it is a great favour done to you, and all may go well."

"But when will he come?" inquired Scrubb eagerly, "for I fear Master Elliot will shortly leave London for some time, with the whole of his family, and then there will be no opportunity left."

"Why, in that case," replied Buckingham, "I could see Sir William to-morrow, and he would come at night. I will let you know exactly, if you will be at the Conduit in the Chepe to-morrow, as the clock of Bow Church strikes twelve. So come, friends, we will even pay our learned astrologer a visit to-night before he goes to rest, to ensure his visit to Master Elliot's to-morrow night."

Seeing the signal was for marching, and feeling rather uncomfortable in such fine company, Scrubb was not long in rising from his seat and making towards the door, the lock of which, seizing in his hand, helped him to support his body in the peculiar performance of a very unique and low bow.

"At the Conduit at noon to-morrow," remarked the duke, "you will be informed of Sir William's intentions: meanwhile, let this be a profound secret with all but Constance herself."

"I will be punctual and remember," replied Scrubb.

"This will tend to keep your memory in good order," said the duke, as he hurled a purse of guineas at Scrubb, who, catching it in his hand, made a still lower bow than before, and not daring to look up, turned on his heel and left the room, muttering to himself, as he jinked the purse in his hands, "This will stock me in pills and ointment for six months, and go towards buying the goodwill of a neat little tripe-shop."

The whole of his thoughts during the journey homewards were fixed upon the fate the fortune-teller would draw out for him. Sometimes he thought he would decline it altogether, fearing he should not have courage enough to hear any bad news; but then the chance of hearing some good tidings overturned all those resolutions, and he considered he was a very fortunate youth in meeting with such an unexpected piece of good fortune.

The next morning Scrubb arose before the dawn had appeared, and hesitated within himself, as he was engaged cleaning and preparing the warehouse and counting-room for business, whether he should tell Lawrence of the intended visit of the astrologer. He also began to ponder on what would be the most likely punishment that he would receive from the hands of his master if he discovered him in such a confederacy; but he soon changed his mind, and resolved to see first what news he should hear at the meeting at the Conduit at noon. Every quarter of an hour was eagerly watched and counted till the chimes of Bow Church tolled the hour of noon, then bolting away like a hare at the first sound of the dogs behind her, he never slackened his pace till he reached the Conduit. After having grown impatient by waiting nearly five minutes (and in his state of mind at that moment five minutes was as a whole day), he was suddenly aroused by a hearty slap on the shoulder, and turning round he beheld a stranger wrapped in a large cloak, who, without speaking a word, pushed a slip of paper into his hand, and was instantly lost in the crowded street.

Scrubb's first effort was to read the mysterious epistle, and upon opening it he read the following—"At nine precisely, this evening, the Great Astrologer of the age will visit you: be cautious, secret, and vigilant! at nine you will hear three taps at the door of the back part of the house; be there ready. To fail will endanger many!"

Scrubb was somewhat puzzled by the peculiar tone of the letter, and it also appeared curious to him how so great a man as Lilly should condescend to come to him. But then he had the purse, and if there was any harm in it he could swear he knew nothing of the parties, which he was determined he would do, for he knew there would be some blows struck if Lawrence or his master should happen to find out that he had secretly admitted strangers into the house upon such a pretence.

As the hour of nine grew near, Scrubb displayed much uneasiness, which showed itself very prominently, and happening to wait upon Constance to convey a message to her from Dame Trivet, he was determined to put in a word for himself, and try and persuade her to honour the fortune-teller with her presence. Having knocked at her chamber door, Constance, who was reading at a table, bade him enter. He accordingly did so, and delivered to her the message from the worthy dame. When Constance had heard the message, she signified to him that she would attend to it, and taking up her book again. showed no signs of renewing any conversation with him ; it was, therefore, left to himself to broach the subject.

"I wonder where we may all be in ten years hence, Miss Constance ?" muttered or rather stammered out Scrubb.

"That is a very strange sort of wonder to indulge in, Scrubb ; and whatever could have brought it into your head ?" inquired Constance.

"Why you see, my lady, I am going to have my fortune told to-night, and if I thought the man could tell me, I would ask him whether I should know you in ten years to come," answered Scrubb doubtfully.

"Going to have your fortune told, Scrubb ! and pray who have you engaged to do it ?" asked his mistress.

"Oh, I dare say you would not guess in five years, and perhaps not believe me when I have told you. He is no other than the celebrated Sir William Lilly himself, for a friend of whom I did a good favour, and he thus rewards me," answered Scrubb with much confidence.

"Is he not reckoned very clever ?" asked Constance, inwardly feeling a desire to see the man of renown, especially as he was about to visit their own house that very evening.

"He would be glad to tell you, I know, Miss Constance, for he told me that he had heard of your beauty, and should very much like to consult the planets on your fate. Besides, he told me I was to pass many of my days with a beautiful lady much above my rank."

These and other flattering epithets did the simple Scrubb pour into the ear of his mistress, to induce her to patronise the affair, and by so doing clear himself of any blame for admitting them into the house.

"I should very much like to hear him, and ascertain his guide in these matters," observed Constance.

"Oh, moons, stars, and bright clouds !" answered Scrubb, in the random recollection of his memory.

"If I thought Lawrence would not be there, and that my father might be from home for an hour, I would certainly see him," replied Constance.

"That objection is soon overcome," replied Scrubb. "Your father is going as far as Aldersgate this evening, and Lawrence must be cheated in some way or other."

"Then be careful, and mention it not to him," suggested Constance. "Let me know when they arrive, and I will wait upon them."

Scrubb having thus obtained his mistress's sanction to the meeting, immediately left the apartment, completely overjoyed at his success.

Leaving the room quietly, he was about to retrace his steps gently and noiselessly back to his own apartment; but Lawrence, who with the eye of an hawk, had traced him into the room, suspected some conspiracy wasafloat, and had basely submitted to become a listener to the conversation. He had heard nearly all that had transpired between them, and seizing hold of Scrubb by the ear, he pulled him up from the ground and nearly twisted it out of its socket.

"So, you cunning villain; I find you at some of your old schemes again, but you shall remember it better this time." So saying, the head of poor Scrubb found itself in collision with the wall.

"If you have heard me, Lawrence, I ask your pardon; for I was afraid to tell you at first," muttered Scrubb, in a tone of apology.

"No matter, sir, I suspect some mischief in this; I shall watch your friends, the 'fortune-tellers,' narrowly; and if I find anything suspicious about them I will have them all kicked out of the house, and locked up in the Compter, and you with them for aiding and abetting their cause. In the meantime, I merely charge you to let me also know when they arrive, that I may be present to receive them. You will not forget that."

And Lawrence, shaking his oaken cudgel in the face of Scrubb to frighten him into obedience, left him.

Scrubb was now placed in a peculiar dilemma; he did not know how to act for the best. The fortune teller would be here in a few minutes; he had informed Constance of it privately, and she had consented to hear the astrologer, provided Lawrence was not there, and now Lawrence had overheard all, and had also declared it to be his intention to be there also. "If I run away," thought he, "I may get into a more troublesome family; and therefore I have resolved that Sir William shall tell me first, according to promise, and if he don't happen to prophecy that Lawrence and Constance are to be married, and have a large family of children, I shall have no peace for the next three months to come."

While he sat pondering in this manner, three low taps were heard at the small gate at the back part of the house, and Scrubb hastily proceeded thither on tiptoe, to usher them into the kitchen, which he had swept and garnished for their reception.

Instead of the gallants he had seen at the tavern, Scrubb now saw before him the form of an old man, who was stooping with age, supporting himself with a long staff, and who was wrapped up in a long blue serge cloak; whilst his hair, which was silvery white, hung in streams down his back. His companion was attired in a loose soldier's mantle. Scrubb scanned their features attentively, but could not discern any resemblance to either of the gallants who had so liberally entertained him at the tavern. Leading the way for the astrologer and his assistant, as Scrubb supposed him to be by his bearing a couple of globes and some bundles of paper, he took them into the kitchen, and pulling out a long table, with two chairs, seated them before a large fire.

"I have prevailed on Mistress Constance to visit you here," said Scrubb to the astrologer, as he unfolded his array of mystery upon the table.

"I am right glad of that," answered the astrologer, "for I have heard she is much prized in the city, and I should like to see what fate awaits her future path through this wearisome world; will you let her know I have arrived, young man?"

"I will," replied Scrubb, and he advanced to the door for that purpose, but his progress was for a short time stayed by his watching the preparations of the astrologer, who having spread a large planetary guide or map of the Heavens over the table, began carefully measuring distances with a pair of bright steel compasses; the globes were placed at each end of the table, and the centre was filled up with Weather Guides, Almanacs of every description, and a "History of Astrology and Foresight into Human Events." Casting up his eyes with astonishment at the sublime mystery of their profession, Scrubb hastened to Constance's apartment.

"They have come, Miss Constance," he whispered through the keyhole; "and are now seated in the kitchen."

"Wait for me, Scrubb, and I will join you," replied Constance, slightly opening the door.

"And I, also," exclaimed Lawrence, stepping forward. "I trust you will not consider my presence an intrusion," he added, to Constance, who had now joined them.

"You must know different to that, Lawrence," replied Constance; "I should have told you of this visit of the astrologer's, but I feared lest your apprehensions might construe it into some plan for my being carried off."

"And was that the *only* reason, Constance," inquired Lawrence of her, smiling.

"I could have no other; for what could I wish to hear, that would not be equally interesting to you ?"

"Nothing, nothing; well, let us not keep our visitors waiting," observed Lawrence ; and taking Constance by the hand, he led her to the kitchen, and Scrubb, carrying a light, followed in the rear.

Although Lawrence was somewhat cool and sarcastic in his address, Constance took no heed of what he had said. He had overheard Scrubb tell his young mistress of the intended visit of Sir William Lilly, and he then inwardly vowed to be present, for he had heard much of his celebrity; he having some few years before predicted the death of Charles I., in a little book, entitled "The last days of Royalty, or Power in Exile." He had also announced the coming of the plague, foretelling that it would happen in the very year that it really made its appearance. Arriving at the kitchen, Lawrence led Constance to a seat near the table, and taking one beside her, locked the door inside, putting the key in his pocket; this caused the astrologer and his companion to exchange looks with each other, which they thought were unobserved by all; but Lawrence kept his eyes fixed on them, and began to form a peculiar notion of them from their mutual glances.

"We did not bargain for a third party, young man," said the astrologer to Scrubb. "Who may he be ?"

"One of the family," replied Lawrence, rather sharply; "if you would rather have my absence, I would rather be present than not, and am willing to pay you any price you may demand, in reason."

"Our rewards are not centered in perishing gold, young man," replied the astrologer, sarcastically; "but however, I perceive by your features that your destiny is connected with that of this lady. I will proceed at once."

Lawrence bowed, and turning to Constance whispered in her ear, "Do you not think him very clever, already ?"

"I do," said Constance.

"The lady's age," inquired the astrologer.

"Nineteen, last May," answered Constance.

"What day of the month ?" he next asked. "And the precise time."

"On the 4th; at seven minutes after two in the morning.

"Good !" remarked the astrologer—"a few moment's silence, and I will soon let you know the most prominent events of your future and past life." Proceeding at once to consult his Planetary Guide, he wandered over several hemispheres of planets, and having fixed the nativity of Constance under the planet Venus, he noted the fact in a little green-cased pocket-book which he took from within his mantle. He then went on turning over the two globes, and making occasional observations in his little pocket-book. This proceeding took some minutes, during which Lawrence was busily engaged in watching every movement they made; and, biting his lip with vexation, seemed to be much displeased with some of their actions. The astrologer's assistant was employed in opening parchments, laying hieroglyphies before

Vide page　8

the astrologer, and making a few occasional references to the Planetary Guide, which was spread out on the table before them.

" You will have much trouble in love affairs ; and if you are ever married, which appears very doubtful, you will have a very jealous husband," said the astrologer to Constance, in a low, solemn tone.

" You hear that," observed the maiden to Lawrence.

He merely turned his lip in contempt of the assertion, and, motioning silence, listened attentively to the conversation which was now passing between the two strangers.

" How rates the position of the planet, doctor ?" said the astrologer to his assistant ? " is it in its ascendancy, in the full, or in conjunction with Mars, for I find the red-coats have much to do here."

" You are right, Sir William," replied the assistant ; " the planet I find was in conjunction with Mars at the exact moment of the maiden's birth."

" I reckoned so," said the astrologer to Constance ; " your husband will be either a soldier, or a man of great courage and daring ; you will live in troublesome warlike times, and will be married or buried at the time of some great public calamity."

Here the ceremony was interrupted by a loud knocking at the door, which upon being opened by Scrubb, proved to be Dame Trivet, who had come to inform Constance that her mother was seeking for her.

" You had better retire for a few moments, Constance," said Lawrence, " and I will occupy the attention of these learned men in the meantime."

Constance immediately left the room, accompanied by the worthy dame. On passing the chair of the astrologer, she felt a slight pull at her dress ; but taking no notice of the event she proceeded forthwith to her mother's apartment.

9.

"Perhaps I should not be exacting too much from your store, worthy sir, were I to solicit your attention to my destiny?" inquired Lawrence of the astrologer. "I have a sort of anxiety concerning my future prospects, and would like to know whether it is probable I shall be Lord Mayor of London, or die a plodding tradesman as I am."

"Humph!" growled out the astrologer, as he surveyed the form of the youth. "Lord Mayor of London, indeed! 'twill be lucky for you if ye 'scape the gibbet! Your appearance promises little. However, let me see: your age, and the time of your birth?"

"Twenty-two next 4th of July—time, quarter past twelve at noon," replied Lawrence.

"Ah! you are an orphan, then, I perceive!" exclaimed the astrologer.

"True—I am," answered Lawrence.

"Most wonderful! is he not, Lawrence?" whispered Scrubb in his ear.

"Silence, idiot!" he replied. "Listen, but say nothing."

"Your love is—or, rather, will be—hopeless!" resumed the man of fate, "for I perceive that with you also the planet Venus plays a prominent part. Your affection will not be returned, and the party upon whom you have fixed it will become a lady of title."

"Indeed," murmured Lawrence sarcastically.

"Your age will never be great; you will travel much, and either die by shipwreck or the hands of an assassin."

"I thank ye, sir, for such fair promises," answered Lawrence to all these denunciations; "and in return have a favour to ask of you, which I trust you will grant."

"Certainly," replied the astrologer, "provided it be not unreasonable."

"'Tis merely that you will allow me to tell you a little of your own prospects, your plans, and your probable fate through life."

"How! would you mock me?" exclaimed the sage, rather angrily.

"I would not; I was never more serious in my life," replied Lawrence. "But I can read a little into futurity myself, and it strikes me, from a close inspection I have had of your features, and that you will admit goes a great way in these matters, that you are not what you pretend to be."

"Do you, then, take me for a juggler?" By my soul, but I would not brook such an insult to be made Astronomer Royal this instant!" stormed the astrologer. "What mean ye, stripling?"

"That you are, in spite of a paltry disguise, either the Duke of Buckingham, or a mean, designing villain—the titles are, perhaps, synonymous; and that your cringing assistant there is some bastard of a Court knave, who does your bidding for the sake of your favour."

As he spoke, Lawrence grasped his cudgel tightly in his hand, and stood on his guard.

"Damnation!" roared out the duke, dashing on the ground his false wig, spectacles, cloak, and globes; "if we are discovered, further disguise is now useless."

"Mother of Life! my friends at the Fleece, by all that is wonderful!" replied Scrubb, as he recognised the duke and Vincent Palmer before him, as the astrologer and his assistant.

"You may retire when you please, my lord," said Lawrence sneeringly; "you have missed your mark this time. I foresaw the whole of your plot. You may deceive old age, but not young eyes. Shall I have the honour of showing you to the door, gentlemen?"

"You may triumph, boy, at this; but, as sure as you live, shall Constance be mine. I would wrest her from a host of friends, and bid them all defiance as I bore her from their sight. Lead on, Vincent; we lose time to prattle here."

"No, my lord duke, or whatever name you please to style yourself, you leave not this house till you have sworn, solemnly sworn, never to enter it again on such an errand."

"Psha!" replied Buckingham, trying to push Lawrence on one side. "Come, Vincent, follow me;" and making towards the door he was about to leave the house, when Lawrence suddenly stepped aside, and pulling from beneath his vest a pistol, presented it full at the duke's breast.

"You stir not till I have gained my point!" he exclaimed, and placing himself near the door defied their attack.

"Hell and devils! are we to be flouted by an unbearded stripling like this? Your sword, Vincent," said Buckingham, at the same time plucking a short dagger from beneath his robe. "Two to one must surely win the day."

"You reckon wrong, my lord duke," replied Lawrence; "though yonder weak-minded lad has been deceived by you, he will not so far forget himself as to turn against his friend. Scrubb! for one or for both?"

"For you, Lawrence, and no other," replied Scrubb, who, as he spoke, sprang upon Vincent Palmer from behind, and wrestling with him for his sword, both fell to the ground.

This attack was answered by the duke making a heavy lunge at Lawrence, who warded off the blow, and gave in return a well-aimed retort with his cudgel, which made the duke recoil for a moment.

"You will surely lose by such measures as these," exclaimed Lawrence; "I will defend this post to my last breath, and if you do not give me the pledge I require, and leave this house quietly, I will alarm the whole family, give you in safe custody to the watch as a midnight marauder, and procure for you some hours' repose in the cell of the City Compter, to awake in the morning to walk through the Chepe, hooted and pelted at, and be rated for your folly, if not punished, by the Mayor. Such honours must be welcome to a duke! and to one who is the boon companion of a monarch, and *such* a monarch, too! Heaven alone can keep virtue from your hawkish grasp! My lord, do you give me your vow, or shall I with the report of this pistol bring a crowd of unwelcome visitors about you?"

"Say it, Buck," whispered Vincent Palmer; "if giving your oath will get us out of this scrape, in the Pope's name give it. Were it my case, I would swear my head was the steeple of Old St. Paul's, and kiss his Mightiness's great toe in the bargain, to make it more binding, so that I could clear myself from a hobble."

"What is it you require?" inquired the duke pettishly of Lawrence. "What would you have me say?"

"Solemnly declare you will never enter this house again for such purposes as you have done to-night."

"I promise," replied the duke.

"By what?" asked Lawrence.

"By my honour!" was the answer.

"'Tis a blank," replied Lawrence. "That is no pledge. Swear by your soul, by Heaven!"

"By my soul's health, and by Heaven, I swear to it!"

"Enough; I am satisfied. You have removed a load of anxiety from my conscience, my lord," replied Lawrence.

"Indeed!" said the duke sarcastically.

"Yes, indeed; as I always hesitated doing an injury to a fellow-creature, so I hesitated from harming you this moment, as it would have been easier for me to have passed a bullet through your brain, than to have used my cudgel on your head. But such scruples are now removed; for as I told you on your oath not to violate these walls again with your presence, so surely wtll I put my threat in execution if I see you in this house from this time ; and think I was doing society a beneât in ridding it of a perjurer !"

"Bah ! keep sermons for grandfathers and grandmothers! We understand each other. When next we meet, may life and death be the only game on the board. Lead on ; I would be gone."

And wiping the blood from his face, which had trickled from the wound caused by Lawrence's cudgel, the duke and Vincent followed him as he led the way to the back entrance ; Scrubb bringing up the rear with the sword he had gained in the conflict, and which he returned to its owner on reaching the street.

"Farewell, my young city marshal," exclaimed the duke to Lawrence. "When next we meet, 'twill be no child's play then !"

Lawrence made no reply, but closed the gate after them.

CHAPTER X.

THE recent tragic occurrence at Old Saint Paul's, in which Dr. Calder and Mother Hagget had been the principal performers, still remained in perfect mystery. The sudden disappearance of the two vergers, who had met with their end through their own avariciousness, had been accounted for by the doctor in the following ingenious manner. He gave it out to all inquirers that the deceased bell-ringer had been a man of some property, and in his dying moments had expressed much uneasiness on the subject, and also seemed to be very suspicious of the two absent vergers. This, with the fact of the forcing of the tomb, and the empty chest being shown in evidence, corroborated his statement ; the unfortunate men were considered as plunderers, and a reward was issued for their seizure, in which Dr. Calder participated largely, well knowing the impossibility of their discovery.

Having thus silenced all misgivings and apprehensions concerning these men, of whose murder he felt himself horribly guilty, and having also conveyed the corpse of the wretched bell-ringer to its earthly resting-place, by means of Gowles's dead cart, for which service, by-the-bye, together with a *comfortable* coffin, which was particularly wished for by the deceased man's friends, the doctor had nothing more to do than issue his bill of costs, which the dean of the cathedral, being a benevolent man, had undertaken to discharge. Still there was a lurking suspicion in the mind of the doctor that the bell-ringer must have had money, and the fact of his having promulgated a report concerning the empty chest which was discovered in the stone vault, and which turned out such a spurious affair, gave proof that it was done merely for a decoy, and the more likely to direct a person's attention from the actual hiding-place, which the doctor himself suspected must be secreted somewhere in the apartment in which he had been living, and in which he so miserably died. Impressed with these ideas, and studying how he might best form a pretext for originating a search, or a wholesale clearance of the room in question, he resolved upon consulting his black and guilty colleagues, the undertaker and the plague-nurse, and towards the residence of the former he bent his way.

It was nearly midnight. The day had been sultry in the extreme, and the increasing fineness and heat of the weather seemed but as favouring the horrid ravages of the plague, when Andrew Gowles was seen urging a half-starved, emaciated horse (which was dropping on its knees almost every ten yards) up Holborn-hill, dragging with him a heavily-laden cart. The undertaker's occupation that night had been more irksome than usual, for he had not as yet gone round one-third of his district, and his cart was already filled to inconvenience with dead bodies. Gowles had ceased to sound his bell, or to bawl forth his usual request of " Bring out your dead !" at the corner of every street, as he was in the nightly habit of doing, and his solitary assistant had gone forward to prepare the place of burial, which was, for the present month, a vacant piece of ground near Finsbury, and not far from Gowles's residence. As he was crossing Smithfield, overcome with his exertions to increase the speed of his horse, and sauntering along at a dogged crawling pace, his hands thrust into his pockets, and his whip under his arm, he was all at once brought to the ground by a heavy stumble which he made over some substance which was lying in the road. His fall was nearly a fatal one to him, for had it not been for the fatigued condition of his horse, and its readiness to stop at the slightest intimation, the black-hearted undertaker would have fallen a victim to his own machine, and have been crushed to death beneath the wheels of his favourite dead-cart !

Resuming his original position as soon as possible, he snatched his lantern from the side of the cart, and looking around him beheld stretched on the ground the form of a man. Stopping his horse, Gowles surveyed the apparent lifeless body with surprise, and wondered what miracle could have interposed to save him from being ridden over and killed by the cart, which had passed so close to his head as to have crushed his gaily-decorated hat, which lay near him. The prostrate stranger, by his dress, appeared to be some gay gallant, who had got intoxicated in some neighbouring tavern, and whose senses had taken leave of him before he was in a state of safety, as by the vibration of his pulse, which Gowles had cautiously and carefully tried, life was strong within him He seemed rich by his appearance, for in addition to a costly dress, a massive gold chain was suspended round his neck, and by his side lay a valuable Spanish rapier, whose hilt glittered with jewels, and by a vigilant search into one of his inmost pockets, Gowles discovered a purse well filled with gold. Delighted beyond measure at such a piece of good luck, the undertaker was for a moment lost in contemplating the luxury of his future prospects, when his ear caught the sound of a distant bell, and the gradual approach of another cart for the reception of the dead, near which district he had by this time arrived. Speedily pocketing the purse, Gowles began to hesitate how he should act with regard to the body, which was soon solved by his giving the prostrate stranger a heavy blow on the head with a crowbar, so as to stun if not kill him ; and swinging the body into the cart amongst the plague-reeking corpses, he once more urged his miserable steed forward on its journey.

As he progressed on his way to the dead pit, which was a large space of ground dug very deep for the reception of a great quantity of dead bodies, and when filled, was securely covered up—Gowles resolved in his own mind not to touch any of the jewels, as they were likely to tell tales ; and he murderously determined to shoot the body with the others into the gaping abyss of death, as he was aware that in a few days it would be closed, being now already filled beyond the limits of the City Commissioner's rules.

Upon his arrival at the wholesale sepulchre in Finsbury, Gowles told his assistant that he might go home for the night, as he should not go another round, his horse being now nearly broken down, having been in constant work night and day, for the last three days ; which boon the yawning menial was not slow to obey, and Gowles was now left alone, to bury the living with the dead ! Previous to doing this he resolved upon taking some token from the young man he had picked up, by which he might be enabled some time after to learn who he was that had so strangely fallen in his way ; and accordingly, after a few moment's search within the folds of his vest, he discovered a golden locket, in which was platted a wreath of auburn hair, evidently some love-token or keepsake from an intimate friend ; and as he drew it from the young gallant's vest, the chest of the owner heaved a deep heavy sigh, which caused Gowles to start back with a guilty consciousness of wrong, and being anxious to rid his sight of so obnoxious a spectacle, he hastily pulled the spring which caused his cart to make a mechanical evolution by which it shot out its contents into the yawning gulf ready to receive it ; and the stupified and senseless victim to the barbarian's villany rolled down, mixing with the rest of the dead and decomposed bodies.

Without waiting to look behind him, Gowles mounted his cart and drove away ; not even daring to look back, lest the murdered youth should appear to his frenzied gaze ; and as he left the precincts of death, he heard or fancied he could descry, a faint cry for help, followed by a low murmuring groan, so dismal and so horrible, that it penetrated even the adamantine fortress of Gowles' black heart, but he paid no heed to it ; and hurrying on his wretched pack, was soon out of hearing and sight of the dead pit of Finsbury !

Upon his arrival at home, Gowles was much surprised to find Doctor Calder and Mother Hagget anxiously waiting his return.

"What news, now ? Who wants a coffin to-night, that I find you here, doctor ? and you, too, Mother Hagget ; any of your friends want the ever-lasting tailor, eh ?"

"No, Gowles," replied the doctor, "we have come to consult you upon an important subject—the money of old Ralph Garland, the late bell-ringer, who——— ?"

"Money, did you say ?" interrupted Gowles—"who then has found it ? I guessed he must have had some—was it much—who is the lucky man ; eh, man, dos't hear ?"

"You prevented me, or I should by this time have explained," answered Doctor Calder. "You are aware of the ill-success of our late attempt ?"

"Rather say the good success," replied Gowles ; "for if you had not quieted your friends who were so anxious to promote your fame, they would have soon had you safely fixed in Newgate. I should reckon it as a lucky, rather than as an unfortunate, attempt."

"Well, as you please to that," replied the doctor. "It is my opinion, Gowles, that money is still to be found ! and whoever finds it will be well paid for their trouble ; for I know there must be a pretty hoard of it, some-where."

"And it is my solemn belief," replied Mother Hagget, "that the old fool lied on his death-bed, by saying it was in the stone vault. I'd wager six months' fees 'tis still about his bed, and will there remain till found out by chance."

"And I trust, then, that chance will be mine," answered Gowles. "If I had not been already paid, and well-paid too, by the dean of the cathedral for the job, I would be glad to seize upon or take his goods as payment of the debt, if they would allow me."

"Or, were I to pronounce the bedding and furniture as likely to retain contagious effects, and insist upon their being removed or destroyed ?" sug-gested Dr. Calder. "I think the plan could not fail ; what say you, Mother Hagget ?"

"No matter how we get in, or under what pretence, so as we get there," replied the hag : "when there, I hope we shall be more successful than in that cursed stone vault."

"It shall be so, then," said the doctor. "I will at once wait on the dean and suggest the subject, and endeavour to have it done in the night-time— eh, Gowles ? that will suit you best, I guess ?"

"Any time suits me when there is money to be had," replied the grasp-ing undertaker : "for instance, although I was engaged upon very important business this evening, in my official capacity, yet I could not refrain doing a little on my own account—see here, this is a pretty looking jewel, is it not?" and as he spoke, he displayed to their view the locket he had taken from the young man whom he had left heaped up with the dead in the pit. It was of pure gold, profusely covered with diamonds, and fastened with an emerald snap, and as Gowles held it up, the light reflected upon it to great advantage.

" Why, what have you here, Gowles?" exclaimed the doctor, taking the locket in his hand, and examining it carefully. " It is of great value, and must doubtless be the property of some nobleman. You had better let me take care of it; I shall soon discover its right owner, for it will be sure to be cried at every gate of the city before two days are past, and I shall most likely be able to obtain a larger reward for its recovery than you would; so that you see your gains would be increased by such a step—do you agree?"

" No!" roared out Gowles, at the same time snatching the locket from the doctor's hands, and thrusting it into his pocket; " I will keep it myself, out of respect to its master, and if it's worth any thing at all, why I shall never be poor while I keep it by me—do you perceive that, master doctor?"

" Perfectly; I am satisfied. I shall now take my leave, and expect to meet with you both at the cathedral to-night—what hour shall we say?"

" Ten," answered Gowles.

" I will be there; for the present, good time o' night to you!" and drawing his mantle close round him, to protect him from the penetrating damps of the night air, the doctor took his leave.

As soon as he had gone, Gowles beckoned Mother Hagget into an adjoining apartment, and lighting a large lamp which hung from the ceiling, over a table in the centre of the room, he drew two chairs towards the fire place, and stirring up the ashes of peat and turf which had been smouldering on the hearth for some hours, there was soon a cheerful blaze in its place, and gave the somewhat gloomy apartment a lively appearance.

The table was soon replenished with various flasks and tankards, in addition to which Gowles brought forward two large bottles from a sideboard chest, filled with sack and canary, and placing them before Mother Hagget added, with a smile, " These are better companions than lying knaves of doctors, Hagget, are they not?"

" Right, old boy, they are," was the response of the nurse, as she poured out for herself a tankard of her favourite beverage, and turned it off at a draught.

" For some time, Hagget," began Gowles in a low tone to his confidante, " for some time, I say, I have not half liked the doctor's doings, and I am half inclined to think that he wants to be rid of us, and to get all the bargains he can for himself, but I'll prevent him, though: perhaps he forgets that although a quieting dose is very handy at times such as these, a ride in the dead cart is better; for there are no searchers there, no tales to be told when you once take your seat in my charming black vehicle, ha! ha! ha! 'Tis the neatest carriage in all London, and is generally pretty well filled. So let Master Calder beware, or he may not be the first or the last live passenger I have driven to the Pit, to rest in peace and quietness with lodgers who will never trouble him."

Gowles ended this harangue by taking a heavy draught at the tankard of sack; and then, drawing his prize once more from his pocket, he began to examine it more carefully.

" What windfall is that, Gowles?" inquired Hagget. " Did it give you much trouble?"

" None in the least," answered Gowles with a grin.

" May I be allowed to look at it?"

" Yes ; there can be no harm in a look ;" and as he spoke he threw the locket into her lap.

" This will create a rumpus, depend upon it, Gowles ; it has come from a good stock, and where there are plenty more remaining. Come, I will make you an offer for it—I will give you my share of the money we shall find at old Ralph's for it."

" Bah ! d'ye think I'm an idiot, then ? Give it me back directly ! I would not part with it for an estate."

" Then you are likely to keep it, I guess," replied Hagget, as she threw it back to Gowles. I should value it at about ten guineas, if I was buying it, and at fifty if I was selling it."

Though the nurse returned the miniature, she resolved in her own mind to be possessed of it the very first opportunity.

" I was speaking concerning Calder," resumed Gowles, at the same time taking a hearty draught at the sack. " I know his determination is to sell us. Look how he kept me from applying to Elliot's for an order, when his wife was ill with the plague. Had it been any other patient, she would have been mine in a week. I could have charged what I like there ; but I won't forget him for it—his friend, indeed ! Of what good are friends, if not to make use of them ?"

" Well and did he not prevent me from going there, too ?" exclaimed Mother Hagget, " I could have made a comfortable thing out of such a family as that ; besides you know a certain duke is in love with Elliot's daughter ; for the matter of a well-filled purse, I would have assisted him to carry her off. 'Twould have set me up for six months to come. Confound his scruples, I say."

" This is my plan to have our revenge on him," said Gowles :—" but drink, mother, drink ; we do not often meet over the bottle."

And pouring out more sack and canary, they each changed glasses and liquors, and drank to each other in the opposite to what they had been drinking before ; the effects of this intoxicating scheme, however, soon became visible.

" He has planned," resumed Gowles, " to meet us at the cathedral to-morrow night ; very well, be it so. Yes, we will go—I will go, Mother Hagget, and you shall go with me. Let us search vigilantly for the money which is hidden, and if possible secrete it immediately, and swear it has never been discovered—that it is as much a hoax as the vault was, or that some one else had taken it before us—eh ! will not that do ?"

" Excellent !" replied Mother Hagget ; although she had secretly vowed in her own mind that if her's was the hand which should discover it she would keep it a secret and have the whole.

The conversation between these worthy contemporaries now dropped off for a time, the interval being filled up by Gowles's first drinking hot canary and water, and then washing it down with sack made into a sort of toddy ; now and then, he broke out into loud and noisy songs, calling upon Mother Hagget to join him in them ; and almost quarrelling with her for not drinking more. Mother Hagget watched her companion with the same keen eye as an eagle watches for the ewe straying from the young lamb, that she may pounce upon her prey with greater security and less risk. She had made up her mind to rob him of the locket, if it was at all possible ; and once her's, it was lost to him for ever.

After about half an hour of noisy revelry, the head of Gowles fell back on his shoulder, the half-emptied tankard rolled from his hand on to the floor, and he was soon in a state of perfect stupefaction ; completely overcome by the liquor he had been drinking so largely of. The first thing Mother Hagget did was to cut the string which he had fastened to the locket, and which

hung suspended from his neck; this enabled her gently to draw the locket from its place round his neck, and thrusting it into her pocket, she said exultingly, "He may charge me with having it if he pleases; but he shall never charge me with being discovered, for I will destroy it before he should have it; and if he is but lucky enough to be smitten by the plague, and I have to attend him—why, his case will then be settled; I will wipe out all old scores with him."

Preparing to depart unobserved, Mother Hagget extinguished the light, and stealing silently out of the room, left Gowles to enjoy his midnight repose.

CHAPTER XI.

AFTER seeing Buckingham and his companion clear of the house, and once more securing the yard gate, and making every outlet safe from further intrusion, Lawrence turned his attention to Scrubb, who he intended severely lecturing for his imprudence in admitting strangers into the house, seeing how the present affair had terminated, though from the first he had had his suspicions that the parties were not what they represented themselves to be. Calling Scrubb into his presence, he severely interrogated him on the subject of the visit.

"So, sir, I find after all the warnings I had previously given you, that you have again acted the part of a traitor to your master, by admitting those into his house, under an idle pretence, who would have robbed him of his best and dearest treasure—his daughter."

"You are too hard with me, Lawrence," replied Scrubb soothingly. "I knew not their intentions, or who they were, at the time of their coming;

10.

I believed them to be the great Lilly, and one of his brother astrologists, till you discovered who they really were. Who would have taken that venerable old man for a villain?"

"It may be as you say," replied Lawrence, "but what sort of an excuse would this have proved, had Constance been carried off by the scheme? Think you it would have pacified her father for your disobedience and folly? It is the second time your stupidity has been the cause of that illustrious vagabond's entry into the house, but it shall be the last, for I will lay the whole affair before your master, and leave him to decide as he pleases."

"Oh, no! for mercy's sake do not that, Lawrence," exclaimed Scrubb, falling on his knees before him. "I will watch all night at the door, take physic by the quart that will prevent me from sleeping, run ten miles on a dark rainy night to serve you—any thing if you will not tell Master Elliot. He will never forgive me; I shall be instantly turned from the house, become a lonely outcast, and shall catch the ague through want of proper nourishment; that will bring on the plague, and, without a penny to buy me a box of ointment, a bit of salve, or a single refuse, I shall die a martyr and a beggar! and then what will become of poor Pauline?"

"I dare not trust you. I should expect the same thing to occur again to-morrow," answered Lawrence.

"Kill me! shoot me dead instantly, if you ever find me do wrong again. I may be foolish, Lawrence, but not ungrateful. Try me once again."

Lawrence was somewhat touched by this appeal from Scrubb. "Well, then," he resumed, "as you are so pressing, I will for the present keep your secret; but remember, it will be always ready to come against you should you break your word."

"That I never will, Lawrence; indeed you may trust me," answered the repentant Scrubb, overcome with joy at the proposed pardon.

"You had better get to bed now," said Lawrence. "I shall want you in the morning, so be stirring at daybreak."

"I will be sure to obey you. Good night," replied Scrubb, as he left the kitchen, and proceeded to his chamber for the night.

"I will try him once more," thought Lawrence, and locking the door he stepped lightly along to his room for the night.

To detail events minutely, we must now retrace our steps back to the Duke of Buckingham and Vincent Palmer, on their sudden expulsion from Elliot's house by Lawrence. Their first step was direct to the Devil Tavern in Fleet-street, where, coming so unexpectedly upon the gay visitors of the dice-room, their presence caused much surprise; especially as the duke on entering threw his astrologer's cap, beard, and gown into one corner of the room, exclaiming, "Away, thou base and false disguise, thou hast betrayed me!"

Then casting his eyes on Captain Blount, who was half overcome by potations deep, he beckoned him towards him, and threw himself into a chair.

Vincent Palmer had imitated the example of the duke in hurling the emblems of his office into the furthest corner of the room, and drawing a chair near the fire exclaimed, "Here, you rascal of a drawer, bring me instantly a long Dutch pipe of the mildest tobacco you have, exquisitely palated with a tonquin, a tankard of canary sack, with a little lemon, plenty of sugar, and a tamarind tart. I will luxuriate in silence."

"Why, sparks and gunshots, what's up now?" exclaimed Blount, as he eyed the duke and his companion, and then their disguises, which lay in the corners of the room.

"We have been serenading," answered the duke.

"And have been discovered, and rather roughly handled," answered Blount.

" In the first you are right ; in the second, nearly ;" said the duke, " However, knowing your ingenuity, bravery, and gallantry in such matters, we have come to lay our case before you, and solicit your aid and advice, as a cunning general."

" A-hem !" coughed Blount, and looked significantly ; " do you say aye to that, Master Vincent ?" he said, addressing himself to the duke's companion. " Are you also a young recruit in want of a brave leader ?"

" Exactly so !" murmured out the person whom he addressed.

" Why, then as a good general, and one who loves to see a well displayed field before him, I must say that, before I can give my counsel on this question, I must see a flowing bowl and a sparkling bottle before me—shall I give the order, cousin of Buckingham ?" he exclaimed pointedly to the duke.

" As you please," answered the nobleman addressed ; " I am ready for anything, even to cut a lover's throat, and afterwards rob him of his mistress."

Captain Blount was not long in taking advantage of the duke's generosity ; for he was a needy man himself, and used these sort of friendly favours to the best advantage : and in the course of a few minutes the table creaked under the load it sustained.

" To commence business, Blount," began the duke ; " we have been foiled in a brave attempt to storm a fortress here, hard by, and to carry off a fair captive who resided within its strongholds—do you comprehend ?"

" Precisely !" exclaimed Captain Blount. " The stationer's, I guess."

" Right !" resumed the duke. " Yes, I own to the defeat, by an opposing party, only our equals in number, though superior in stratagem ; and all through the want of a brave gallant, and intrepid leader."

" Would I had been with my noble duke," replied Blount, pompously ; " I would have cut down the opposing party from the crown to the chin but what I would have carried off the prize my leader ventured for !"

" Bravo, general !" shouted the duke ; which exclamation was answered by his companion Vincent Palmer.

" Name any plan : say how you require my assistance, valiant leader, and I am yours ever to command, through fire, water, earth or air !" said the captain vauntingly.

" 'Tis briefly as I will state, Blount," answered the duke. " Fill up your glasses, pass them round, and I will go on. It is now, I reckon, the third time I have been foiled from carrying off that charming, sweet-consenting piece of virginity, the stationer's daughter ; and all through the cupidity and jealous watchfulness of a cursed serf in her father's house, who has had the audacity to fall in love with her himself !"

" What !" roared out Blount, half drawing his sword, " has he had the presumption to become the rival of a duke ? Mountains and earthquakes ! but I would swallow him up alive !"

" There is no occasion for that ; which you will find if you listen," said the duke. " I have a plan to lay before you, which I wish you to assist me in to carry out, that I think will equally serve our purpose, by disposing of him without either swallowing him up, or chopping him up. It is this— Master Elliot's house, you well know, has lately been a condemned house by the plague commissioners ; and I understand it is Elliot's intention to remove into the country ; so that any plan we have in contemplation must be put in force at once. My scheme is this : as it has now become a frequent occurrence in some parts of London for houses that have been once blockaded by the plague to be fired by the owners as the only and last resource of obtaining their liberty, and either leaving their bed-ridden relatives to fall victims to the devouring flames, or if possible carry them away with them, so is it my intention secretly to fire Elliot's house in the dead of the night, to bear off Constance in the confusion, and if the meddling cur, the apprentice, comes in our way, to hurl him back into the flames to perish."

"But how is such an attempt to be accomplished, my lord duke?" inquired Blount.

"Leave that to me," was the answer given by Buckingham; "only let me insure the assistance of one or two brave and trustworthy companions, like yourself and Vincent here, and I would undertake to fire the City of London, and pull the Lord Mayor himself from his chair."

"You may cordially reckon upon my strenuous aid," replied Vincent, "for I have some long odds to settle with that youth you speak of."

"Once possessed of that divine creature, I should moralize for a twelve-month, and bid adieu to the follies of a court to bask in the sunshine of love."

"Then when will my noble leader require the services of his devoted slave!" inquired Captain Blount.

"I have fixed it for to-morrow night," replied the duke; "they may chuckle at the chagrin they have caused us to-night, but let them beware how I retaliate!"

"Well, my lord," said Vincent, "I have a little business to settle in the Temple here, hard by; will you stroll with me, and we can talk further upon the subject?"

"With all my heart," replied Buckingham. "Blount, meet us here to-morrow night at the hour of nine precisely. Bring your pistols with you, and let them be well loaded; you may require them. Adieu! I shall expect you."

"And not in vain!" exclaimed the captain; "I am too fond of storming in the breach to be absent from the scene of action."

And thus these three conspirators plotted and parted; vowing vengeance on the house of Master Elliot, and death to most of its inmates.

        *   *   *   *   *   *   *   *   *

It was at the close of a fine summer's day in June, that Master Elliot's house had been one uninterrupted scene of congratulations and visits of rejoicing between himself and his neighbours, which had caused the whole family to be stirring much after their usual time. However, long before the hour of ten, everything bore the stillness of death, and nothing was heard but now and then the hoarse and feeble voice of the city watch crying the hour. The night was the extreme contrary to the day; dark heavy clouds were filling the whole horizon around; the moon which was two days past her full was not visible for a moment; and the wind was just getting up into a shrill searching blast. At this critical juncture the forms of three men, dressed in long black mantles, were visible scudding towards Lad-lane, beneath the jutting points of windows and under shelter of doorways; these were no other than the Duke of Buckingham, Vincent Palmer, and Captain Blount, who had arrived at the scene of action, to carry their plot into effect.

The private entrance in Lawrence-lane to Master Elliot's house was well known to the duke, having once entered into the house that way clandestinely, and having been twice forcibly ejected from it by that very door By the aid of Captain Blount's shoulder, he easily scaled the wall, and alighting into the yard, looked about to gather information. The house was quite dark and silent; not a sound or soul was stirring; he marked well the window by which he had entered Constance's apartment, and he was in doubt now to conclude whether it was really her bed chamber or not.

Not being able, however, to obtain any answer from the repeated sallies upon the glass, by means of small pebbles, he turned back, and opening the door with a private spring under the latch, which he had watched Lawrence doing, he escorted his companions into the yard. The forcing of the house door was now the next job which gained their attention; the duke was for cutting out a hole sufficiently big enough to insert an arm, and draw back the lock but Blount dissuaded him from that, and attempted to try the lock, by means of a long piece of wire, by which he might pick or destroy it at leisure.

"Cutting away the door would be a more speedy manoeuvre," urged the duke, who was too impatient to wait for anything like trifling with a stubborn lock. "Cut away, I say; let us lose no more time here; 'twill be morning before we enter!"

"But had ye better not enter at all, Buck," replied Vincent, familiarly, "than to enter and be discovered; which you assuredly would do if you attempted to cut away that pannel!"

"Bah!" exclaimed Captain Blount, throwing open the door in question, whilst the two friends were disputing which way it should be done, either by forcing or cutting away the pannels. "There, you see, I have settled the knotty point, while you have been arguing it; who will be the first to enter?"

"I," replied the duke. "And I trust also the first to return, bearing with me the lovely Constance, still deep in her innocent slumbers!"

"Proceed, then," exclaimed Vincent. "We wait but to follow your footsteps."

Accordingly the duke stepped slowly and cautiously into the house; leaving the door open in case any urgent retreat might be necessary. They first proceeded to the warehouse, where they found a profusion of waste paper; this was all gathered up together by them, and placed in a side cupboard under a flight of stairs communicating with the upper part of the house. This was done to cut off all communication between the upper and lower part of the house, in case any of them should venture to interfere or cause a rescue to be attempted.

To prevent any confusion or disarrangement of his plans, Buckingham ordered that Blount should now go round to the front door in Cheapside, and at a given signal, which was to be a pistol shot, he was to knock violently at the door, and raise a cry of fire. Blount accordingly left his companions, and directed his step towards Cheapside. The first they fired was the paper which had been disposed of under the stairs; then leaving open a slight partition between one of the lower rooms, which was merely composed of thin boards and laths, they placed a small lump of tow saturated with oil, which soon blazed up fiercely;—a door which led into the alley behind the house was also opened wide by Vincent Palmer; this gave a fresh breeze to the flames, which now began to burn rapidly.

"This will soon enlighten their dreams," exclaimed Buckingham, in a tone of jocularity. "You may as well give Blount the signal, Vincent; for I think that by the time he has beat up a row at the door, the house will be too hot to hold us all!"

"I will," replied Vincent; and pulling a heavy dragoon's pistol from his belt, he fired it off with a loud report.

"There, that will set him to work; we must be quiet till he has made his way through. Come, let us get a room farther off, it is unpleasantly hot here, already. "And following up these instructions, the duke and his companion retreated a few stairs away from the flames which were now spreading rapidly to come forth at the proper period.

Blount, stationed in Cheapside, was not slow in acting upon the orders he had received from the duke, and the very moment he heard the report of the pistol, he applied his eye to the key-hole of the door, and could plainly see the red flare making its way slowly towards the front of the house, accom-

panied by a loud cracking sound, as if of wood breaking and giving way by
the heat. Looking up towards Cornhill, he beheld one of the night patroll
on his way towards the house, shouting forth at the very top of his voice.
" Fire! fire! help! here is Master Elliot's house burning!" and knocking
and kicking violently at the door. The patrol was soon on the spot, and a
large mob, composed of benighted 'prentices, strolling vagabonds, drunken
gallants and their low female associates, soon congregated before the door.

" Break open the house!" exclaimed the captain, " or the inmates will be
roasted to a cinder. I have been bellowing here this half hour. Break it
open, I say; here, lend me your staff, constable; I will soon effect an entrance." And snatching the staff out of the hand of the patrol, he dealt
several heavy blows at the largest pannel of the door.

The noise awoke Master Elliot himself, who, jumping out of bed and finding his room full of hot smoke, had much difficulty in reaching the window,
which he immediately threw up, and demanded what they wanted by knocking so violently at the door.

" Up, man! if you wish to be saved!" replied Captain Blount to his demands; " your house is in flames! come and let us in, that we may assist
you to escape!"

" Gracious Heaven! my wife! my children! save them, save them all,
and I will reward you handsomely! Wife! wife! rouse up! we are burning! we are in flames!" and staggering into the room, he seized his wife by
the arm, and tried to awaken her; but she was so sound asleep that it gave
him much trouble.

The bombardment at the street door had by this time met with success,
for by Captain Blount's repeated attacks upon the two lowermost pannels of
the door, they at last gave way, and he being the first to spring through the
aperture, unclosed the fastenings, and opening the door admitted the watch
and his companions. The fire had now reached the first floor or landing,
and the passage way to the street was filled with burning smoke, and the very
boards beneath the feet were like hot cinders to walk upon.

" We must first rescue the inmates," exclaimed Blount, as soon as he could
draw his breath from the stifling effects of the smoke, which was now filling
the house in volumes; " Follow me! Quick, men, or all will be lost!" and
dashing up the staircase, he was followed by several men, whilst others of
the watch and assistant night constables were engaged in fetching water in
buckets from the Conduit in Cheapside.

The whole family were now on the alert; Master Elliot having aroused
his wife, next directed his attention to Constance, and going to her chamber-
door, without waiting for admittance, he caught her in his arms, half asleep
in her night dress as she was, and carried her to her mother's apartment.
Lawrence had awoke by the noise, and starting from his bed was at first re-
pulsed by the fiery vapour which had hung heavy and thick around him;
kicking Scrubb from his bed, which was in an adjoining closet, he flew to the
chamber of his master, where he found all the family by this time assembled.

The flames, totally unimpeded by the paltry attempt of two or three
buckets of water to extinguish it, were now winding their snaky-folds up the
staircases. Already was the lower part of the house one sheet of flame, and
any egress by that quarter was totally impossible. Beams and heavy partitions were falling in every direction; the glasses of the windows melting and
throwing the casements open with the air, the flames rushed out at these
outlets in volumes; for the house being a very old one, its wide staircases
and massive wood work only assisted the progress of the flames in their overpowering course.

In the confusion which now prevailed, Blount, by a given watch-word
managed to join his companions, who were anxious to know the state of the

family. They were informed by the captain in a brief hurried whisper that they were all in the room above, whither the three incendiaries proceeded.

The head constable of the ward and a body of men were now in attendance, who strenuously exerted every effort to extinguish the flames, but without success. Finding this to be the case, all force was now to be employed in saving the inmates, and for that purpose the constable, offering a high reward to whoever would follow him, dashed headlong through the fire, which was now blazing with fury through all the lower doors and windows, and ascending the staircase, reached the chamber of Mistress Elliot, which being the largest room in the house, and situated on the back landing of the first floor, now contained the whole of the inmates ;—in his venturesome flight, however, the constable was only followed by two of his men, four others having given up the attempt.

" Four minutes more, and this floor, which now glows like a bed of fire, will give way," exclaimed the constable. " Have you any outlet on the roof ?"

" Alas, no !" replied Elliot.

" Then there is but one course for you to take, and that speedily," replied the constable. " Let every one make the best of their way to the front room above, and we must gain the street by ropes and ladders. Come, lads, take the women in your arms ; the men can shift for themselves. Now lady," said the man to Constance, " let me conduct you !"

" See to the old lady behind," replied Lawrence ; " I will conduct this person myself."

Master Elliot had now taken his wife, who had fainted in his arms, and as he left the room he gave a solemn charge to Lawrence to preserve Constance safe

" Depend upon it I will not leave her ;" answered Lawrence ; and lifting her in his arms, he implored her to take fast hold of him round the neck.

"Dear Lawrence, this heat overpower's me ! heaven's how faint I feel ! Oh, water ! I die ! I burn !" and uttering these lamentations she swooned in his arms ; while Lawrence, clasping her closer to his bosom, darted up the stairs through a shower of sparks and scorching smoke, after her parents ; leaving the constable and his men to bring up Dame Trivet and Scrubb.

Buckingham had witnessed Lawrence bearing Constance swooning in his arms, up the stairs, and would have darted upon him and rescued her, but he was withheld by Captain Blount.

" Keep quiet, my lord, or we are lost ! Remember, this is no child's play. Let them all go to the room above, in front of the house ; we will wait in the one behind, and I can ensure us a safe retreat that way from a low lattice window, that looks on to a building, from which we can descend in safety."

" By Heaven ! I remember you are right !" exclaimed the duke ; " the very window I entered by on a late occasion. But come, this place is unbearably hot, let us up after them." And the trio accordingly ascended, and lay in waiting at the room adjoining that from which the family were then escaping.

By means of long ladders and ropes it was deemed possible to gain the street from the windows, and the first person who was to descend was Mistress Elliot, who, wrapped up in a large canvass, was safely lowered into the street, which was duly announced to those above, by a tumultuous shout from the populace below who received her.

" Now, Constance, my dear child," exclaimed Elliot, " let me place you on the ladder."

" I will not move till I know your are safe, my dear father—not a step ;" answered Constance, who, having recovered from her swoon, was leaning near the window to gain a breath of air.

" Be quick! the flames are gaining upon us," cried the constable ; this room will not stand much more ; you, Master Elliot, go down ; the youth here will see your daughter safe, and I will bring your son."

" Heaven speed me, then," replied the agitated man ; " but my servants ; where are they ?"

" All are in safety, dear master," replied Lawrence ; for Dame Trivet, locked fast in the arms of one of the watch, had some minuaes before descended the ladder ; and had joined her mistress below ; while Scrubb, not waiting to be told, had made his escape the same way.

" Hold fast, and you are safe !" exclaimed the constable, as he lowered Master Elliot down the ladder with a rope ; and watching him carefully to the bottom, shouted out, " He is safe ; he is safe !"

" Kind Heaven I thank thee!" was the reply of his affectionate daughter, as she heard this intelligence.

" We must now save ourselves ; we have already dared too long the stability of this apartment ; I feel it shake beneath our feet," said the constable ; and mounting one of the ladders, prepared to descend with his men ; having directed Lawrence to cary Constance down the other ladder, which was standing near the left window of the apartment.

Lawrence and Constance were now left to themselves, every one having secured his flight by escaping into the street by the ropes and the ladders.

" Cling fast to me, Constance, I conjure you : and with Heaven's assistance we shall reach the ground with safety," said Lawrence soothingly to his lovely burden.

" It seems a fearful height ! I am giddy with gazing," replied Constance.

At this moment a loud shout from below urged them to make haste and descend ; for already had the flames from the lower rooms began to show themselves between the boards of the flooring of the room in which the lovers were remaining. Lawrence now mounted the casement and clasped Constance tightly in his arms ; he had thrown a loose mantle round her, which would save her from the scorching of the flames. Already had he placed his foot upon the ladder, when at the instant he was about to descend the floor of the room partially gave way, and a furious body of flame and smoke filled the apartment. Constance shrieked with alarm, and springing backwards with fright, fell upon the burning boards ; this caused Lawrence to step backwards into the room to extricate her from the fiery envelope which now surrounded her. When he returned to the window, however, to rush down the ladder, he found to his horror it was gone ! The flames had consumed the fastenings and it had fell to the ground.

" God of mercy !" exclaimed Lawrence, staggering with the intense heat of the apartment—"is there no help ? Must we remain here and perish ?"

" There is help !" exclaimed Buckingham, rushing into the room and disguising his voice ; " give us your hand, friend ; be steady and resolute, or all your footing will give way.

Lawrence waited not to inquire who the party was, but giving him his hand, he suffered him to lead him from the room. while Vincent had taken Constance in his arms. They had now safely reached an outer landing at the back of the house where the fire had not made any way ; and Lawrence being somewhat recovered, asked for Constance.

" She is here, and is safe !" answered Buckingham, and taking the senseless maiden from Vincent Palmer, he pressed her to his heart, and leaping on to the adjacent out-house, safely reached the yard, by the gate of which he escaped with his still fainting burthen.

Vincent Palmer and Captain Blount having now secured the retreat of their gallant leader, thought of nothing else now but their own safety ; and Lawrence having fainted in the captain's arms, from his great exer-

tion and the excessive heat he had been enduring for the last half hour.
Making the best of their way out of the window down into the yard, by the
same path as the duke himself had taken, they disposed of Lawrence in his
senseless agitated state by fastening him up in a small building at the further
corner of the yard, commonly used as a store-house or extra kitchen by the
family; and barring the gate after them, left the exhausted Lawrence in
solitary and unknown confinement.

The building was now one sheet of flame, which poured out at every window and outlet in the front part of the house; for the wind being set in a
quarter that played on the back of the house, kept the fire in the front;
consequently, the hindermost part of the building was the last to fall a prey
to the devouring element.

It was now two hours since the fire had first broke out; and all attempts
to extinguish it by carrying water by hand from the Conduit having been
abandoned as useless, it was left to burn itself out.

By midnight the flames had somewhat lulled—nothing being left to burn
but the bare walls. As the chimes of Bow Church struck the hour of four,
the remnant of the once handsome edifice fell in with a loud crash—and the
house of Master Elliot was no more!

CHAPTER XII.

In accordance with his promise to Gowles and Mother Hagget, Dr. Calder
paid a visit early the next morning, after their conference, to the Dean of Old
Saint Paul's, one Reverend Gregory Bridgeman, to lay before him his views
and plans concerning the intended search of the late bell-ringer's apartment.
The doctor had painted in glowing colours the fearful dangers that might

II.

ensue from articles of furniture and other things being allowed to remain undisturbed and breed contagion ; these prominent reasons, which were sufficient for any prudent man's ideas of safety, together with an offer on the doctor's part to purchase the lumber, soon won consent from the dean, upon condition that he alone should receive the fee, and no mention whatever should be afterwards made concerning it. Having agreed to these proposals, it was finally arranged for the doctor and his assistants to come that evening at ten o'clock to clear out the apartment lately occupied by the unfortunate Ralph Garland ; and a written order to that effect was then signed by the dean and given to Doctor Calder, for his warrant and permit to fulfill the same, according to agreement.

At the appointed hour that same evening the three contemporaries of death and crime met at the door of the South Gate, leading to Paul's Chain. Each party, however, though giving their actions the semblance of unity and friendship, had predetermined inwardly, by fraud or deceit, to become possessor of the treasure, unknown to his fellow-searcher. For instance, Doctor Calder had formed a plan in his own mind, that if he lighted upon the treasure he would immediately secrete it, and keep its discovery still a mystery, and at a more convenient time, remove it to his own house for greater safety. Gowles and Mother Hagget, as it has been previously stated, had made a compact jointly to rob the doctor of his share ; and to do the coffin-maker justice he was the only one of the three who was sincere in his intention to keep the word of agreement, for he actually did intend to share his portion with Mother Hagget, though she in return clandestinely intended to conceal the whole in the event of her finding it ; to threaten the doctor into silence with the late deed in the stone vault, and to get Gowles plague-stricken by the best means in her power, and then, by *careful* nursing, to dispose of him.

" You are punctual to your word, doctor," observed Gowles, as the former joined them at the gate ; the chimes at the same moment tolling the hour of ten.

" I always strive to be so," replied Calder, "especially when I have business of moment in hand ; such as the present, to wit."

" Ah ! ah !" sneered Mother Hagget, "whether a death by the plague, a birth, a broken leg, or a diseased alderman, requires the doctor's presence, it signifies nought, for it all fills his purse,—'tis all grist to his mill."

" And is it not the same to yours, you sarcastic wheedling beldame ?" inquired the doctor, rather pointedly. " Does the doctor ever have patients without their always requiring a nurse, and sometimes unfortunately an undertaker ?—eh, is it not so, mother ?"

" Yes, it is so, I confess ; unless, indeed, they are particular friends, such as a certain stationer seems to be ; and then they are allowed nurses of their own."

" And no undertaker at all !" growled out Gowles, interrupting Mother Hagget. " No, no ; the doctor reserves the fees of his friends to himself."

The doctor felt these remarks keenly, but suppressing his real opinion, he observed—"Why, our employment and profit would soon be at an end, if *all* my patients required the dead cart. That would procure for us a very unprofitable fame, in the end, I think. But, come ; no more of this, let's in, and reap such a harvest from our last patient, as shall satisfy us for our late losses."

So saying, he pulled a bell at the side of the door lustily for some minutes, which was soon opened by a verger, who had been appointed door-keeper in the room of those who now slept soundly in the vault below. Looking out, he demanded their business.

" We come, with an order of the dean's, to remove the furniture and goods from the apartment of the late Ralph Garland," answered Doctor Calder.

" I must see and read such order before I can let you pass," replied the verger. "Will you hand it to me?"

"It is here: you will perceive the reverend gentleman's signature on the left hand corner." said the doctor, as he handed over the certificate to the official.

" I am perfectly satisfied," exclaimed the verger, after having perused the document; "you may enter; but I must keep this order.'

"Agreed," replied Calder. "Come, friends, we have much to do yet Let us enter."

And following the doctor's footsteps, the trio now walked slowly down the centre aisle, followed by the verger, who bore a lighted torch in his hand, whose flickering rays but cheated the darkness which prevailed, by dancing from pillar to tombstone, from altar-piece to monument, as if it was the dance of death in its grim midnight gambols.

Arriving at the apartment of the late bell-ringer, the three friends were soon left to themselves; and Mother Hagget, after making sure of the cir cumstance, pulled out from a large pocket she always wore on such occasions, a small flask, and filling a horn with some of its contents, turned it off hastily.

"Now I can breathe freely," she observed. "Shall I help you, doctor?"

" What is it, Hagget?" inquired the doctor.

"'Tis nothing but a decoction of my own making: a mixture of carraway, poppies, and juniper berries; sweetened with the milk of almonds, and honey."

"Ah! a capital preventive, indeed," answered the doctor, "'twould be difficult to procure better—but I have taken an antidote already, and require nothing at present. But I would recommend Gowles to try it," replied the doctor.

"What say you, death and cross-bones; will you have a sip?" said Mother Hagget, addressing Gowles in a tone of vulgar familiarity.

"I care not if I do—I need something, if it is only to revive my spirits," replied Gowles; and having received a bumper from Mother Hagget, he drank it off eagerly, with an appearance of much relish. "By all the corpses in Finsbury dead pit! but that is excellent," exclaimed Gowles, as he drank off the beverage. I would have tapped that before, sweetheart, if I had known of it, I can tell you."

" I doubt, I doubt," replied Hagget; "we have come to search, not to revel, remember; so let's to work. Come, Calder, how will you begin?"

"That bed and its appurtenances must be our first object to remove," replied the doctor, "for in that jumble of lumber I put my best hopes."

Accordingly the clothes and mattress, together with the rug which had proved so useful to Mother Hagget, were seized upon, and two or three severe shocks and wrenches bestowed upon the slight fabric by Doctor Calder, soon brought the whole to the ground. Every joint, nook, and crevice attached to the bedstead was strictly searched, but nothing was discovered likely to give a clue to the anxiously sought for treasure. Gowles suggested the propriety of exploring the recesses of a large closet, which stood in the wall in a corner of the room. Doctor Calder, acting upon the suggestion, was not slow in entering it; groping his way into the nook, he ordered Gowles to take his station at the door, holding the lantern, whilst Mother Hagget was directed to rip up the mattress and pillows of the bed, to see if anything was concealed in them, preparatory to their being thrown on one side.

Nothing could have been better suited for the plan of Gowles and Mother Hagget; for while the doctor was in the closet, and therefore could not see anything that transpired without, Gowles from the entrance peeped out at intervals, and making signs with the nurse, directed her attention to a place in the partition of the room where the woodwork seemed to have been recently removed. Stealing silently from her occupation at the bedstead, the nurse crept across the room to the place pointed out by Gowles. A pannel was visible in the wainscoting, and by cautiously inserting a small piece of iron she thrust it open, when, to her surprise and pleasure, two bags and a roll of paper stood on a shelf opposite the door. Covering the entrance of the secret opening with her body, to prevent the penetrating eye of Gowles in detecting her lift out the two bags, she caught one in each hand, and by a skilful manoeuvre, hastily secreted one of them in a large leathern wallet that she always carried suspended to her side, beneath her outer clothing. Holding up one bag and the roll of money, she nodded significantly to the undertaker, and closing up the sliding pannel returned to her task beside the bed, having swung the remaining bag round her waist, and concealed the roll of paper in her high-crowned hat.

At this moment the doctor came from the closet, cursing and swearing at his ill success: he was covered with dust and cobwebs, and looked more like a negro than a man of physic.

"May the old miser never rest in his grave till the treasure is discovered!" he exclaimed angrily. Then turning to the nurse he inquired of her how she had succeeded.

"No better than yourself," was the reply. "I believe the miserly old wretch was so fond of his money when alive that he has charmed it away after him."

"Some one has charmed it away, that is quite evident," remarked the doctor, very peevishly. "I know positively that he had money, and I also know that it was secreted in this room at the time he was taken ill—I could have sworn you must have seen it, Hagget."

"You seem to be very uneasy, doctor," replied the nurse; "if I had discovered it, I should have equally divided it, and that is more than I can say of you; 'twould have been like some of those handsome presents which you have lately received from families for effecting cures of the plague, and have never been generous enough to give me, who shared all the danger of infection, and did a greater part towards curing the patients."

"Or like the burial expenses of the whole family in Dowgate-hill," added Gowles, "where you was commissioned by the parish to see them under ground, and charged liberally for it, at the same time telling me to hurl them into the dead pit. I have not forgotten this, Master Calder, and now I have brought it out—I care not for your frowns or threats: if I am black with mud, you are up to your neck in mire; so I care not for your blab! The two vergers in the stone vault beneath will cover any thing you may know concerning me, and that is enough to bring any man to the gibbet!"

"And look you, Master Doctor," added Hagget, whose malice seemed whetted by the turn Gowles had taken in the affair, "Had it been any other family than the Elliot's, of Cheapside, with whom you pretend to appear such an intimate friend, I should have been introduced, and have gained a good month's salary, besides other perquisites."

"And should not I have had some ten or fifteen pounds for undertaker's bill as well, if it had been any one else? But I'll be sworn there has been a good round sum given there as a bonus; which, forsooth, you think proper to keep to yourself, without saying a word to us about it, and this is keeping up a friendly contract, indeed! To the devil with such contracts, say I," exclaimed Gowles maliciously.

"So say I," muttered Hagget.

"Hell-crew that ye are!" answered the doctor, who had stood paralysed with astonishment during this attack upon him by his confederates. "And is this the reward that I receive for making you both what you are? for dragging you from a position of poverty and wretchedness, and placing you in a way to make rapid fortunes? May you both rot on a gibbet before I hold further dealings with you! And you, Gowles, who I took by the hand from being a common water-side porter, lent you money from my own purse, and worked you into a first-rate connexion as a coffin-maker, now to turn upon me in this dastardly and ungrateful manner. And you, Hagget; what did I not for you? Did I not save your life on a bed of death, starving and emaciated with disease, and introduced you into the houses of respectable patients as nurse, where you might have gained gold like rain, could you but have kept your cursed fingers from other people's property. To charge me with secreting the profits, too! I will not parley with you any longer; it is clear to me that the treasure of old Garland has found an owner ere this, and our compact ceases from this moment. I suspected as much, but lacked the proof. To jail with ye both! where you can dwell in silence and solitude over your past stupidity."

"Take heed you are not there first," replied Gowles.

"We understand each other now, remember," exclaimed the doctor to his companions. "I leave you for ever; I shun you as I would the plague: one, for a villanous wretch who would not hesitate meeting a drunken man, robbing him, and hurling him into the dead pit! the other, for a hag of Lucifer's own breeding, who in nursing invalids strangles them with one hand, as she administers relief with the other! I know ye. Dread and for ever avoid me!"

As he pronounced these words, he rushed from the apartment, and hastily descended the flight of stone steps that led towards the outer gate of the cathedral.

"Well," exclaimed Gowles, after he had recovered from the effects of the surprise which the doctor's speech had caused him, "he has left us in a sweet temper, I must say. We cannot mistake, now, his intentions towards us, and so our only plan must be to meet them. He has no proofs, however, that can do us any harm."

"But," replied Hagget, "I know where to find plenty of proofs that will sink him so deep in the pit of guilt that all his cunning shall not be able to extricate him—the two vergers beneath; besides several lotions that he has given me to administer to patients, which would sleep them off in an hour, and which I have kept for myself, and disposed of them equally sure and safe by a way of my own. He should have been the last man to pick a quarrel, for if he is the cause of our adorning a gibbet, the same wind that swings us to and fro will blow him high between heaven and hell, never to reach either!"

"But the money, Hagget, the money; let's count it over, and see the ex tent of our gains," said Gowles.

"Here it is," replied Hagget, drawing a single bag of gold from her pocket, leaving the second one secreted in its hiding-place round her waist. "It seems well filled, any how: is it gold, silver, or copper, I wonder?— Gold, by all that is bright and good-looking?" she exclaimed, as she poured the pieces into her lap in a long yellow stream.

"And think you this is all of the old bell-ringer's wealth, mother?" inquired Gowles.

"I do," replied the nurse. "There was no more to be seen, and I call this a pretty tidy saving for one so poor as he seemed to be. But let us count it out."

Seating themselves at the table, they proceeded to count and divide their gains, which they did speedily, and with very great satisfaction to both, but especially the nurse, as she had the remaining bag still untouched in her possession. They then packed up the furniture which was in the apartment, according to the agreement that had been made between Dr. Calder and the dean of the cathedral, and loading each other to the extent of their strength, they left the vault, and stole out of the church by the most secret and lonely passages, partners alike in guilt and fear, and trembling alike for any impending consequences.

CHAPTER XIII.

BEARING his fainting burden in his arms, Buckingham and Vincent, who had by this time joined him, made the best of their way to Temple Bar, a coach being in waiting for them. Hastily unfastening the door, Buckingham leaped in with Constance still senseless in his arms, directing Vincent to mount the seat in front and keep a sharp look out, for he anticipated a pursuit, and in the event of such a circumstance had provided both himself and companion with a supply of arms. Dealing out a variety of maledictions to the yawning and half-drowsy post-boys, who had now taken their seats on the horses, he threatened to shoot them if they did not proceed at full gallop the whole of the journey. Pulling up the wooden shutters of the coach, he thus prevented any ill effects from the night air, and amid the lumbering of the heavy vehicle as it rolled or rather danced over the rough and uneven streets towards Charing-cross, he endeavoured to revive Constance to a sense of her position and companion, but for the present all his attempts had been useless.

Drawing a thick mantle round him, and cocking two large dragoon petronels, Vincent rolled himself up into a heap in his garments to keep warmth in him, for the night air was piercing cold. Giving his gruff orders to the drivers, by growling at them every now and then for the creeping pace they were going at, and singing and cursing at intervals, he was at last lulled into a sort of doze by the swinging motion of the coach, which was now dragged along over mounds of mud and sinking into deep-furrowed ruts and holes, of which the roads at that time abounded, at a rattling pace of four miles an hour. They had passed the quiet hamlet of Charing, and turning down by the side of the mall, round St. James's Park, made for the Tyburn-road, along which, by dint of whip, spur, and bellowing, the post-boys urged their snorting steeds at a galloping and furious pace.

Buckingham, although a thoughtless, reckless man, began to grow alarmed at the swooning state of Constance, who, as yet, save by one or two heavy sighs, gave no signs of animation. However, after a lapse of about half an hour, her eyes opened, and in a low faint voice she called upon her mother, for her confused ideas were still wandering on the fire, amidst the blazing folds of which she had sunk into her present state of unconsciousness.

"Light of my soul! look up and bless me with thy smiles," exclaimed Buckingham, pressing her to his heart.

Slowly casting her eyes around, and fixing her vacant gaze upon him as he spoke, she uttered a piercing moan, and again relapsed into her former state of senselessness.

By the dull light of a horn lantern, which hung from the roof of the coach, Buckingham administered a little relief in the shape of a glass bottle of chemical scent, which seemed for the moment to revive her. He chafed the palms of her hands, her temples, and her forehead, and lowered down one of the shutters to give entrance to a gust of cool air. These means, after some moments, had the effect of once more reviving the fair captive Buckingham had so villanously dragged from her friends and her home.

Her eyes again opened, discovering to his view their blue orbs streaming with tears of woe and anguish. " Where am I ? For Heaven's sake tell me of my parents! Are they safe ? Lawrence, too, is he saved ? Tell me, I implore you, are they safe ?"

" Your parents and friends are all safe and well, dearest Constance," replied Buckingham. " 'Tis I who have saved you and your family. I rushed into the burning gulph only just in time to save you from the devouring element, which had already began to enfold you within its deathly arms. Look up, dearest, fairest of maidens, and bless me with but a smile in return—one look of love is all I ask."

" Can it be ? Arthur! Buckingham! heavens, how is this ? What mystery is it that brings me here, and with you, away from all my friends and kindred. Lawrence, too, where is he ? Now I pause, and look back, I remember being with him ; the room was on fire beneath our feet, the atmosphere was scorching hot, loud cries and shouts met my ears, mingled with the suffering voice of my dear mother calling for her child. The flames thickened round us, and I sank senseless into the midst of them, only to be released by a miracle."

" And that miracle was performed by me, Constance," replied Buckingham to her reverie.

" But Lawrence, who saved him ? or has he fallen a victim, and met his death in trying to save me ?"

" Fear not for such as him, lovely Constance," exclaimed Buckingham. " He is as safe as all such cowardly poltroons generally are in the time of danger."

" How ! what mean you by that, sir ?" interrupted Constance indignantly. " He was at my side in the moment of extreme peril, and might have easily effected his escape some time before had he chosen to have done so without me. But he refused to move till he had conveyed me to a place of security, and I fear his generosity has cost him his life."

" Quite the reverse, I assure you," answered Buckingham. " My friends and myself met him leaving the apartment as we were approaching ; he called out that all was lost, and that help was useless ; and then making the best use of his activity, fled far from the scene of danger to leave the perilous though heavenly task to me of saving the life of one for whom I would gladly give my own to preserve from harm. Dastard, coward as he is ! I thank him for the deed, since it has given to me the person of my beloved and dearest Constance !"

Clasping her familiarly in his arms, Buckingham was about to strain her to his heart, and drink the joys of love in kisses from her lips, when Constance, raising her voice to its highest pitch, uttered a loud and piercing scream, which her companion tried to prevent by placing his hand over her mouth, and with the other closing the shutter, lest the noise should reach the ear of any traveller who might be curious enough to ascertain from what cause it originated. Constance, completely exhausted by her efforts, sank back in her seat, and sought relief in a flood of tears.

Buckingham was instantly at her feet, and taking her hand humbly sought forgiveness.

" You injure yourself and me by these outcries, Constance," he exclaimed. " I only bear you to a place of safety, whither in a short time we shall arrive. Suffer me, then, dearest Constance, to pour out before you the ardent love of my heart, which I here swear will never know rest or true happiness till you become mine."

" My lord duke," replied Constance, somewhat haughtily, " the only reply I can make to language of this sort is, what I have told you before, that since I have found you capable of the base deception of which you was guilty towards me, in denying your name, that must be your answer now and for ever. Besides, I have solemnly and truly, in love, honour, and gratitude, given my hand and heart to another, which promise, if I forget, may heaven for ever forget me ?"

"And may every hope of happiness be snatched from me ; may Heaven also forget me if I forgive the hand that dealt so fatal a blow to my peace !" exclaimed Buckingham in anger. "Constance ! mine you must be, shall be, in spite of friend, lover, or foe ! I have tried to win you fairly and truly, but I have been thwarted and crossed by a menial, lowly slave. But as there is a power who watches and reigns above us, I will deal a death blow on that head that has dared to come between me and my heart's choice. Constance, despair not, but in love and duty yield to me, and sure as the morning sun is slowly travelling to lighten up these dark clouds in beams of glory, so sure shall to-morrow see you the Duchess of Buckingham, and wife to the man who adores you."

"No, my lord, that must never be !" answered Constance with such firmness that even the persevering audacity of Buckingham itself was taken aback. "As Arthur Latymer, a tradesman, citizen, or merchant, I confess with truth you had won my girlish heart ; but the instant you were revealed to me in your true name and colours, that moment was all love or esteem for Arthur Latymer, or the gay, deceiving, worthless Duke of Buckingham for ever banished from my heart !"

"Say not so," exclaimed Buckingham, imploringly. "I did but make use of the disguise to win your heart by my own efforts, and not the attractions of my wealth. Believe me I had no other motive—could have none !"

" Did not conflicting circumstances give such an excuse a flat denial and positive falsehood, I might be inclined, as the simple, easy girl you took me for, to give ear to it. But, my lord, when I found from clear substantiated evidences that not even *your* easy-shifting tongue could deny that you had adopted this plan with others, and some of them, to your shame be it spoken, had met with a sorry return for their confidence, I denounced you at once for a trifler, and a villain ; for in no one instance where your real name and position in society was made a secret, did any feeling or act of honour appear connected with it ; and I have too good reasons for saying that I believe even as the Duke of Buckingham your conduct will never add a honourable tint to the title hereafter !"

" Nay, nay, Constance, you trifle with me. Some hypocritical priest has been reading sermons to you, sure ;" and breaking into an affected laugh, he tried to give the conversation a jocular turn.

" I do indeed trifle, and too long," replied Constance. " But whither am I being carried ? sure we must have travelled some distance, and I have no friends but those I have left in such dreadful suspense. Say, my lord, do you intend to kidnap or imprison me that I am thus hurried whither I know not —turn, I beseech you, and let me but once more enfold in my arms my beloved parents, and insure them of my safety, and I am then ready—"

" To what, Constance ? ready to what ?—say but the word, and your wish shall become law."

" Ready to deliver up my life to him who gave it, rather than thus be made an object of care and strife !" answered Constance, sorrowfully. " And if you possessed but a single atom of that affection for me which you so plentifully boast of, you would not commit an act that gave me so much pain. Return, my lord, I implore, I entreat you on my knees, I supplicate to you, who say my slightest wish is your supreme command !"

" This must not be," replied Buckingham, raising her up, and placing her by his side.

" Then stay our progress ; let us return ; let me at least have my liberty !"

ejaculated Constance with energy; and rising to put her wishes into execution she lowered the window, and screaming forth for help was instantly forced back from the door by Buckingham, and pushed into a corner of the coach.

At this moment the horses started by the appalling shrieks of Constance, or grown enraged by the constant application of the whip and spur that had been bestowed upon them for the last four or five miles of their journey, began to grow unmanageable and desperate; they plunged, swerved from the right course, suddenly slackened their pace, and then as suddenly rushed on with the furious speed of madness; and, at a sharp turning of the road, brought the carriage with such tremendous force upon an adjacent bank that the forewheels were dashed to atoms, the coach thrown over on its side, and the drivers were precipitated several yards from the spot. The horses speedily disengaged themselves from their incumbrance, and dashing forward with the terror and fury of wild beasts, dragged after them a large portion of the lumbering vehicle; which, swinging and rattling at their heels, only served to increase their speed to a pitch of greater frenzy.

This disaster immediately put a new face upon circumstances. Vincent Palmer, being at the moment of the accident fast asleep, was carried along with that part of the carriage which remained attached to the horses heels; and after performing many very extraordinary and uncomfortable evolutions in his progress, was at last hurled, by the friendly interposition of a mile-post, into a swamp near the road, where for some time he lay stunned; but soon recovering himself, he perceived by the glare of the two front lamps where the carriage was lying, and to the assistance of its inmates he at once directed his way.

The two drivers lay in opposite directions, severely mangled and wounded by their fall, but without waiting to look at them, Vincent, taking the carriage lamps in his hands, proceeded to the door of the coach which was up-

12.

permost. Upon opening it, he discovered the inmates both senseless, and inanimate ; for Constance was bleeding from a severe wound in the forehead, caused by her coming in contact with the sides of the carriage ; and the sudden lurch which the coach had taken in overturning had pitched Buckingham on his head, and for a while had stunned him. Lifting them both from the coach, Vincent seated them on a bank, and fetching some cold water from a small stream which was running at the foot of a hedge by the road-side, soon succeeded in restoring Buckingham to a state of consciousness.

The first inquiry Buckingham made was after Constance ; and being informed that she was by his side, wounded and senseless, he caught her in his arms, and called upon Vincent wildly to fetch a surgeon.

"That would be a vain and a foolish attempt, Buckingham, depend upon it," replied Vincent. "For we are not in sight of any human habitation, and a tender female like her might perish during my errand !"

"Heaven and earth ! what is to be done ?" exclaimed Buckingham in a tone of great affliction ; "she cannot remain here ; this penetrating night air will kill her."

"I will suggest a plan. This road is as well known to me as if I was a highwayman ; and by my calculation it is not more than two miles across yonder meadows to your house at Harrow. Thither let us at once direct our steps, and leave these awkward hell-hounds to recover themselves, in the same manner as they have left us. Come ; I will bear one of these lamps with us ; take the girl up in your arms, and when you are fatigued, I will releave you—hark ! Some one is coming this way that may assist us !"

After both straining their eyes in the direction pointed out by Vincent, and after listening attentively for some minutes, Buckingham, catching Constance in his arms, exclaimed, "It is some one coming this way, as sure as life ! They are horsemen ; and, if I guess right, are our pursuers. Let's begone ; we have not a moment to lose. Lead the way down this hill ; it being shaded with trees will cover our retreat for a full half-mile."

"And by that time we shall be safe, for all their speed. They are coming at the rate of thunder-bolts ! let 'em alone—this narrow road, this sharp turning, and this old coach, lying here in the middle of the road, will bring them to a halt as sudden and as unexpected, and perhaps as inconvenient as ours—come, I am with you. One light will suffice us ; I will leave the other as a legacy to lighten the darkness of our followers. Will you give me your hand in descending this hill ; it is very steep ?"

"No, you go first, and cast your light on the ground that I may pick my way. Constance is recovering—she breathes easier and more frequent. Shade your light, man, for Heaven's sake, or else they will mark it as a beacon, and be down upon us in an instant. I hear their horse's hoofs rattling like hail-stones ; they are not far behind, and will be up with us in a few minutes. I am ready."

Taking the coach-lamp in his hand, Vincent cautiously led the way down the hill-side, which sloped off away from the road, across an open meadow country. He had much difficulty in opening the way for himself and his companion, for the brushwood and thick-set hedges ran so high and were so strong, that it much impeded their way. After about ten minutes' careful, slow walking, however, they reached the bottom of the hill, and found themselves in a plain, or open field, whither, for a few moments, they paused to rest themselves, and try and listen if anything was to be heard from their pursuers.

The sounds of horsemen which had been heard by Buckingham and his companion was no other than Lawrence Wood, the constable of the watch, and one of the city marshal. On they came with the speed of demons, never heeding anything before them, or behind ; and as they neared the spot where the carriage had been overturned, the constable, who was first, had just time to call out for his companions to halt when his furiously driven steed unable to slacken its pace, rolled headlong over the carriage as it lay in the road. The marshalman, who followed next, shared the same fate, though with more disaster, for being a heavy man, he fell with his horse, who rolled over and over with him, till they both quietly reposed in a ditch by the road-side. Whilst Lawrence, who was last, had just time to rein up his steed, to prevent any mischief; and he immediately descended to the relief of his fallen companions.

CHAPTER XIV.

WE must now return to Lawrence at the time of his imprisonment by the duke and his companions. Coming somewhat to himself, Lawrence began to grow uneasy at his confinement, the place of which happened to be a brewery or out-door pantry, and used by the family of Master Elliot for other domestic purposes. After kicking, plunging, and calling at the very top of his voice, he gave up the idea of gaining his liberty by fair attempts, and he therefore made up his mind to force the door. Groping round his cell, he had the good fortune to find a strong club, used as a masher of malt: with this he began to belabour the door most lustily, when after several heavy blows one of the panels gave way, and forcing his club between the aperture made by his battering, he pushed out the wood-work sufficient to enable him to get out. Throwing away his club, and mounting a small stool, he soon gained the yard by jumping through the opening in the door. Casting his eyes up towards the house, he was surprised to find the back of it so entire: for the wind having been blowing strong from the north-east all night, had kept the fire all to the front. Without waiting to consider, he rushed out at the back gate, which was standing open, determined upon seeking Constance and her parents, feeling convinced that they were protected by some kind neighbour. On his way round to Cheapside, he tried to bring his memory to the circumstance of leaving the windows with Constance in his arms : he could remember first mounting the ladder, Constance fainting in his arms, and the rushing up of a terrific body of flame through the flooring of the room, the suffocating smoke, and his sinking into the midst of it with his mistress firmly clasped to his breast, and then all was lost to memory and reason: these circumstances he was enabled to tell over successively to himself in his contemplation, but no further; he had not the remotest idea of what befell either himself or Constance afterwards. "Sure," thought he, " they never left her to perish !—though by Heaven, now I think of it, there was no one left to rescue her ; the city constable and his men had descended by their ladder into the street, and we were the only persons left in the house. Well do I remember their hoarse words in exciting us to haste, as the floor was sinking, and all would be lost ! Oh, Heaven ! merciful provider for the helpless and the innocent, grant that it may have been otherwise !"

Thus ruminating, he worked himself up to such a pitch of feverish excite-ment that he had not hope sufficient to allow him to put any other construc-tion upon the affair. " I could have been saved only by a miracle," he ex claimed to himself ; " snatched, no doubt, from the jaws of death by some kind hand, and hid away for security in the place I have just escaped from. But then could not the same hand have rescued Constance ? 'Tis plain that some one was in the room after the bursting in of the flames. It must be so ; for no one would save me, and leave an angel like her to perish ! I will hope for the best. Heaven grant it may be so !"

By this time he had arrived in Cheapside, but owing to the smoke, and the crowds of men who had gathered round the house, and who were now busily engaged fetching water from the Conduit in large barrels and casks, to throw upon the still smouldering ruins, he was unable to get near the premises. He busied himself, however, in asking questions of those around him, to ascertain where and what portion of the family were lodged in safety.

"All, I believe, are safe of Master Elliot's family," replied one of the watchmen who was keeping the crowd; "though they do say his apprentice, who is a fine daring lad, has fell a victim to the flames, for no one has seen him since he showed himself at that second story window, where you see the flames were hottest. They do say, too, that he had a female in his arms, and that they were both seen to sink down together."

"Is that all the information you can give me?" replied Lawrence, rather pettishly.

"Is that all! yes, it is all," answered the man gruffly. "You can't expect to know more than I do myself, can you?"

"Excuse my being so pressing, friend," said Lawrence calmly. "I am Elliot's apprentice, and the person you saw at the window. There was a female in my arms—Constance, his only daughter, and I fear she is lost in the flames."

Darting forward from amidst the crowd, Lawrence now mixed with the constable's men, who were in charge of the house. Forcing his way through rubbish and over fallen beams, he encountered the chief constable, whom he immediately recognised as the man who had charged him to descend the ladder when the room was in flames. Making towards him, he begged of him in earnest solicitations to inform him if any tidings had been heard of Constance.

"Alas! no," he replied. All hope is gone; she must have fallen a prey to the flames. Her poor old father never left the burning ruins till a short time since, when he was forced away by a neighbour, and taken to the residence of Master Buckthorp, the hosier, in Friday-street.

"Poor old man! his sufferings must be dreadful—he was so fond of that girl," answered Lawrence. "But I will never leave the spot till she is found."

"How were you saved?" inquired the constable. "I left you in yonder room, which is still burning. I saw both ladders fall directly I left the room, and judged that both you and the girl were perishing in the flames."

"I know not, indeed, by what miracle or by whose hand I was saved," replied Lawrence, "but when I recovered my senses, I found myself fastened in an outhouse."

"Fastened up, did you say?" That is a strange way of preserving a person's life. Had the wind but changed a point, your place of safety would have been your death. Some one must have entered the room after I left it, and have borne you out, and they must have seen the girl, and surely would never have left her. Do you know that man stealing along under yonder wall?" inquired the constable, pointing to a person who was walking over the ruins under the shade of the wall: he was enveloped in a large black mantle, wearing a soldier's hat and feather, and by his side hung a long Spanish rapier.

Lawrence looked long and steadfastly at the figure pointed out to him, and after having carefully scanned him from head to foot exclaimed as he rushed towards him, "Villain! I will tear the secret from his lips, with my life I will purchase it."

The next instant, and before the constable could interfere to prevent it, Lawrence and the stranger were struggling with all the fury of madmen. The mysterious person was no other than Captain Blount, who having missed the retreat of his companions by not being let into the secret of their place of refuge, had tarried on the spot to see what might turn up in the event of the girl being missed.

" Mother of heaven !" roared the captain, having disengaged himself from the grasp of Lawrence, who had seized his throat with such fury and earnestness that had not the interference of the constable released his grip, the wretched man he had so roughly handled would never have spoken more. " Mother of Heaven !" he repeated, "for what do you clapper-claw a man after that style ?   Draw out your rapier, and let's have steel to steel ; or a petronel, if you have a mind for a trial of skill that way. No matter for why or for what, a quarrel is always welcome to me, but let me not suffer a fowl's death, with a twisted neck and a fling on a dungheap. Out, man, I say ; have ye no good blade at your side to serve your purpose ? or here, if you will be so courteous, take which you please of these two petronels ; their triggers never fail, I assure you."

Here the captain handed two pistols to Lawrence for his choice and acceptance, which Lawrence dashed aside, and was making another attempt to rush upon his antagonist, when he was forcibly held back by the constable.

" Tell me then, villain, what you and your dastardly accomplices have done with the lady you have been here watching for. Now I see you here, a new light breaks in upon me. 'Tis a plot—a vile scheme to rob a citizen of his child. This calamity is a premeditated affair. Have you seen this man before ?" said Lawrence, turning to the constable.

" I have," was the reply. " I saw him and two other persons, richly dressed and wrapped in cloaks, going up stairs during the fire, but I guessed they were members of the family."

" Members of a crew of debauched villains and incendiaries ! Constable, I charge you in the king's name, and in the name of my master, to detain that man as an accessory in this hellish deed. He is a companion of the Duke of Buckingham's, who, I am well aware, to gain his purpose in such an event as this, would fire a whole town, and stand smiling by. Seize him, I say !"

This was putting quite a different view upon the subject than Blount either expected or liked, and drawing his rapier stood upon his guard.

" You are rash, young master," reasoned the constable with Lawrence. " The Duke of Buckingham, bad as he is, could never have been guilty of so villanous an action.   Yet still I think this fellow must know something about your master's daughter."

" I am fully assured that he does," replied Lawrence, agitated and trembling with rage, " and though he be armed to the throat in steel, I will wrench it from him."

Saying this, he sprang upon Blount with the fury of a tiger, and seizing hold of his sword wrenched it from his grasp, and forcing the captain back a few paces, he brought him to the ground, when placing his knee on his chest he demanded of him what he knew concerning Constance.

" Release me, I implore you," said the captain, " or the point of the sword will be through my throat before I can draw another breath."

" I care not," was the reply of his angry captor ; " you move not an inch till you have told me all you know concerning your accomplices."

The constable and several of his men, who had now gathered round the spot, seeing that Lawrence's object was to gain information respecting Constance, rather than to do him any serious bodily harm, stood looking on, and laughing to see so tall and gaunt a looking man as Captain Blount begging for mercy at the hands of a stripling like Lawrence. Some of them, in their jest, besought him not to hurt the good gentleman.

" He dies by his own sword on this very spot, if he does not confess the truth," exclaimed the infuriated youth, "though I swing high on a gibbet the next hour."

"Remove the sword from my throat, and I will tell you all I know," said the captain imploringly.

Assenting to this request, Lawrence raised the sword in such a position as to bring it to bear again in an instant if required. "Proceed instantly," he said, menacing his antagonist.

"You may stand a good chance, then, of catching the girl if you can find good horses to carry you some twelve miles on the Harrow road such a night as this. At the duke's country-house there, on the hill to the right of the town, no doubt you will find them at breakfast. They did not choose to let me accompany them, but they shall find I can send them visitors for all that," and with an oath he called down curses on his own stupid head for having allowed himself to be prevailed on so far as to have assisted them in their project.

"The hell-hound!" exclaimed Lawrence; "I knew it was his doings. I wonder I had not guessed as much before. May I depend upon what you have told me?"

"As my life!" replied the captain.

"You are free, then," said Lawrence, withdrawing from him so as to allow him to rise. Then turning to the chief constable he exclaimed, "You have heard his tale; will you join me in pursuit? I will ensure you a handsome reward in the event of our chase proving successful; as I suppose this fellow will not accompany us."

He alluded to Captain Blount; but on turning round to gain his assent to the proposition, he found that he had gone. "Cowardly wretch?" exclaimed Lawrence, "he has fled and left his sword in my hand. No matter; I will use it with interest against his friends. What say you, constable?"

"With all my heart," replied the man, "provided you obtain horses."

"That shall be done," answered Lawrence. "'Tis now two good hours to day-light, and with some good cattle we may gain upon them a little in that time. As Master Elliot and his family are safe lodged, I shall not disturb them with my errand, till I can restore their daughter to their arms. I should like a third party, though—"

"For what, and for why," exclaimed Rough Gabel, a stout brawny built man, of seven foot standing, who having entered the house at the moment, and overhearing Lawrence's last words, had made the above remark. Jem Gabel, or Rough Gabel, as he was more familiarily called, from his uncouth, blunt, hardy ways, of herculean strength and courage, was one of the city marshalmen, a body at this time of considerable note in the city. "What treason is hatching here," he demanded sharply, as he broke upon the conversation of Lawrence and the constable of the watch.

"Why, 'tis a job, Gabel, that will just suit you and me, I have no doubt but what you will gladly assist us. 'Tis to recover a lady who has been forced from her parents by titled court-going villains, that class of the community you are so particularly attached to, Gabel!" remarked the constable pointedly.

"It is my master's daughter;" interfered Lawrence, in explanation. "During the confusion of the fire, she has been clandestinely and forcibly carried off by the artful and designing Duke of Buckingham. I have gained information of their route, and trust, by the assistance of one or two brave companions, and some sure footed steeds, to be able to overreach and recover her—have you a mind to become possessor of a good reward, by joining us in pursuit of her?"

"Not the least! I'm your man. Anything to be revenged on a court-gallant! Oh, that he may strike at me with his sword, and give me fair cause for chopping him down from the head to the loins—I would split him in two as a cooper would a stave, with all the comfort imaginable. But when do we start?"

At once, now, come with me! we lose time;" replied Lawrence. "I can procure horses at the Castle in Aldersgate, where my master is well known · come, come, every moment is of object to us."

As he said these words, Lawrence led the way, accompanied by his two companions, down Cheapside, towards Aldersgate-street. Each person was well-armed, for Lawrence, besides his glorious trophy won of the captain, had a brace of heavy pistols which had been given to him by the constable,— and they were a match for any light party of four or five men.

Arriving at the Castle Inn, after a few minutes of pulling and tugging at the old cracked yard-bell, which was accompanied by the loud barking of a watch-dog, the gate was opened by a drowsy ostler who demanded their business.

"Horses, instantly," replied Lawrence. "Have you some good bloods in the stables—is your master stirring?" he inquired of the yawning groom, who stood shaking before them.

"Oh, is it your master, Lawrence?" drawled out the ostler, after a few moment's glance at all their faces with his lantern. Come in, come in, I dare say I can find you some dancing blades; but wherever can you be going this time of night, I wonder?"

"Never you mind, sleepy-head," answered Lawrence. "Only you be quick and start us off, and put the guinea safe in your pocket, which you may have if you are civil and speedy."

This had a magical effect on the ostler, who skipped away nimbly to the stables to execute Lawrence's bidding.

Master Elliot in his wholesale trading did a good deal of business with the Castle Inn, by sending large quantities of paper every week to his country customers, and also by receiving a great quantity from his mills in Lincolnshire; so that his name was well known there, and the commands of even his apprentice obeyed as promptly as if they were his own orders.

"If we get some good flesh and keep the right road, we may chance to run them down by day-break, now;" exclaimed the marshalman. "For heavy carriages are lumbering affairs behind horses, in bad roads, and at night time especially."

"Yes, so I should guess," argued the constable. "Let's see—they have not more than an hour's start of us, and Harrow-on-the-hill is not more than two and twenty miles from Charing-cross; why we ought to be upon their heels in less than an hour and a half from our starting."

"Well, I hope I shall find your calculations right, my friend," returned Lawrence to the well-meant remarks of his companions; "for here comes the boy with the horses."

The trio now mounted their horses, which were brought ready saddled to them; and to do the innkeeper justice his supply was excellent; for the cattle presented on the above occasion were in good condition, sleek and eager to throw the ground behind them. Throwing the promised fee to the ostler, as he held the gate open for them to pass, Lawrence led the way, and they all started off across Newgate-street at a brisk canter.

"Double fees for the man who lays first hold of the bridle of one of their horses," exclaimed Lawrence, encouraging his companions. "Lay to it, my boys, and we shall soon be on their track!"

This intreaty was answered by a shower of blows from whip and spur upon the steeds of his companions, and they being fresh and young horses, took to the road in first rate style, leaving Lawrence for a while terribly in the rear, Sweeping down Holborns they gaily bounded up the hill opposite, and leaving the lights on the banks of the Thames, and the hedges and ditches of Gray's Inn Lane behind them, they were rapidly making for the neighbourhood of Tottenham Court. Passing on with their horses heads towards Tyburn, they soon reached that famous spot, and the road here being very dark, and the obstructions but few, they trusted to their horses more than to their own judgment; and sticking the spurs deep into their sides, and awakening them up with the whip, they actually flew along, over pond, brake, or bank that came in their way.

Lawrence was not quite such an experienced horseman as his two companions; but, however, he managed to keep them in tolerable view, and as his horse was one that did not require much urging on, it kept him employed in holding safely on, while his companions lost much time and underwent much labour with flogging and coaxing their cattle along. At this pell-mell rate they had hurried along for more than an hour, when the foremost horse, who was the marshalman, discerned lights in the distance, dancing, as he thought, to and fro.

This gave them new hopes; again whip, voice, and spur, were in requisition, and again was their speed mightily increased. Lawrence had been all the way along still kept in the rear; but his voice was frequently heard urging his friends onward, while they were laughing at him for not keeping pace with them.

The night, as yet, had been bleak, cold, and cloudy, the moon only appearing at intervals from behind dark clouds, so as just to enlighten surrounding objects by a glimpse, and then as suddenly disappear, leave all in gloomy darkness as before. It was at this moment, that the marshalman, crying out that he saw lights moving onward, that the moon peeped out from behind a thick black cloud that had obscured it for more than an hour, and throwing around her silver rays discovered to the horsemen some dark obstacle in the road before them, besides figures moving with a light across the road.

"We are on them," shouted the marshalman; "they have been stopping for something or other, and are now preparing to start again. Five minutes more and we shall be up to them—to it, lads!"

The three horsemen now exerted every effort and energy they possessed to overtake the objects they had in view; and at this juncture of their proceeding the moon was once more more encased in darkness, and left them without a guide. Speeding onward, full cry, without having any other object in mind but the captive and promised reward, the marshalman being the foremost of the troop was the first to meet with the concussion before spoken of, as he rolled over the carriage which lay before him, followed by his advancing companions.

Lawrence being the only one who had not met with a collision, groped about in the dark to find his associates who lay scattered around him.

"Give me a hand, for the love of Heaven!" implored the constable; "my horse is lying across my breast, if he plunges, I am a lost man!"

Pursuing his footsteps in the direction of the voice, Lawrence managed to reach the unfortunate man's hand, and with a steady pull released him from his perilous situation, and assisted him to raise his horse. The marshalman now occupied their joint attention, for he had pitched forward over the neck of his horse, which stood quietly by. Raising him up, and putting questions to him, they discovered, after a few moments, that he was only stunned by his fall.

"Here has been a spill here, besides us;" said the constable, "for see, here are wheels laying here broken, and the carriage is laying across the road. 'Tis a miracle we were not smashed to atoms!"

"How shall we act," inquired Lawrence; "if we proceed onwards we must sure overtake them; if they have not however taken a cross-cut to some

village.   Perhaps some of the party are hurt—Constance herself, likely, may have been injured by this accident, and I not near to help her! Or has this been a trick, think you, constable, to deceive us?   Doubtless they heard our approach!"

"Not at all likely, man," answered the party spoken to. "Why, here lies one of them on his back in the road; this doesn't look like a trick, I think :" and turning over the body of one of the postilions with his foot, he was answered by a low groan.

"Gracious Heavens! who is this?" exclaimed Lawrence in surprise, as he placed his hand on the man's breast: "he breathes, and is quite warm—he cannot be dying!"

"Come to this side of the bank," called out the marshalman, who had now so far recovered as to be able to speak. "Here is a man lying by the side of me either dead or dying!"

"Another!" cried out the constable; "why, we shall find the lady next if we go on this way."

"God forbid!" replied Lawrence. "But let us look to these wounded men. Here is a coach lamp at my feet; is there any possibility of getting a light, constable?"

"Only one, and that is with my pistol. I will try if you will hold the lamp."

Lawrence held up the lamp to the pistol of the constable, which he snapped off, and by placing a little powder on the wick, it had ignited by the flash. Holding it forth to cast a view over the surrounding group, Lawrence was horrified to behold a man lying bleeding at his feet, senseless, and apparently much injured. Directing his attention across the road to the object which had been spoken of by the marshalman, they discovered another body, the second postilion, who lay stretched on his back, with a deep gash on his forehead, from which the blood had been flowing copiously, and had clotted in a

13.

pool around him. In the centre of the road lay the duke's travelling carriage, rent into several parts; the wheels were separated from the vehicle,
two of which were smashed to atoms; all signs of the horses or the harness
had totally disappeared, and every thing around presented the picture of de-
vastation and confusion.

Confiding the charge of the two postilions to the constable and the marshalman, Lawrence pulled the steps of the coach down, and managed with
much difficulty to creep into the interior of the carriage. The first thing
which met his eye was the scarf or mantle which Constance had thrown over
her shoulders upon being aroused from her chamber by the alarm of the fire.
On searching the pockets in the cushion at the back of the seats, he discovered in one of them a large pair of holster pistols, which he placed in his
own belt, and in the second one a bag of gold, which he also secured. Having diligently searched every part of the coach, he leaped out and communicated to his companions his success, for holding up the mantle he exclaimed,

"See! we are on the right track; they have been disturbed by our approach, and have fled hastily; for this, with some money and a pair of
pistols, I have just found in the coach. But how fare his servants—are they
recovering?"

"They will soon be sensible," replied the marshalman, who was busily
engaged washing the dirt and blood from the face of his patient, while the
constable was pouring down the throat of the man in his charge some few
drops of brandy, which he always carried about him in a small flask on such
occasions.

"Here are striking signs of recovery," exclaimed the marshalman, as he
noticed the eyes of the postilion whom he was attending unclose. "A few
moments, and he will be on his legs."

After a little more attention on the part of Lawrence and his companions,
the two postilions were so far recovered as to be able to walk a few paces with
assistance; this soon gave them new strength, and enabled them to rumi-
nate upon their late disaster.

"You were conducting the Duke of Buckingham, I presume, by the appearance of that shattered carriage?" demanded Lawrence of one of them.

"You guess right, sir, for no man but the duke would have kept us flying
along at such a pace down a road like this, and in such a dark and bleak
night, too."

"But was he not accompanied by some one on the journey?" eagerly inquired Lawrence.

"He was—a lady was with him, but I know nothing of her. We took
them up at Temple Bar, where we had been waiting three hours."

"Did you hear any thing that transpired between them?" said Lawrence.

"No: merely a scream or two at first; but we heard very little after we
began to move along the road."

"Whither were you directing your course?"

"To Harrow Hall, the duke's seat: it lays about two miles across the
meadow there," replied the man, pointing in the direction that the duke
and Vincent had taken.

"Not a moment must be lost, then," exclaimed Lawrence. "Come,
friends, let's away:" and heading the procession, the whole body followed
him down the hill.

CHAPTER XV

Master Elliot and his family, on the morning after the demolition of their house by the fire, were assembled round the breakfast table of their friend Buckthorp, the hosier; but in spite of the kindness and attention shown to Elliot, the present absence of his daughter Constance threw such a damp over his spirits, that it was in vain for his wife or neighbour to attempt to soothe him.

"Depend upon it, neighbour," urged the hosier, "your daughter is safe, but not yet knowing your place of refuge, it is impossible she can visit you. Besides, there is that brave youth Lawrence Wood also absent—a conclusion that she is safe, for surely both could not have fallen victims to the flames."

"It may appear strange to you," replied Elliot to the kind soothings of his neighbour, "but the very reasons you urge for her apparent safety, appear to me to be the ill omen of her death. What did I glean when wandering over the burning ruins last night but the very same facts, only more dangerously applied—that Lawrence and Constance were both seen at the window of the front room, and that at the very moment Lawrence took her in his arms to descend the ladder, its fastenings gave way and fell to the ground; at the same moment both of them sank backwards into the room, as if overcome by the excessive heat, and the whole room was immediately one sheet of flame, the floor having given way beneath. Could any thing short of the hand of Heaven itself have snatched them from a death so certain? I feel it—I know it; yes, yes, my mind tells me, too true, that my dear child has met a terrible death, and that the brave lad has fallen a victim in attempting to save her."

Overcome by his feelings, Master Elliot sank back in his chair, and gave way to the excess of his grief in heavy and afflicting sobs of anguish.

"Paint not such a fearful picture, dear husband," exclaimed Dame Elliot, whose bosom was wrung with the contrary pangs of hope and fear, for she was more sanguine than her husband of her daughter's safety in the hands of Lawrence. "Let us hope for the best: for myself, I place every hope in Lawrence, and trust that they may have reached some friendly shelter, unknown to any one at present but themselves."

"Heaven grant that such may be the case," responded the stationer with fervency. "If Lawrence has really saved Constance, and still retains her in safety, I vow by the interposing goodness of the all-powerful Creator, who has assisted them in such an attempt, that at the expiration of his indentures he shall take her for wife, and become an equal partner in my business, and thus be a prop to me in my declining years."

"And most heartily do I agree with it," answered Mrs. Elliot, "for he truly loves her, and I am sure would make her a happy partner, and then all my fears about the intrusions and attacks of that titled villain Buckingham would be at an end."

"Name not that man to me, wife, I entreat you; he has already caused me more anguish than the whole of my family. I have solemnly and positively forbidden him to enter my house, and the next time I encounter him under similar circumstances, we shall not part so easily; it will then become a matter in which the king himself may perhaps be concerned. Friend Buckthorp, will you accompany me to Cheapside? I am anxious to make every inquiry about my child."

"Most willingly," replied the worthy hosier : and in a few moments he was equipped and ready to start.

Taking an affectionate leave of his wife and son, and bidding Dame Trivet also be of good cheer, for as yet no tidings had been heard of poor Scrubb, he withdrew with his neighbour, to clear up all doubts by a vigorous and earnest inquiry.

The origin or cause of the destruction of his house by fire had never once created a doubt in Elliot's mind, for his business being that of a stationer, and the immense ware-rooms being filled to the ceiling with paper, it was by every one attributed to accident. Fire insurances there were none, or at least the few individuals who might be said to compose a solitary company of the sort, had only as yet ventured to insure ships and merchandise in exportation, so he could look for no remuneration in that way, but as good fortune would have it, his stock at the time of the fire was of very trifling value compared to that of former years, and his household furniture he considered as nothing in comparison to the safety of his family. For Master Elliot, to do him justice, was as wealthy a citizen as any in the ward.

Proceeding to the ruins, they there found the alderman of the ward and the city marshal examining the spot. Cordially greeting Master Elliot, they accompanied him and his friend Buckthorp to the interior, more for the purpose of ascertaining that the fire was totally extinguished, than through any other motive.

"Your family are all safely housed, I trust," inquired the alderman of Elliot.

"Alas ! no, sir," replied the stationer; "my daughter Constance and my apprentice are still missing."

"Good heavens ! is that the case ?" exclaimed the alderman. Then turning to the marshal he said, "Have the ruins been searched ? have any bodies been found ?"

"Not as yet, your worship," replied the marshal, "for we have not had sufficient warrant to do so: if any of the inmates are missing, it does not follow that they met their death. Besides, there is one of my men still absent, and I do not believe he was inside the house at all. There is some mystery about the affair, that wants clearing up."

"Is that the case ?" inquired Master Elliot eagerly. "A new light is breaking upon the affair, I perceive."

"I have also a man missing," exclaimed the chief constable, who had now joined the party, and overheard the latter part of the conversation. "I have ascertained from one of the constables that he was seen speaking with your apprentice, some time after the fire had been extinguished: soon after which they disappeared."

"Thank Heaven, then, there is at least one life saved !" exclaimed Elliot fervently. "After the fire, friend, did you say ?"

"Yes ; it was some time after it."

"Bring that man before me; this purse shall become his if he corroborates the statement clearly."

"He is here somewhere," answered the constable. "I will seek for him, and bring him to you."

"If Lawrence was seen after the fire, I am convinced that my daughter is safe," exclaimed Master Elliot in a tone of joy.

"How so, master ?" inquired the alderman.

"I know he would never have left the house without her," answered the glad-hearted father.

"This is the man who gave me the information, Master Elliot," said the chief constable, again joining them, and introducing one of his men to the worthy citizen.

" Do you know Lawrence Wood, friend,—my apprentice ?" he asked very eagerly.

" By sight as well as my own child," answered the man.

" And did you see him last night ?"

" I saw him this morning, just after we had ceased throwing water upon the fire : the roof had fallen in, and we were about to leave the spot—the day was beginning to break."

" How did he look ?"

" Much excited and agitated."

" Well, what took place ?"

" After a few words with one of our men they both left the street in great haste."

" Take this purse, my friend," said the worthy citizen, pressing a well-filled one into the constable's hand. " Your information has relieved me from the most painful doubts. I am certain now that my daughter lives."

" And we have ascertained that there is another of your servants now at the Fleece in the Old Jewry. I saw him this morning : he says he only escaped by a miracle."

" Indeed, friend ! then we will repair to that house immediately," replied the stationer, and accompanied by his neighbour they proceeded to the Old Jewry.

The servant spoken of by the chief constable was no other than the poor unfortunate Scrubb, who on the night of the fire, without waiting to assist any one else, or to ascertain if any one was lost, hurried on an outer garment, and half awake and half naked, flew on the wings of fear to the Old Jewry. It being the dead of the night, of course the whole of the tavern was closed, and its inmates safely at rest for the night. Without the least consideration, he proceeded round to the kitchen entrance, in a room over which Pauline slept, and by thumping at the door and ringing the bell, accompanying his efforts with cries of " Murder ! Fire ! Plague !" he managed to wake the poor little terrified damsel from her sweet and refreshing slumbers. Jumping from her bed in a terrible fright, Pauline made sure the house was in flames, and throwing a loose mantle over her trembling limbs, she opened the window to call for help, when she was almost petrified with fear at beholding a man half naked jump into the room.

" Oh, Pauline ! save me ! save me. Fire ! fire ! 'tis worse than the horrible plague !" as leaping into the room he seized a blanket from the bed, and wrapped it round his shivering person.

" Gracious-a-mighty, Scrubb ! is this you ?" shrieked the terrified damsel. " For Heaven's sake leave this room, or we shall be discovered and lost, and that will be worse than being burnt. Do jump out of window again, there's a dear Scrubb, and I'll join you in a few minutes," said Pauline in an imploring tone.

" No, but I don't, though," answered Scrubb sulkily, and immediately sat himself down in one corner of the room, drawing the blanket closer around him. " I'm very comfortable here. But the house is on fire, Pauline, and I have come round on purpose to tell you of it !"

" Then for Heaven's sake, Scrubb, let us fly," answered the now equally terrified maiden, and wrapping an extra cloak around her delicate little form, and before Scrubb could prevent her, or explain in which house the fire was, she lifted up the sash of a window which overlooked the yard beneath, and jumped down, calling on Scrubb to follow.

" Stay, Pauline, stay, I don't mean this house !" cried out Scrubb ; but the caution was lost to the ears of his lady love, who had leaped before she looked, and had now safely alighted on the pavement beneath. Without waiting for further explanation, but being determined if possible to prevent

her running through the city at that time of night, half-dressed and unpro-
tected as she was—a step he verily believed she was about to take—he made
a sudden spring from the window-seat to join her ; but, alas ! not knowing
the anchorage of such a narrow harbour so well as the maiden who had set
him the daring example, sad to say, poor Scrubb fell head foremost into a
great cistern of rain water, which had been accumulating for weeks for the
use of the tavern laundry.   Here he lay struggling, kicking, and plunging
for some minutes before he could speak, for the water not being deep
enough to drown him, just reached to his neck, and the top of the cistern
being above his grasp, he could do nothing more than bellow at the top of
his voice for help, which he did most lustily, at the same time standing
quietly in the cooling stream, till assistance should arrive.

"Is that you, Scrubb ?" responded Pauline to the appeals of her lover.

"It is, Pauline.   Flying from the dangers of fire, I am now likely to die
the death of a martyr by water.   Here I am up to my neck shivering in this
cursed pool of water.   Help, help me, Pauline, or I shall be drowned, and
you will die a widowed maid !"

"Keep your head above water, dear Scrubb, till I can come to your aid,"
answered the industrious damsel, who was struggling under the weight of a
foot-ladder to place against the cistern, with which she might help him out.
Bringing the ladder to the side of the cistern she mounted it.   The darkness
of the night would only enable her to see the white night-dress and red cap
of Scrubb bobbing about at the top of the water.   "Give me your hand,
dear Scrubb," she exclaimed encouragingly.   "I will try and help you,
though I am almost afraid it will be useless."

"For the love of Heaven, hold tight, Pauline !" implored Scrubb, "for if
I am not drowned this will be a sure provocative for the ague, and the ague
is sure to be succeeded by the plague, and then it won't matter whether I
am burnt, frightened, or drowned !   O Lord ! oh Lord ! miserable martyr
that I am !"

And with such like exclamations as these did the poor half-drowned, half-
terrified-to-death Scrubb rend the still midnight air.

"Don't go on so, Scrubb, but give me both your hands," replied Pauline.
And stooping for the purpose, by a careful and almost over-balanced position, she managed to grasp his hands.   Exerting all her strength, and imploring her lover to keep his mouth shut and spring up, Pauline pulled heartily upwards to save a life precious to her as her own.

Scrubb faithfully kept the commands of his energetic mistress, at least as
far as the springing up part of it, which he did in right good earnest ; but as
to keeping his mouth shut, that was quite out of the question ; for having
with an herculean leap brought his whole body nearly out of the water, and
leaving hold of Pauline's hand to catch at the sides of the cistern, he missed
his hold and sunk with the velocity of a stone ; at the same time gulping a
great quantity of water, which caused a shrill through his whole frame.   On
rising again to the surface, he exalted his voice for help most manfully,
which, to do him credit, was not unavailing.

"Oh he's drowned ! he's drowned ! we shall be discovered, and I shall be
ruined !" exclaimed Pauline, in piteous accents, as she peeped into the dark
abyss of waters that flowed beneath her gaze ; but could perceive nothing but
the red night cap of poor Scrubb being tossed about by the waves.

At this critical juncture, Dame Sirloin being aroused from her peaceful rest
and pleasant dreams by the loud appeals of Scrubb to her or any one's
sympathies, had risen from her couch, and summoning to her aid the persons
of two porters to the tavern, came into the yard to discover the cause.
Judge of her surprise, however, when, instead of meeting with ferocious
ruffians, or burglarious vagabonds trying to effect an entrance, she beheld the

person of her scullery maid, who was screaming most lustily for help, and exposed to the rude night air, standing upon a ladder, endeavouring to reach into the cistern !''

" Mercy, come save us !" exclaimed Dame Sirloin, holding up the lamp to show sufficient light upon the object of her surprise—" why, who have we here ? Pauline, as I live ! Seize her, John, Arthur, she is meditating self-suicide—look ! she walks in her sleep, and is about to jump into the cistern, and spoil all my rain water ! Seize hold upon her, I say !''

Inspired by such an oration, the men who had accompanied Dame Sirloin to the scene of action, grasped her round the waist, and lifted her down from the ladder, though Pauline, taken by surprise, plunged and struggled with all the resistance she could muster to her aid.

" Why, what's all this, hussey ?" demanded Dame Sirloin of her juvenile assistant, " that you must be disturbing quiet people, like this, in the dead of the dark night, I should like to know ? Drag her in, drag her in, she shall pay for all this to-morrow !''

The men were about to fulfil the orders of Dame Sirloin, had not the beseeching accents and piteous looks of Pauline prevented them, as she implored them to rescue Scrubb.

" Oh save him ! save him ! I beseech you—he's dead, dead, drowning !''

" Drowning ! who, what !" exclaimed Dame Sirloin in surprise.

"My poor Scrubb ; he has fell into the cistern ; don't hurt him, pray don't ; he could'nt help it, indeed he could not !''

" A man in my rain water !" roared out Dame Sirloin ; " here's a pretty go ! what fine doings are these, hussey ? pull him out ; pull the vagrant out !''

And accordingly poor Scrubb was pulled out by the hair of his head ; and by the time he reached dry land again, he was so terrified and exhausted that his tongue (as the romancists say) refused him utterance.

" What ! you were about to make off in the night time, you baggage, were you, along with this sneaking hound again ! Bring him in—bring him in ; I said if I caught him here again he should suffer for it, and so he shall. I'll vow my chastity there's plenty of broken victuals and silver plate packed up for this occasion ! A pretty affair, truly ! sweethearting in the night time, I did not think my rain water would prove such a good trap. Bring the dripping hound in !''

" Oh don't hurt him ! pray don't hurt him !" exclaimed Pauline, urgently ; he only came to tell me of the fire, and to help me to escape !''

" Fire ! what fire ?" inquired Dame Sirloin.

" What fire did you mean, Scrubb, dear ?" asked Pauline of her trembling lover.

" Oh don't talk about fire ! see I am nearly killed with water ! I feel the ague creeping over my body already !''

" Bring him in doors ! this shall be examined into to-morrow," said Dame Sirloin, authoritatively. " I'll see if quiet respectable people are to be disturbed in their sleep on a night like this for nothing—bring him along !''

Leading the way, and dragging Pauline by her side, Dame Sirloin marched to her room, and having placed poor Scrubb in durance vile, and locked Pauline into her room again, retired again to her slumbers to dream of tender things, resolving in the morning to investigate the whole affair.

Master Elliot and his neighbour Buckthorp arrived at the Fleece in the midst of the investigation, and having explained the circumstances which tempted Scrubb to such an unaccountable proceeding, and being answerable for his future behaviour, he was given over to him, but no tidings of Lawrence or Constance could be obtained of the terrified Scrubb, who thought of nothing else than his approaching ague fit. Nothing discouraged, Master Elliot and his friend returned homewards.

CHAPTER XVI.

MAKING the best of their way across the meadows, under the guidance of one of the postilions, Lawrence and his companions, after about an hour's sharp walking, reached the villa of the Duke of Buckingham. It was a noble looking mansion of the ancient time, surrounded by a moat, and reached by a drawbridge, and was a building well worthy of a better master. After many loud knocks had been bestowed upon the gate, it was opened by a military looking servant, who at first denied his master to the inquirers ; but Lawrence, having anticipated such a reception, pushed past him, and ordered his two comrades to follow him. Seizing upon the false-tongued domestic, they locked him in a neighbouring apartment, and slowly and cautiously crept up the wide staircase that lay open to their view. After a fruitless and silent search through the corridors, halls, and banquetting rooms, they at length reached a detached building, which had the appearance of an armoury or private library to the mansion ; and by applying his ear to the keyhole, Lawrence could distinctly hear voices in solemn consultation at a distant part of it. He intimated his suspicions to his companions that the objects of their search were secreted there, and as it was useless to attempt to seek an admittance fairly, they must force an entrance. Without any further delay, Lawrence drew his sword, and having previously primed and cocked the two heavy pistols which hung in his belt, he caught his sword by the blade and with the iron hilt and two or three heavy blows, he shattered to pieces a handsomely painted door, and leaping to the opening he had thus made, soon gained the interior ; in which attempt he was instantly followed by the marshalman and the constable.

Proceeding along a short passage, they gained a staircase. Upon reaching the summit, they entered a magnificent looking hall, at the extremity of which, round a sort of temple or altar they perceived several persons standing, in the midst of whom were two females. Urging on his fellows to follows to follow him, Lawrence rushed in the midst of the group, when to his surprise and indignation he discovered that they were engaged in the celebration of the matrimonial service ; and seeing Constance reclining on the shoulder of Buckingham, he made towards her, but the duke recognising him, and anticipating his intentions, stepped back one or two paces, drew his sword, and encircling Constance, with his remaining arm stood on his guard.

" Cease this unholy and blasphemous ceremony, I conjure ye !" exclaimed Lawrence to the officials who were acting in holy robes ; " you know not what you do ! This lady I demand from the hands of her captor ; he is a villain, and shall not escape me ! Seize upon him, comrades !"

" Out and upon them !" exclaimed Buckingham ; when to the surprise of Lawrence and his companions, the attendants at the ceremony and even the officiating minister himself, threw off their robes, drew swords and pistols, and attacked Lawrence's party.

" Stay, stay ! peace ! strike not, I implore you ! Lawrence ! Arthur !— men, will you shed innocent blood !" screamed Constance at the top of her voice ; I alone am the cause of this !" Then violently struggling to free herself from the embrace of Buckingham, she sank swooning in his arms ; and he, being desperately beset by Lawrence, sword to sword, could not support her, and she fell with a heavy weight upon the marble pavement beneath.

The marshalman and the constable were busily employed in repelling the attacks of the pretended pastor and his attendants; the second lady, the companion of Constance, having fled from the scene of strife.

With the body of Constance laying prostrate between them, did Lawrence and Buckingham for some minutes contend; but the former, not being such an expert swordsman as his antagonist, and also somewhat fatigued with his hasty pursuit, his blows fell less frequent, and with greater force. Buckingham, taking advantage of this, stepped forward, made a false parry, and passed his sword through Lawrence's left shoulder. He had directed the thrust at his heart, but by a fortunate movement on the part of Lawrence, it had taken a direction somewhat higher, and less likely to be fatal.

Lawrence reeled, made a grasp at the sword of Buckingham, and then fell by the side of Constance, the blood flowing from him staining the snowy robe of her for whom it had been shed.

Buckingham now threw aside his sword, and was in the act of raising Constance in his arms, when he was withheld by the marshalman, who, forcing him back with a heavy blow, he fell to the earth stunned.

The conflict between the officials and attendants and the constable and the marshalman was of short but severe duration. One of the attendants had breathed his last in the fray; the others had taken to flight, and the holy man himself, who was no other than Vincent Palmer, not being able to contend against the prowess of two foes, had also made good his retreat, having fired off a random shot at the head of the constable; but, happily fo. him, without effect.

Taking advantage of the senseless state of the duke, the marshalman and the constable bore away Constance and her lover to a small cottage, hard by. A medical man having been sent for, Lawrence's wound was dressed, and he was left to enjoy that rest and quietness so essential to his present distressed condition.

14.

Constance soon recovered from her swoon, but was nearly distracted at the condition of Lawrence, whose death, should it ensue from the wound he had received, she laid to her own charge. Turning a deaf ear to all entreaties to leave her present abode, the marshalman and constable prepared to return to their duties in London; having previously charged the inmates of the cottage not to admit any one, on whatever pretence they might come. Promising to give a full account of her safety to her father, they took a respectful leave of the agitated maiden, and departed on their journey homewards.

The inmates of the cottage closely pressed Constance to take some refreshment and repose, but she returned their kindness with almost uncivil coldness. Towards evening the doctor paid his patient another visit, and gave it as his opinion that the wound was a very dangerous one, and that unless the sufferer was kept strictly quiet and composed, it might turn to a fever on the brain, and death would inevitably follow.

The whole of that night did Constance watch at the bedside of the youth who had so nobly fought and bled in her rescue, nor would she allow, even for a moment, any one to take her place. His medicines were administered by her hand alone, and the bandages on the wound kept moist by her applying a lotion for that purpose, frequently every few minutes, to keep up a perpetual coolness. She administered drink to his parched lips, and applied leeches to his throbbing and burning temples. At times he would rave as if engaged with the duke in the conflict, dare him to the encounter, and call loudly for Constance. Again, he would fancy himself in the burning ruins of his master's house; call madly for water to be thrown on him, for that he was burning! Then he would picture the falling roof, the hot flames encircling his body—"Save her! save Constance! and leave me to my fate," he would exclaim, and then sinking back on his pillow, as if overcome with his exertions, would doze for a long time.

"Merciful Father!" cried Constance, as she looked upon the writhing and distorted countenance of her lover, which betokened internal agony, "I beseech thee to save his life as the greatest boon thou couldst grant! Never more shall this bosom know joy or peace if I am bereft of thee, my own dear Lawrence!"

And Constance, overpowered with eager watching and the rapid flow of tears, sunk unconsciously into a slumber, from which she did not awake till the glaring beams of the sun shone into her chamber.

The constable and the marshalman lost no time in performing their promise made to Constance, for without dismounting from their horses they proceeded at once to the hosier's house, and laid the whole affair before the eager family.

"Gracious Heaven!" exclaimed Elliot, "to what villany are we subject that our children are to be snatched from our presence, and forcibly detained by a herd of such titled ruffians as these. The whole matter shall be laid before the king. I will have ample satisfaction and apology for this treatment, with strict assurances to guard against a repetition."

"The poor dear boy, too," added Mrs. Elliot, "to be in danger of his life in her cause! I knew he would not leave her. Heaven grant that his life may be spared, that I may live to clasp him in my arms as my son, and the protector of my child."

"I will proceed on my journey at once," replied Elliot, "and if he can be removed with safety, I will not return without him; for doubtless his life will be beset by the villains whom he has thwarted by his bravery."

Liberally rewarding the men who had brought him the information he had so ardently longed to possess, he also gave each a letter of recommendation to the officer of the ward, for he was a common councilman, and a man in high repute. Having received from the men in return a solemn promise that they would come forward and testify to the truth of their assertions, whenever he might think proper to call upon them, they departed; having lightened the hearts of the stationer and his wife by their timely arrival.

"Dame Trivet must accompany me," said Master Elliot, "for if I find Lawrence not sufficiently recovered, I will not leave him with strangers; Constance, I presume, is his attendant, and if I remove her I must fill up her place; and I am sure no one could be a better substitute than the dame, for I believe she loves the lad as her own son, and would do any thing to serve him. Mrs. Elliot cordially agreeing with the proposition, the worthy dame was summoned to their presence, and informed of their wish, to which she cheerfully acceded. By noon the worthy stationer and his housekeeper, seated in an open carriage, were on their way to the relief of the young sufferers.

It was evening before they arrived at the place of their destination, for travelling at that time was somewhat different to the present day; and a journey of twenty miles was considered a tremendous undertaking for one day's performance. When they arrived at the house to which Constance and her lover had been conveyed, they were warmly received by the landlady, who knowing the whole circumstances of the case, had taken as much interest in the affair as if she were more nearly related.

"The patient," she added to the inquiries of Master Elliot, "was improving rapidly, but she feared they must not be too sudden to see him, or it might destroy all that had been done for him."

Constance was soon in the arms of her father, and it was a long time before she was able to give utterance to her joy by the convulsive sobbings of her heart, which prevented utterance.

"And so the villains would have torn you from me?" exclaimed the agitated but overjoyed father. "But, as sure as there is a power above, I will be revenged!"

"How, my father? You surely will not endanger yourself against that wicked man."

"Not in the way that you imagine, my child," answered her father, "but I will lay the whole affair before the king, and if there is justice to be had in England, I will have it for this gross outrage upon a citizen's liberty."

Dame Trivet now entered the room, and informed her master that he might now safely go up and see Lawrence, for she had just left him: "his fever had abated, and he was much better than she expected to have found him."

Profiting by the information, Elliot, accompanied by his daughter, proceeded to the chamber of the sick young man. At the entrance of his kind master, Lawrence had well nigh sprung out of bed to grasp his hand with joy, but he was gently restrained by Constance, who entreated him to keep himself quiet and composed. Kindly and affectionately greeting him by the hand, and suppressing too much speaking on the occasion, Elliot examined the wound as well as the bandages would allow. He pronounced it a dangerous wound, but gave it as his opinion that it was going on as favourably as could be expected.

At this moment the doctor who had been attending Lawrence paid him a visit. He was surprised to see so many persons in the room, but on being informed who they were, he entered familiarly into conversation with them on the subject.

"Lawrence," he said, "would not be able to be removed for some days. He was happy to say that all traces of fever had left him, but that his present weak state would not permit of any exertion—it might prove fatal."

It was finally resolved that Dame Trivet should stay and attend upon him in the place of Constance; but although this piece of information was a pang to Lawrence, yet he knew Constance was no where so safe as in the midst of her own family; this caused him to suppress any remark he might have thought of upon the subject—for he trusted soon to join her in the family circle at home.

Handsomely remunerating both the doctor and the mistress of the house, Elliot prepared to take his departure, which was fixed for the next morning early.

Previous, however, to taking even a temporary leave of her lover, Constance paid him a visit in secret, and alone. At the expiration of it, Lawrence's eye possessed a brightness it had been a stranger to since his illness; and his countenance bespoke a gleam of joy which nothing but the genuine return of a youthful loving heart could have inspired.

By sunrise everything was ready for departure, and Elliot, accompanied by Constance, once more took a formal farewell of the sick youth, trusting to have his presence in a few days amid the family circle.

Upon her journey home, Constance informed her father of everything that had passed between herself and Buckingham; of the attempted forced and fraudulent marriage, which was so fortunately frustrated by the arrival of Lawrence and his companions. Elliot was more incensed than ever against the duke, and resolving in his own mind to seek the advice of his friend the mayor, on his return home, he was silent for a time on the subject.

The after part of the day brought the travellers to the City of London, and a few minutes more Constance was safely locked in the embrace of her tender mother, who shed tears of joy for her safe return; and inwardly offered up a silent prayer to the Disposer of all events for his mercy and goodness in preserving her child in the hour of danger.

While all was love and joy with the family of the Elliot's, Lawrence, under the treatment of his excellent and kind nurse, was daily recovering. Three days had enabled him to gain strength sufficient to leave his bed; three more and he left his room: and by the end of a fortnight from the time of Constance's departure he was enabled, by easy stages, to return to London, which he did safely; and reached the abode of his master on the day month that he left the one which had been destroyed.

CHAPTER XVII.

The first thing which engaged Master Elliot's attention upon the return of Constance and Lawrence to London was, the representing the case to the Lord Mayor, and soliciting his protection and support to lay the matter before his Majesty. Accordingly the day after Lawrence's return, they both waited on his lordship, and Master Elliot pourtrayed in a striking outline the character of the duke, and also the annoyance and depredations he was in the habit of committing upon his family.

The Lord Mayor gave a patient hearing to Master Elliot, and then informed him that he was sorry to find that so worthy and respectable a man as he was should be ranked amongst that class of persons, to which the duke was a perpetual annoyance. He believed him to be a most hardened and abandoned character, and fitted for any villany that might enter his wicked imagination. Lawrence also informed the Mayor of his suspicion concerning the fire, namely, that it had been done by Buckingham's party, or by his orders, as they were discovered secreted in the house at the time, and made such good use of the confusion afterwards.

" That," replied the mayor, " would be a dangerous question to handle;

for if you failed in proving that the duke himself fired the premises, you could have no lawful hold on him for the acts of others, although they were his companions. That is a subject you had better let drop, and adhere to the one on which you have such good evidence to bear you out. Believe me, the duke is no friend of mine; I have suffered much both privately and publicly by his slanders and his injuries to my character; but I have never thought them worth while meddling with; however, if you wish to press this case, and feel yourself aggrieved as a citizen, I am bound to see you righted; and the aggressor being a courtier, and one of the royal cortege, I will certainly do my best to lay the subject before his Majesty in its true light.

"My warmest thanks be yours for your concession," replied Master Elliot, to the reply of the worthy mayor, and having given instructions to a lawyer of the Lord Mayor's Court to draw out the petition which was to be laid before the king, and having unanimously agreed that the next day should be fixed for the deputation, Master Elliot and his apprentice took their leave.

It having been Master Elliot's intention, ever since the recovery of his wife from the plague, to take a house in the country, that they might in some measure be free from the infections, and the fire and destruction of his house in Cheapside having turned that doubt into a necessity, he started off that very afternoon to look at a neat cottage at Dulwich, which a neighbour had to dispose of; being determined, if possible, to obtain it.

During his absence, Constance and Lawrence walked over to survey the ruins, and contemplate the scene of their former perils. Lawrence pointed out to Constance the window and the room in which they were situated at the time the fire broke in upon them. He also pointed out to her the place where Buckingham and his companions must have secreted themselves. Constance, in this engaging stroll with her lover (for she had entirely blocked out Buckingham from any share in her affection, since she had found him the dissipated and false character he proved to be), informed him of her father's intention to unite them at the first opportunity, and to take him into partnership with him at the expiration of his indenture.

"Kind, generous man!" exclaimed Lawrence; "how shall I ever repay him for such a gift?"

"You have purchased my hand by becoming my protector, Lawrence," answered Constance. "It is no longer a gift under such circumstances; but if esteemed at all by you, you have a claim on it for your determined conduct in rescuing me from danger and peril."

"Name not that as a service which I took to be a pleasure," answered Lawrence. "I should have been undeserving the name of man had I not done so? Had I perished in this burning fabric, Constance, think you the Duke of Buckingham would not have won you over to his wishes, and have gained your hand, and title to a coronet, if he had not gained your affection?"

"No, Lawrence," replied Constance, with ardour and affection; "nothing should ever have persuaded me to have become his; I own at first I was dazzled by his appearances, by his manner and fascinating behaviour; but his heartless, dissolute conduct wiped out for ever every idea of affection with which he might have inspired me."

"The affair is to be laid before the king to-morrow!" exclaimed Lawrence. "The Lord Mayor has consented to accompany your father, who will be attended by the alderman of the ward, and the City Marshal, who were so active in making the inquiry after you in your absence."

"I trust this proceeding will not draw down upon us the vengeance of that persevering tormentor! I fear he will be much enraged and lay wait for you, Lawrence; for you are his bitterest enemy, and the one he seems most desirous of getting rid of."

" Fear not, Constance," replied Lawrence; "the Duke of Buckingham may be a persevering gallant, but he is not a bold, daring man, and would tremble for his life, and seek safety in flight, if resolutely opposed: as in the case of our conflict at his house. His number was no match for us. While touching upon this subject, Constance, I would ask what were your thoughts during your flight in captivity? Did you not expect a rescue from my hands?"

" Alas, Lawrence !" she replied, " I was senseless nearly the whole of the time: I had, it is true, hurried ideas of the fire, of my parents, and of you; but no sooner did my senses even for a time return than my inveterate tormentor was at my side, pressing me with his loathsome caresses !"

" Unprincipled ruffian !" exclaimed Lawrence; " we may be on even terms yet: although, without taking an overdue to myself, I think I may say the duke has received as much as he lent to me, and with interest, too ! But the marriage, Constance, the marriage ! how did he persuade you to that ?"

" I knew not of it till I was brought to the spot where you found me. I gave no answer to the questions put to me, and had it been even a proper and sacred ceremony, it never could have been binding. I was dragged half senseless to the scene, and when there, treated as a cipher; others answering for me, and forcing me to remain. I was resolved not to sign my name, and I was contemplating what death I should die to escape further villanies from my oppressor, when the sound of your voice opened a new light upon my hopes !"

" Then had I not arrived, you would not have looked upon him as a husband, Constance ?"

" Never, by Heaven ! Death should have been my husband and my rescue—as the only remedy !"

" Then do I offer to Heaven thanks for its kind assistance in helping me to trace you out; for had I not discovered the place of your probable retreat from one of the duke's associates through fear, all help would have been lost to you, and you must either have become his victim, through being succourless, or have met a dreadful end by your own hand! Gracious Heaven ! how I thank thee for this marked interposition of thy power, in the cause of the innocent and the injured !"

" My dear parents, too, must and did suffer many hours of tormenting suspense in my absence !" suggested Constance.

" Your father most," he replied; " not because your mother loved you less, but because she placed such a strong reliance in my absence being caused by yours, and that I was with you wherever you might be."

Now that every thing was once more in its original position, and Constance and her family safely restored to peace and tranquillity, Lawrence in his own mind was not sorry the circumstance at the fire had happened, for it had given him a chance of proving to the parents of his beloved Constance the ardour and integrity of his attachment towards her, and to the maid herself it also furnished a sufficient proof, if any was wanting, of his utter disregard of life and injury to rescue her from danger. With Mrs. Elliot, as has been before noticed, no such proof was wanting: she having long before in her own mind resolved upon Lawrence as the husband of her daughter; but her husband being a man more occupied by his counting-house and his papers, had not entered so earnestly into the idea, for Constance being as yet only eighteen, he considered the affair in a less serious form. These circumstances justly weighed in his own breast made Lawrence feel a degree of selfsatisfaction in what he had done, which he never before experienced.

Upon their return home, they found Master Elliot had arrived from his journey; he informed his family that he had taken the house he had been in search of, which was pleasantly situated between the luxurious hills which lay on the borders of Surrey and Kent, in the delightful village of Dulwich, which being in a south-east direction from London, was the most free from infection of any quarter round the metropolis; a south-westerly wind having raged ever since the appearance of the plague in the City of London!

Three days was fixed for the departure, and with the exception of the family and one or two particular neighbours, it was to be kept a profound secret;— and the next day being the day appointed by the Lord Mayor to visit the king, preparations were now being made for the necessary equipment of Lawrence and Master Elliot.

Early next morning every thing was hurry and bustle in Master Elliot's family. As Warden of the Stationer's Company he was richly attired, and wore suspended round his neck a large silver medallion, the insignia of his trustworthy office. His apprentice Lawrence also had a silver-satin sash suspended diagonally across the breast, with a small star attached to it, to signify that he was a Master Warden's apprentice in that company, which was a note of much honour amongst the apprentices of those days, entitling them to a gift of ten guineas upon the expiration of their apprenticeship, and an exemption from duties on stamped parchments in the process of taking up their freedom. Lawrence was also attired in a new suit; his silver-buckled hose, and silk jerkin, added to a well made person, set him off in no unenviable position.

Having arrived at the Mansion-house, they were most graciously received by the Lord Mayor in person, who was dressed ready to depart. A parchment document had been drawn out as a memorial by the City Recorder, who was to accompany the deputation to read it before his Majesty.

It was nearly noon before everything was ready for their departure. A carriage of the Mayor's drew up to the door and received within it his Lordship, the Alderman, the Recorder, and Master Elliot. Lawrence, with several petty officers, marshalmen, and constables, brought up the rear on horseback, and the procession started off down Cheapside, at a sharp pace. They passed the ruins of the stationer's house, near which stood a group anxiously watching the cavalcade, and Lawrence thought he could perceive in the midst the figure of Buckingham; as immediately on their passing a horse was brought, on which the suspicious person seated himself, and keeping at a wary distance dogged the procession during its route to Whitehall, where he disappeared in the direction of Westminster.

Having disposed of their equipages, the whole deputation, officers marshalmen, &c., entered the Palace of King Charles the Second. They were met at the outer hall by one of the guards of honour, who having learned their business, turned them over to the care of the king's chamberlain; the worthy official then placed the officers and marshalmen, together with Lawrence, into a splendid antechamber, and led the way before the deputation to the grand hall, where they were to wait till the king's pleasure should be known.

The Court of Charles the Second, as history testifies, was notorious for its luxury and splendour. The apartment where Lawrence and his friends were abiding, although expressly used for such purposes as the present, was, nevertheless, of a splendid nature. The floor was covered—first, with a rich India matting, over which was spread a gorgeously-worked carpet, and the centre was ornamented by a flowery circlet of silk and satin, so wove in colours as to represent, within a circled border of flowers of every hue and description, the birth of Venus, with the attendances of her graces, rising from the sea. Looking glasses of full length hung round the apartment, and from the ceiling hung three splendid glass drop chandeliers, of a massive and costly description. In cornices and under sideboards were placed, as if to shade them from the gaze of all observers but the most curious, several pictures, of a nature which though pleasing to the king and his court, often disgusted those who happened to direct their glance in the direction. Chairs of burnished gold frames, and rich green velvet seats, were the common-place furniture of the apartment. A large old-fashioned table, with carved lion claw feet inlaid with gold, silver, and ivory, constituted the remainder of the accommodation; which was well stored with biscuits, pastry, sweetmeats, and several flasks of sack, canary, and hock, for those who thought proper to avail themselves of it: and at the pressing invitation of the chamberlain, the newly-arrived citizens regaled themselves with the king's bounty.

The grand hall, which was set apart for the principal visitors and private councils, was a most magnificent and superb apartment; it was one complete round of windows, except the entrance, reaching from the ceiling or dome to the ground; these windows were of manufactured stained glass, each alternate frame bearing an exquisitely painted representation of Heathen Mythological History, the lasciviousness of which was well suited to the taste of the owner of such a place. The dome was one large arch of glass, through which the sun poured his burning rays with concentrated force; and the clear blue sky floating above gave the room, which was very large, the appearance of being uncovered from the canopy of Heaven. Pictures of every description adorned the room, though they were of a nature far more repugnant to modest minds than those in the anteroom; satin and velvet couches, inlaid with pearl and gold, stood round the room, with splendid ottomans or footstools of velvet, with silk tassels, lay at their feet. A sideboard filled with bottles and flasks, with silver and ivory tankards, and flagons of the choicest viands, from burgundy and sack, to canary, cream jellies, and custards; with made dishes, fowl and game of every description, ready for the appetite of the most refined gourmand. These were drawn out and placed before the visitors, who being somewhat fatigued by the heat of the day and the dusty road they had to travel, fell to with a perfect good will, and genuine relish.

Turning to the king himself, he had not awakened from his repose of the night previous, or, to be more correct, of the early part of the present day; he never thinking of retiring from any pastime or folly he might be engaged in till the daylight fairly put out the glare of candles and lamps; and by that time he would either be so fatigued with his exertion of dancing, or fencing, or struggling—or perhaps overcome with wine, that he was generally carried to his chamber by pages, and was soundly snoring in their arms before his clothes were taken from him. In this state he would lay frequently till evening (except on levees or cabinet councils), and then he would be more fit for a hot bath, than for legislating in a council chamber with his ministers.

The king's grand chamberlain having informed the private secretary of the arrival of the Lord Mayor of London and some of the corporation, that person waited on his Majesty immediately on his appearing at the breakfast table to inform him of the event. The king was graciously pleased to apologize to his lordship, and sent down a message to say he would be ready to receive him in a short time.

It was not with many that Charles would have used this condescension; but the corporation of London, and particularly the Lord Mayor, had been so prominent in their endeavours to aid the Royal cause at the time of the civil war against his father Charles the First, and the present Lord Mayor (when alderman) having raised a troop of volunteers at his own expense, was for such deeds a favourite with the king, and had received many marked favours from him besides being knighted and having a pension of 800 guineas a year granted to him, with the rental of an estate in Westminster for him and his heirs for one hundred years to come.

After having extended their patience, and supplied their appetite during about two hours' heavy-going suspense, the king's secretary at length informed them that his Majesty was ready to receive them, and politely requested them to follow him. Walking in due form and state after the secretary, they were led through grand lobbies, libraries, drawing-rooms, and banqueting-rooms, till having arrived at the Scarlet Closet, so called from its being hung all round with scarlet velvet, the alderman, Elliot, and the Recorder were desired to wait there, while the Lord Mayor waited upon the king and made his business known to him.

Ushered into the presence of his sovereign, the mayor bowed his knee to the earth; but the king rose to receive his favourite, and having raised him up by the hand, led him to a seat.

"Well, master mayor, and what is the news in the city that I have you such an early visitor this morning?"—(it being the hour of two in the afternoon). "Any band of rebel apprentices broke loose; is the corporation in want of new leases; or is it for the repeal of some heavy tax you come to solicit me, including at the same time a sly hint that I ought to keep my Court up at half the present expense, these bad times. Is it so, my worthy mayor?"

"No, my liege, it is not," replied the mayor very respectfully. "It is neither for the repeal of a tax, for the suppression of a riot, or for a renewal of city lands that brings me here before your Majesty in the character of a supplicator. It is for redress and justice for injuries received by a worthy and loyal citizen from some of the members of your court."

"Ah, ah!" exclaimed the king, "what is going on now? Any Rochester or Buckingham fray, my worthy mayor. Have either of the vagabonds been at their gambols again? Some wench has been decoyed away from her parents, I suppose, and married with a wooden bible and a soldier parson! Is that the case, my lord?"

15.

"It is something of the sort, your Majesty. In the apartment adjoining I have waiting our Recorder, with our grievances drawn up, together with one of our aldermen who has been a witness in the affair, and the citizen who has been wronged."

"Bring them in, Exmouth, by all means," said the king to his secretary. "I am devilish miserable this morning, and this affair may help to enliven my spirits."

The secretary now entered, leading in the Recorder, the alderman, and Master Elliot, who having been introduced to his Majesty, took his seat at a table a little distance apart.

"So, my Recorder, I understand you have something to read to me there. In the name of fortune, let it not be tedious or solemn, but witty, sharp, and to the purpose, and then perhaps I may keep awake. Proceed.

The Recorder, making a low bow, and advancing from his seat to the centre of the room, read forth in a loud voice as follows :—

"May it please your Most Gracious Majesty :

"We, your Majesty's loyal citizens of London, do most humbly beg and entreat your Majesty's most gracious ear and condescension to our petition and prayer.

"Whereas, at divers times and places, we, your Majesty's most loyal and dutiful citizens of London have been sorely pressed and grievously injured by the conduct of George Villiers, Duke of Buckingham, Grand Steward of your Majesty's household, who, together with some loose and viciously-inclined companions, doth make incessant inroads and intrusions into the privacy of our dwellings, to the no small inconvenience and grief of the owners thereof.

"Whereas, also, we, your Majesty's most loyal and faithful subjects, most humbly beg and request your Majesty's most kind and gracious attention to the following instance of insubordination and aggression shown towards one of us, your Majesty's most worthy and loyal citizens of London.

"On the night of Thursday last, July 17, George Villiers, Duke of Buckingham, together with the aid of other wicked persons, was the cause of a fire being kindled in the house of Master Matthew Elliot, citizen and stationer of London, to the destruction thereof, and to the immediate peril and danger of the surrounding dwellings.

"And also further state, that the said George Villiers, Duke of Buckingham, assisted by his dissolute associates, did forcibly carry off, against her intention, the said Matthew Elliot's daughter Constance, a maiden of tender years, and did bear her away to a country-house, near Harrow, belonging to the said George Villiers, Duke of Buckingham, and by means of a false priest and villanous confederates had nigh finished a mock form of matrimony, when the damsel was rescued from his hands at the danger and peril of your loyal subject's servant's life.

"Now we, the citizens of London, and your Majesty's most loyal and obedient subjects, do earnestly pray that your Majesty will use your influence and authority to check and restrain the aforesaid Duke of Buckingham in his malicious conduct towards your Majesty's loyal subjects generally ; and by seizing upon the goods and effects of the said Duke of Buckingham, give and allow some remuneration to the parties who have sustained such injury at his hands.

"And your Majesty's most loyal and obedient subjects will ever pray."

"Hey-day! why these are pretty doings, indeed!" exclaimed the king.

"Is that the father of the fair maiden, master mayor?" said Charles, point ing to Elliot.

"It is, so please your Majesty," answered the Lord Mayor.

"And what would you, friend, that I should do for you in this case?" asked the king.

"To issue your Majesty's royal order and command to authorise your loyal and dutiful subjects to punish the said Duke of Buckingham, when he may be guilty of such crimes," answered Master Elliot bowing.

"Retire with me to my cabinet, my Lord Mayor," and I will arrange every thing," said the king.

Accordingly, the king and the mayor retired to an adjoining closet. leaving their fellow delegates in the room. The king then gave the Lord Mayor positive orders, by virtue of a warrant signed by himself, to imprison the Duke of Buckingham or his accomplices for any offence they might commit, and not to liberate them without his express command, but urged him to keep the secret to himself. He then made out an order of value to the full amount of damage done to the house and trade of Master Elliot, which was to be paid by the Lord Treasurer out of the allowance to the duke from the king as Grand Steward of the Household.

Having effected such amicable and liberal compensation for the injuries they had received, the deputation took their leave, and returned to the city in the same order as they came.

CHAPTER XVIII.

DEEPLY cherishing the spirit of revenge in his bosom, Dr. Calder, on the day following the quarrel that had taken place between himself and his two guilty companions, proceeded to the office of the commissioners of the Board of Health, and laid the whole affair before them. The consequence of this disclosure was, that the commissioner laid it before the sitting alderman, at that time Sir John Boydell, who immediately issued a summons for all the parties to appear before him the next day.

Calder having taken this step, and learning that his friend Elliot was about to rerire into the country, lost no time in soliciting his assistance as a witness to his character and reputation, for whatever might be the doctor's opinion of himself, he was well aware that he should require a few substantial witnesses to bear him out in his honesty and respectability. Besides, he had this great advantage over his confederates—he was busily engaged preparing a defence for the purpose of confuting anything they might bring against him, whilst on the other hand they were not even aware of the accusation having been made; and by their being arrested separately, without any correspondence whatever being allowed between them, would go far to confuse and criminate them.

Although the plague was still fearfully raging in the city of London and its suburbs, yet the breach of confidence that had taken place between the doctor and Gowles had occasioned a great falling-off in the undertaker's business: he now only employed two carts instead of four, and had discharged three of his men, and he began to look upon this falling-off in his trade as the first effects of his disunion with Dr. Calder, which affair he now much lamented.

One evening, long after the busy hum and toil of the day was over, two of the city marshalmen were seen proceeding along by the old London Wall, near Moorfields. Arriving at White's Alley, the place already described as

Gowles's residence, they knocked several times loudly at the door, without receiving any answer, and at first concluded that the habitation was either empty, or that the inmates had fled through fear of arrest and punishment. But they were, however, soon deceived by the appearance of Gowles himself, who opening the door and holding up a dimly-burning lantern, inquired of them their business.

"You must come with us," replied one of the marshalmen, "and that quickly, too."

"Ah !" exclaimed Gowles with some glee, for he believed the invitation to allude to some wretched victim to the plague, who required his aid to deposit him in the embrace of his mother earth. "Who is it that is no more ? Shall I need any assistance, or a shell, or is a coffin already prepared ?"

"We answer no questions," replied the man who at first addressed him. "Our orders were short but peremptory : you must follow us !"

"Well, well," answered Gowles, "I'll not be particular in times like these : as there is such importance and such secrecy in the affair, no doubt there is plenty of pay !" Wrapping round his slim and sepulchral form a large black mantle, which was his usual death-looking covering, he stepped from his house to join them. "Now, gentlemen, I am ready," answered Gowles, leading the way, little dreaming what would be the issue of the adventure, or the place he was about being conducted to. His companions, taking each an arm, hurried him along with rapid strides.

Without returning any answer to the many pressing inquiries made by Gowles, the men held steadily on their way till they came to the door of the City Compter. Here the courage and confidence of Gowles for a moment forsook him ; but he soon rallied, for he thought that perhaps it might be some secret affair, to put under ground the bodies of some of the wretched prisoners who had died of the plague, or some other cause. It was not till he had entered an inner room, and had been requested to seat himself, and to deliver up his mantle and staff, that the fearful truth flashed upon him.

"There is your man," exclaimed one of the marshalmen, "but to do him good truth, he has not given us so much trouble as I thought he would, considering his class. But I rather suspect that he had made up his mind for a different termination to his visit—had you not, my churchyard ploughman ?" said the man, addressing Gowles.

"For what am I brought here, and at whose warrant ?" demanded Gowles of the man who seemed to be head turnkey or warden of the prison. "Am I a visitor or a prisoner here, and for what crime ?"

"For which out of so many I suppose you mean," answered the party addressed. "I dare say you are much surprised ; though, if the truth was known, you have expected this every day !"

"That is no answer," muttered Gowles in a dissatisfied tone. "I have a right to know for what I am accused, and by whom."

"Well, then, my worthy carrier of worm's meat," said the turnkey, "you are here on a charge of conspiring to murder, rob, and pillage, and at the request and instigation of Dr. Calder, together with a whole troop of substantial evidence."

"May the plague seize him, and may he fall a victim to its deadly folds !" ejaculated Gowles bitterly.

"Oh, oh !" roared the turnkey, "then I perceive you know him ?"

"I do," answered Gowles, "for a villain and an impostor. He may not triumph ; though, doubtless, he will have recourse to every stratagem and falsehood that his malicious brain can conjure up."

"Well, this matter is for wiser and longer heads than ours to determine," replied the man. "You must go to your cell for the night, and to-morrow you will be taken up before the alderman, when you will learn something more of the affair, I must now bid you good-night." And turning on his heel to an inner room the speaker disappeared without giving Gowles time to reply, by asking him any more questions; and the men who had escorted him from his own house, now took him by each arm and led him down a flight of stone steps, across a paved yard, and pushed him into a dark damp cell, and told him to make himself comfortable for the remainder of the night.

Left to himself, all the horrors of guilt and fear haunted his stricken soul. He doubted of Mother Hagget's faith towards him, whether she had been bribed to this; or whether she had been already arrested—perhaps she was now an inmate of the same prison, and like himself, suffering from the revenge of Doctor Calder.

To pass the night in sleep was quite out of the question, and to endure with sanity the horrid torture and working of his mind was alike impossible; and he paced his cell in hasty strides as far as its limited partitions would allow, calling down every horror and curse upon the head of his persecutor—till the faint rays of morning called him to a sense of his approaching examination. Overcome by his anxieties he for a short time found a little rest in sleep.

Departing next for the abode of Mother Hagget, which was situated in a low narrow alley running down to the Thames from Paul's Wharf near Watling-street, they ascended the stairs of a mean-looking habitation to the very top of the house and without waiting for any invitation or request, with a blow of his foot one of the marshalmen shivered the door to pieces and they entered the room.

Mother Hagget was in the act of stirring a posset for her supper, having just received a summons to attend upon a lady of fashion who was taken with the plague in Bridge-street; she was therefore preparing for her departure. On the table lay a poisonous draft given her originally by Dr. Calder to sleep off poor old Garland, who had fell a victim to their villanies in Old Saint Paul's; also a manuscript or dirty parchment headed—"Directions for effectually removing the plague and all other evils in cases of emergency."

Starting to her feet, she demanded what they wanted of her, and how they dared force their way into a quiet lone woman's private apartment in that manner.

"Why you must come with us, Mother Physic," replied the foremost of the men, "your old chum the undertaker, Gowles, I think, is his name, has requested us to visit you, as he should like to have the favour of your company."

"And where is Gowles, that he wants and sends for me in such a manner as this," demanded Mother Hagget.

"Safely lodged in the City Compter, where all such destroying vagabonds ought to be," replied the marshalman; "and where you will be in less than an hour. So, come on; get yourself ready;—we can wait five minutes or so."

Saying this, the men seated themselves by the table, one began stirring the posset to hasten its boiling; the other took up a manuscript which lay on the table and having read the title with an exclamation of surprise began to read the contents. This however he was prevented from doing by Mother Hagget snatching it from his hand and hurling it into the fire; but the man who was directing his attention to the posset immediately caught it up and put it into his pocket. Mother Hagget then tried to secrete a phial of medicine on the table, but the man perceiving her intention, darted towards her, and struggled with her for it; the wicked woman kept him at bay for a few seconds, while, she held the mouth of the bottle downwards, hoping by that manoeuvre to destroy all traces of its nature. The marshalman perceiving that the contents of the phial were staining the floor, and suspecting her motive, made a violent effort, and succeeded in wrenching it from her grasp in time to save enough of its contents to discover its nature, if wanted.

"So, so, mother fury! this is your fun is it!" exclaimed the marshalman; "I will prevent this. Come sit down in yonder chair; here is your hat and cloak, put them on, and be off with us, or you shall go without them."

"Surely you don't mean to take me to prison to-night, good fellows;" said Mother Hagget, coaxingly. "I can have till the morning, I suppose; I am always to be found here, where I have lived for the last ten years."

"No you must tramp with us at once. Come, Gilbert, pour out that posset, it must be done by this time," he said directing his attention to his companion who was gently stirring it on the fire, "and then we can be off—for I guess that the doctor and the constable himself will be here to search the room, soon.

"Doctor Calder!" exclaimed Hagget, sullenly, "need beware how he comes here to search; let him look to himself; I think I can tell him a little more than he is aware of; and if he makes any charge against me I will bring one against him, that shall for ever stop his plague practice, clever as he is!"

No remark was made to this allusion by the men; in fact they hardly heeded it. Their business was nothing more than to take into custody Gowles and Mother Hagget, and it mattered very little to them if either or both were innocent of the charges imputed to them; that weight resting with those from whom they received their orders.

"Come Hubert," exclaimed the man who had been making the posset on the fire; "this stuff will warm us as we go out into the night air; it looks as tempting as a sillebub, and smells as savoury as a custard—to your health mother," and turning off a tankard of the foaming beverage, with a loud smack of his lips, he handed one to his companion and one to Mother Hagget, who did not refuse the proffered draught thinking that a little friendly feeling with these men might help her cause.

"What do you mean to do with that phial of medicine," she said to the marshalman Hubert, who had prevented her from throwing it away, by secreting it himself?—"it can be of no use to you give it to me I will pay you well for it?"

"No mother, it will not do; I must show it to the constable first, and if he thinks you may have it, why I have no objection. But between you and me, I think there must be something in it not right, or you would not have tried to throw it away."

"As you will, for a surly hound:" replied Hagget, and turning round from them proceeded towards the door; but she was immediately brought back, for the men having drank up the posset of sack were ready to start; and taking Mother Hagget between them they led her away, having first safely locked up the room and brought the key away with them.

On her journey to the Compter, Hagget maintained a sullen silence; and upon her arrival there would not answer a single question put to her by the receiving turnkey; and she was accordingly locked up in a seperate cell from Gowles, for the night.

Early next morning Doctor Calder accompanied by the two officers who arrested Gowles and Hagget, and the marshal himself, proceeded to the house of Gowles, for the purpose of searching it. Proceeding to his workshop, amongst the many coffins there piled up it was very evident from the appearance of many that they had been used frequently, and had been put in the ground and taken out again in a few days afterwards, and the corps they had contained hurled with others into the dead cart; a most alarming process for the extension and aggravation of the plague.

"I will merely take a note of this fact," said the marshal; "we can do nothing with it ; for not knowing by whom they were purchased, and from whom they were stolen, we could not prove a case of felony ; but, however we can prove sufficient to procure him a heavy punishment for such conduct, under the " Rules and regulations for the City of London, during the raging of the plague." *

Their attention was then directed to the private apartments of the house, and after a search of two hours they were about to withdraw, when Doctor Calder, happening to open a secret drawer in a beaureae, discovered to his great joy a bag of gold ; and upon the bag in red letters was stamped the name of " Master Ralph Garland, 1660."

" This," he exclaimed, holding up the gold to the marshal, " is what I was most anxious to discover. It will prove the case of the murder of this unfortunate man by these wretches for the sake of the money he had scraped up by his hard earnings, during many years of toil !"

" Excellent indeed ;" replied the marshal, taking the bag of gold into his possession and making a memorandum of its discovery in his book. " We may now depart to the womans dwelling ; for a more convincing proof we could not wish to find here."

Accordingly the whole party started off to the residence of Mother Hagget ; which after about twenty minutes sharp walking they reached, and Hubert the marshalman giving up the key, they entered her apartment, which only consisted of one room, and locked the door after them.

" These are the only things I took charge of upon the occasion of our visit," said the marshal, opening a small drawer in a table and producing the phial of medicine he had so much difficulty in obtaining from Mother Hagget, and the parchment manuscript. Both of these he turned over to the possession of the marshal who took a note of the circumstance, together with the resistance made by Hagget on the occasion.

Doctor Calder was somewhat disconcerted upon beholding the phial which the marshal had now the possession of, for it was the identical draft he had given to Mother Hagget, to compose Ralph Garland to a deadly slumber.

" I should like to examine that phial," said the doctor eagerly to the marshal. " I should not at all be surprised if it contained some poisonous decoction."

" You can do so," answered the marshal, " while I examine the room ; and when you have done so give me your opinion upon it."

Glad of the opportunity of destroying such a dangerous evidence, Doctor Calder took the phial to the window, and pretending to look at and taste the contents threw it down upon the floor, and dashed it to a thousand atoms.

" Confound my stupidity, see what I have done," he exclaimed, with apparent vexation to the marshal, " I do believe from the taste that its contents were poison !"

" Yes, a great pity," exclaimed the officers addressed ; " but cannot now be helped ; the best way will be to take it out alltogether in the evidence, now it is destroyed—but it might have been of great importance," he muttered in no very pleasant tone as he scratched his pen through the remark and told his men to take no notice of such a phial.

" It might have proved of more importance than I should have liked," muttered Calder to himself—" I might have been implicated by that very phial for by Heaven it was one which had my private mark upon it, and the contents of it were from a drug that could be purchased only by medical men

---

* An act passed in the Lord Mayor's Court, June 1665; which imposed certain restrictions upon the citizen's for cleanliness, and the preventing infection.—See Chronicles of London, vol 2 ; No. 186.

—a thousand thanks to my perception." And without taking any further notice of the affair, he joined the officers in their search.

"This manuscript," said the marshal folding it up, is of most important use ; we can see by this how she has been in the habit of treating her unfortunate patients."

Opening a small box which was standing upon a shelf, the officer. in routing out its contents, pulled forth, with an exclamation of surprise a small gold locket, with hair plaited in it. This was the very same locket that Mother Hagget had stolen from Gowles, and which he had taken from the person of the young man whom he had found in the road some few weeks back.

"Here is something of value, I guess," he exclaimed, as he held it up to the light : "and not honestly come by, either. It has been stolen from some of her patient's toilets ; it seems a females hair, and doubtless has been the property of some gallant. We must trace whom she has had to attend upon, likely to have been the owners of such a trinket," he observed, as he wrote it down in his book, and folded it up carefully in his pocket.

Again the search was vigorously resumed in every crook and crevice of the room : till Doctor Calder more persevering than the rest (perhaps because he had a greater interest at stake) in rumaging over an old box of lumber underneath the bed, pulled forth the identical bag of gold which Mother Hagget had secreted from Gowles ; and was also marked in a similar manner with the owner's name upon the outside.

"Here is what I searched for !" exclaimed Calder with an air of satisfaction and malicious pride, as he held up the bag of gold—" the fellow to the other, only better filled—the lady seems to have had the better portion of it, I think !"

"And here is more money wrapped up in this old piece of cloth ;" rejoined one of the officers, holding up a bundle seemingly of rags, but containing a great quantity of gold coin.

"There seems to have been something like an unfair division here," exclaimed the marshal looking over the money. "This loose gold is exactly the same amount as we found in the bag at the coffin makers house. It seems to me as if one bag only had been divided and this second one has been kept sly aside."

"A trick worthy of the woman who possessed it," replied the doctor. "Yes ; that is it, true enough, in dividing the money she has managed to cheat that arch-rogue Gowles himself. How he will curse and swear when it is made known to him."

"This piece of old cloth too, bears the cathedral mark ; the same as is stamped upon the clothing of all the servants of the dean !" said the marshal, pointing to a mark in the cloth of a mitre and sceptre.

"Right !" replied Calder, "it is so ! and if I mistake not—in fact, I will swear to it—that is a part of poor old Garland's coat. I remember seeing him wear it the day he was seized with the plague ! This, also, may prove something important."

"I think we have found evidences enough to prove what is wanted ; and as I have taken an inventory of every thing in the room, I think we may now pay a visit to the dean himself, and make some inquiries respecting this money of old Garland's ;" and closing his memorandum, the marshal prepared to depart.

"I think so too," replied Calder—" 'tis the best step we can take, and will go farther towards criminating the parties than any other evidences we may gather."

Now Calder in his own heart, would sooner have gone any where else than to Old Saint Paul's, for knowing how deeply he was concerned in the affair

himself; he feared lest he should hear things which might fix some degree
of guilt upon himself; but having gone so far into it, he could not now re-
tract; and it was with a trembling heart, and a guilty conscience that he
entered the precints of the sacred edifice; and the muffled heavy tones of the
vesper bell rung on his heart as a funeral knell, to tell him of the death that
awaited him.

Announcing their presence they were soon joined by the Reverend Edward
Smee, the Dean of the Cathedral, who ushered them into a private room,
and lent a patient and attentive ear to the statement made by the marshal.

"This intelligence surprises as well as shocks me!" exclaimed the dean;
"to think that deeds so atrocious, and so wicked should be perpetrated here,
in the very face of Heaven itself. I will call up old Oliver the verger, who
has had to do poor Ralph's duty since his lamented death.

In a few minutes they were joined by the old man: to whom the marshal
read over the accusation against Gowles and Mother Hagget, together with
the circumstances that had occurred as evidences in their search.

Old Oliver heard the tale, and the depositions of the marshal and men;
with the opinions of doctor Calder, also; and with a melancholy look and a
solemn shake of the head, he exclaimed, "Ah! this confirms what I feared
to name!"

"Speak your suspicions freely on this occasion, I beseech you, friend,"
said the marshal kindly; "I will promise you a handsome reward!"

"I court none," replied the verger. "I am sorry that it has come to this,
for words of mine to condemn my fellow creatures; but it is Heaven's doings,
who has made my eye to see and my tongue to speak—God's will be done."

Upon being questioned by the marshal as to his opinion of Ralph Garland's
wealth, he replied:—

"That he had money, I was sure of: but where it was kept I never knew.
He was a suspicious and a miserly man—it was generally supposed that it
16.

was hidden in some of the vaults; and Master Garland, whenever he was questioned jocularly about it, always said it was with the dead, and there let it rest. But the sudden disappearance of two vergers, his fellow servants, immediately after his death, led me to suppose that they had found his treasure, and fled with it!"

"That treasure, we can prove," replied the marshal, "was discovered and carried away by the nurse who attended him, and by the undertaker who carried his remains to their last resting place!"

"Heavenly powers! is it so?" exclaimed the verger; "then may God forgive me for my suspicions, as I trust he will them for their misdeeds—they have then caused his death, and not the plague! although he might have been attacked, yet he was so far recovering that his safety was deemed certain by all, especially by our friend Calder here, who was more sanguine than any of us."

"Murdering hell hounds!" exclaimed the marshal in a rage; "who knows how many other deaths, yet undiscovered, lay at their door—what think you of it now, doctor?" he inquired of Calder, who sat a silent hearer of all that passed.

"I am horrified and astounded!" he replied. "But let the old gentleman proceed."

The old verger then resumed his statement. He said that it had been a matter of much surprise to him, the sudden manner in which Ralph's death had occurred; but that he had taken the opportunity, the day that he was fetched away by the dead cart of Gowles, to lift from over his face a cloth when to his horror and surprise, he saw that Master Ralph, had fallen a victim to strangulation, and not the plague! for his eyes were lying out of their sockets, his tongue nearly bitten in two in the agony of the moment; and his face one blotch of congealed blood; presenting to the view the most horrible and ghastly object that he ever witnessed.

And further that on the same morning, early, just before the hour of prayer, he was surprised to meet the woman who had been attending upon Master Garland, come stealing through the middle of the cathedral with a lantern in her hand. Seeing her, he had hidden himself behind a stone pillar, and she passed by, as he thought, without observing him. Paying a visit to the stone vault some hours afterwards, he found that it had been disfigured by repeated attempts to force it—which must have been done by the woman herself. And this it was, together with the appearance of the corpse, which caused him to think Master Garland had come to an unfair end. The mysterious disappearance of the two vergers, now that Gowles and his associate had been found guilty of the robbery, as far as evidence went, he was at a loss to say; and the only cause he could suggest was, that they must have fallen victims to their cruelty, by discovering them in their atrocious attempt.

This closed the evidence of the verger, and the marshal observing that he had collected quite enough, and in fact much more than he had expected, respectfully withdrew with his men—requesting the verger to hold himself in readiness to attend any summons that might be issued for his evidence at the ensuing examination.

Each one now seperated on his way: the verger to his cell; the officer, and his men to the City Compter to lay before the governor the fruits of their search; and Doctor Calder to his home.

If the dean and the verger were shocked and surprised at what they had heard in this examination concerning the death of old Garland; and the officer and his men were pleased at the success their efforts had been crowned with; there was one who was soul-stricken and alarmed; one whose heart writhed with all the pangs of a guilty conscience, and who feared to look a stranger in the face, lest he should point at him and exclaim—" Behold the murderer !" And this one was Doctor Calder.

From the encrimsoned nature of his crime; and the prominent part he had taken in it, he feared lest all these evidences should bring him in for a share of the guilt. He found that much more had been noticed than he was aware of, concerning the old man's death—but then it could not be proved to him ! The verger had examined by stealth, the corpse of the old man—good. There was nothing to criminate him in that; for it could be proved that Mother Hagget had strangled him, which he himself knew full well was the case, and would also assist to bring such conclusion about, why then he was free of that death, for luckily he had destroyed the only evidence in this affair which could implicate him, by breaking the phial of poisonous medicine, which was the mixture he had given to Mother Hagget for the purpose of putting a period to the old man's existence, but which he found she had reserved for some other purpose; thus consulting within his own mind, he breathed once more freely.

But then again the murder of the two vergers was a difficult affair, and by far more dangerous, as the bodies were still lying at the place where they met their death; and where, should Mother Hagget denounce him as her accomplice, of which there was little doubt, they would be found according to her statement. He would have given half his fortune could those bodies be removed ! for that would render all her arguments and accusations against him groundless. Suspicion, it was true, favoured him; for as the money was found in the possession of Gowles and Hagget, the murder would follow as a matter of conclusive evidence that nothing could disprove; and which, fortunately for him, the case of Hagget having been discovered coming from the vault by the verger, would strengthen.

Sleep for that night was out of the question: he almost repented having quarrelled with Hagget, for she knew the most in the affair, and was a dangerous and an unforgiving woman, possessed of much craft and cunning. But then he considered that he could not have bribed her as evidence against Gowles; they were too closely leagued, and were more nearly connected than either of them were with him. The imputations they would throw out against him, he feared, would materially injure his reputation; as people would naturally believe such assertions coming from the mouths of a plague-nurse and an undertaker, persons with whom medical men must be acquainted and concerned. Should he leave the city and retire into some lonely village, that would go far towards criminating him, and would allow any charge to be brought against him by Gowles or Hagget, unanswered and un-defended. Secretly and firmly resolving these matters in his mind, he proceeded to his private surgery, where he mixed up a draught of poison of so destructive a nature that a drop on the tongue would destroy life in an instant, without any signs of violence; this he resolved to administer i the could to either of his foes, or if in case of himself being suspected and captured, to end his own life by the same means.

CHAPTER XIX.

If the Duke of Buckingham and his accomplices were astounded when the news reached them of a deputation from the City of London having waited upon King Charles to represent their conduct to him, they were doubly so, when they heard the decrees which had accompanied it; for besides the reparation which the king had ordered should be made to Master Elliot, he had also intimated to Buckingham that his presence at court could be dispensed with for the next six months.

It was this that cut the duke to the quick more than the fine which had been imposed; to think that he should be dishonoured through a mere citizen's daughter; or rather through the plebeian interference of her family; and he swore deep and bitter revenge towards the Corporation of London; which, together with the aid of his dissolute associates he resolved at once to put in force.

Since the removal of Master Elliot and family to the residence of Buckthorpe, the hosier, in Friday-street, strange alterations had taken place in the behaviour of Constance towards Lawrence, for she had secretly been in the habit of receiving letters from the Duke of Buckingham, through the interference of his spies, who it seems had bribed Scrubb and Pauline (who had now joined the Elliot family as an additional servant,) to deliver them to her. These letters contained the fondest and most impassioned declarations of love, for in them he assured her that he would marry her, solemnly and according to the rites of the established church, if she could obtain her father's consent to the union; and he also painted to her, in striking colours, the conduct and motives of Lawrence, who, he insinuated was, only urged to the tenderness he showed for her, through the hopes of a fortune, which he expected as a dowry.   He also well knew the cord on which to be most pressing; and he tried to wound her feelings against Lawrence by hints thrown out of jealousies and inconstancies, which he observed to her as every day occurrences; and to these letters did the heart of Constance, (true woman-like, ever leaning to the man whose protestations are the most high-flown and flattering, and whose condition in life is somewhat noble or exalted above her own, seriously inclined; and she considered that all favours shown to Lawrence by her, as graces of such a condescending nature, that for him to spurn them was more than she could bear.

Now this Master Buckthorpe, the hosier, had a very beautiful daughter, about eighteen years of age, or rather older than Constance, who though surpassing fair was still shaded by the resplendent beauty of the " Fair Stay of Friday-street," as she was called.   Constance had most cordially hated her for the very many favours and compliments she had seen paid to her since she had been a visitor in her father's house; and now that the duke painted to her an attachment existing between this beautiful damsel and Lawrence, her hatred for her was doubled; and all her love for Lawrence turned into loathing and contempt.   For Constance was a very passionate girl, and she could hate as bitterly as she could love devotedly.   While contemplating these things she called to mind some observation she had heard her father declare concerning the duke, to the effect that if he had courted his daughter fairly he should have been proud to see him win her; for to say the truth Master Elliot, was an aspiring tradesman and thought as much of the honour of a coronet as his vain and lovely daughter; and was it not in her power to let the duke know these sentiments of her father's ; and if he indeed loved her, as he pledged himself so fondly he did, he would lose no time but seek her fairly and honestly of her father. " Yes," she exclaimed ; " I am resolved, since I am treated with disdain by him whom I had condescended to favour, to fix my love on the man who first won my heart, for I will never bend to meek submission, or share the affections of another woman in any man's esteem ! Arthur, my first, my only love, for Arthur shall I ever call you ; I am yours in life, or wedded to death in the grave !"

This wonderful and unaccountable change in the sentiments of Constance Elliot was brought out, partly through some slight offences she had imagined had been trespassed against her, by Lawrence showing too much attention to the fair Helen, the daughter of the hosier. For Lawrence who had no other motive, but gratitude and kindness in his heart, considered that in being respectful to his master's friends, he was fulfilling his master's duty, had paid many slight attentions towards Helen by teaching her the art and mysteries of the chess-board, colouring in water colours, and several light and elegant fancy accomplishments in which Lawrence being naturally an ingenious youth, was an adept. Constance had frequently interrupted and observed them in these conversations, sometimes she would make a pettish remark and suddenly retire without being followed by Lawrence, and that had sorely vexed her ; and at others, she would watch them in silence and in secret, and although even her jealous heart could discern nothing in the conduct of Lawrence above a friendly or neighbourly feeling, she could not help noticing the long glances and ardent gazing of Helen upon him, as he sat opposite to her at a table busily employed sketching some design for her copying : she would notice her, sit and feed as it were upon his features ; dart love in every look, and sighing turn her head in another direction. That Helen secretly loved Lawrence, she could safely assert, by the throbs of her own heart in the affection for Buckingham ere she had found him so false as he had proved ; and she had therefore now fixed her fate on him and happiness ; or without him, misery, death, and despair. And thus in the space of three short weeks was the affection and the confidence which Constance had expressed for Lawrence completely lost, and for ever banished from her heart.

Lawrence, however, was an utter stranger to all that was transpiring in the mind of Constance during the last few days that she had laid herself open to the artifices and correspondence of Buckingham unknown to her father or the family.

The next morning, after the receipt of a letter from the duke, in which Lawrence's duplicity and inconstancy was strangely pourtrayed, she stood gazing through a small window into a room where Lawrence and Helen were seated. Lawrence, who had repeatedly sent several messages for Constance to join them, was giving lessons in landscape drawing, being a very fair amateur artist himself, and he had just completed his design and presented it to his fair pupil, who loaded him with kindness and thanks for his care and attention, and had also taken her hand to lead her forth to another apartment where they were in hopes of finding Constance, Lawrence through a youth's frolic at being alone with so fair a damsel, had allowed his arm to encircle the ivory circlet of her neck had also further ventured to press upon her lips a kiss, when Constance not choosing to brook more, entered the room upon them.

As Constance entered the room Helen was leaving it by an opposite door, and Lawrence was following her ; but seizing his arm and closing the door after Helen, Constance desired him to stay,—

" This is as I wished," exclaimed Constance ; " we are once more alone, Lawrence, and I beg you will this once grant me my favour ; I may not ask another of you !"

"Speak, Constance, I implore you;" replied Lawrence in an eager tone, as if alarmed by the manner in which Constance had addressed him.

"I will, but on one condition only, Lawrence," she replied; "and that is that you do not interrupt me till I conclude—do you agree?"

"Exactly, I will remain silent," answered Lawrence.

"You may, doubtless, Lawrence, conclude my sudden entrance at this moment as a work of chance, but I take this opportunity of convincing you to the contrary. That young girl who has just left the room, although the daughter of my father's intimate friend, and my own, yet is she regarded by me as a viper in my path, and I look upon her with a hate so fearful, that I curse myself when I think of it."

Lawrence was about to reply—

"Not a word, at present, I beg you, Lawrence," exclaimed Constance as she saw his effort. I can see by every action, word, or look of her's toward you that she loves you, secretly, but deeply Lawrence; I could say she had taken my place, but alas! Lawrence, my heart is not my own to give: curse me not when I confess it to you, you whom I have most cause to be grateful to, that whoever owns my hand, yet will that worthless man Buckingham still claim my heart!"

"Curses on him!" exclaimed Lawrence in the anguish of his rage.

"Blame him not, but me, dear Lawrence; I come here to rend asunder from your eyes the cloud of mystery with which you are enwrapped; my mother is favourable to our union, wishes, nay, prays for it; my father, however, is not so eager for it, for he has whispered to me in confidence, Lawrence, that if the Duke of Buckingham had in the first instance fairly wooed and won me, he should have given his consent; and his words intimated to me that if he were to do it now, as a man and an honest one, in spite of all the maledictions and curses he had bestowed upon him, he might be tempted for my future welfare, mark that Lawrence, for my future welfare, he might be induced to consent. For Buckingham stands so high with the king that he would be the making of any family for ever, with whom he should contract an alliance!"

"But what says the daughter to these suggestions of her father?" inquired Lawrence of her pointedly.

"Alas! Lawrence, how can I act! I am still pursued by the importunities of Buckingham; his spies beset me move which way I will, even in this very house. And whenever they are absent I have him in my mind's eye, and in my heart."

"There is but one way to make you mine, Constance; and but one way for you to prove your love for me, Constance; and that is to leave this house with me to-morrow, and return not till the holy ceremony shall have made us one, for ever."

"Lawrence, it cannot, it will never be!"

"How, Constance? Cannot? You amaze me! Explain I conjure you."

"Would you willingly, in binding to yourself my lost and bankrupt heart, rend that of another's in twain?" replied Constance.

"Another's! whose! what others? Who can possibly be so much interested in my welfare, as to feel any emotions by such an act?" eagerly demanded Lawrence.

"Helen! who has just left us."

"Helen!" replied Lawrence, in amazement. "Helen, the daughter of our host and our friend; impossible Constance, you jest with me."

"You do with me Lawrence, if you plead ignorance of it; but I do not upbraid you with it, believe me, on the contrary. I am happy to see that an object has attracted your attention, in preference to her who has no worth to give you for your affection. My die is cast, and I fear my lot is a miserable one! Oh, man! man, did you but know how joyful or fatal it is to a woman's happiness in this life when she bestows on you her first gift of affection, her maiden unpolluted heart, you would value it as a gift of greater worth."

"Constance," exclaimed Lawrence, raising her in his arms, and wiping away the tears as they chased each other down her lovely cheeks—"What act of mine, or what thought of your own has led to this outbreak of your heart. Can you for once believe that I have slighted or given up the love for you which I was ever proud to maintain, and which was the greatest joy of my heart to see returned by yourself; speak, tell me I beseech you, Constance, who has prompted you to this; it is so different from the sentiments of our last meeting. The maiden you have mentioned, our friend's daughter too, I have been grateful and kind to her, but only as a duty for her father's kindness to us; before Heaven, nothing more! My love for you Constance, is as strong and as ardent as ever, then why not yield to my prayer, and make me happy, by consenting to a speedy union?"

"Lawrence, such a step must not, shall not be taken by me; and for two most potent reasons, which when you can remove I will agree to it."

"Name them, Constance, I entreat you." he implored.

"The first is my father's eternal displeasure, which I am certain would follow such a step, even was he willing for our union. The next is the life of our host's child, the lovely Helen, for if you esteem her not at present, in the same value as she adores you, I trust you soon may. Such a step would break her heart. Convince me to the contrary of that, and I am yours."

"Why, I have never breathed of love to her, Constance, believe me," asserted Lawrence.

"Very likely: but that could not blind her eyes or close the portals of her heart. Ah, Lawrence, you are but a novice in love if you think that a woman waits to be told she is loved, ere she loves herself. The love that young creature bears for you, was as deep and as unrootable at the first moment you eyes met, as it is at the present moment, and will gain new strength every-day. No Lawrence, the step you suggest must not be!"

"You distract me, Constance," replied Lawrence with great emotion: "you cannot surely be in earnest."

"As the grave," replied Constance, firmly. "Let not my lot interfere with your happiness, Lawrence. I implore you; I am but as a cast off reed, shaken and bruised by every wind that blows. And above all let n ot this conversation pass your lips. Had I a heart to give you, Lawrence, believe me it would be yours, and yours only; but mine was decoyed from me ere I knew of its flight, and it is now left to throb and break in silence and contempt. For the present, farewell Lawrence, my kind benefactor and my preserver; and if you really esteem my memory and study my wishes, try to obey them by giving your heart and hand to her who so eagerly craves it, and who would doubtless make a better return than I am able to do."

Reaching out her hand to Lawrence, but averting her face, which was bedewed with gushing tears, Constance was about to leave the room; but Lawrence holding her by the hand, tried to detain her.

"But a few moments Constance, in brief explanation;" he entreated.

"Not a moment! I dare not, I am called," she answered hurriedly, as she broke from his grasp and left the room.

Lawrence left to himself, he paced the room in deep thought, scarcely knowing whether what had passed during the last few moments was a dream or reality.

"How her heart clings to that villain!" he murmured to himself, moodily. "There is no chance for me winning her hand, much more her heart, while he exists. So easily is the affections of woman dazzled and entrapped by a flattering display; and once allured it will never leave its fowler. Helen, too! she in love with me! impossible! wonderful! Oh love, how mysterious and contrary are thy ways; I would have given ten years of my life to be sure that Constance returned my passion."

As he was thus ruminating and wandering up and down the apartment, his eye caught a letter which lay on the ground before him, and which had evidently been dropped by some one unknown to them—"it must be either Constance or Helen," he exclaimed, as he stooped down and picked it up; but his doubts were soon set aside by reading upon it the direction, which was for Constance. He paused ere he should open it; and considered it would be a breach of honour, but as it was not sealed he ventured, and unfolding it devoured in greedy whispers its contents.

The letter which Lawrence had thus discovered was the last one which Constance had received from Buckingham; it was written in an elegant and impressive style, imploring forgiveness, urging his suit and protesting the sincerity of his love; it concluded too, with no very flattering description of Lawrence's pretensions to her hand, pointing out his motives as base and false, and alsr hinted at his secret meetings and engagements with their hosts daughter Helen, and the letter concluded with a fervent prayer for Constance to meet the writer that evening at the conduit.

"Shall I return this letter to Constance, or shall I take it at once to Master Elliot and show it him," considered Lawrence to himself, pondering which would be the most honourable and prudent step for him to take. "I will do neither," he exclaimed, as he folded it up and placed it carefully in his vest, "I will keep it by me, and watch the issue of it." So determining he left the room.

CHAPTER XX.

THE day was now fixed for Master Elliot's departure to his country seat at Dulwich, and this through the organization of spies carefully placed in many directions was speedily and promptly conveyed to Buckingham, who lost no time in consulting with his associates, Vincent Palmer and Captain Blount, how they should act, to make one more desperate effort ere the family left London.

The hour of appointment named in the letter was long since past, and the dull shades of evening were fast drawing round the earth its dusky envelope, when Buckingham and his accomplices came creeping down Friday-street, and secreted themselves, as they thought, from public gaze by turning under the gateway of the Old Bell Inn yard, which stood nearly opposite to Master Buckthorpe's house.

This movement however was watched by Lawrence from a garret window, for whether in cloak mantle or court dress the figure of Buckingham was too familiar to Lawrence's eye to allow any disguise he might adopt to deceive him.

Lawrence had made known his fears and his surmises to Master Elliot with whom he had long communed on the subject of Buckingham's present attempt; and he called him to the window, and pointed out to him the three men in ambush, who were now and then peeping out from their hiding-place, and betraying themselves.

"Relentless villains!" exclaimed Elliot, "how my hand trembles to grasp their throats, but as you observ Lawrence, stratagem succeeds best with them, so let your plan proceed, I am confident of success, and if so, we act our own game immediately. It is an excellent bait, and one which they are sure to snap at."

Lawrence and his master now withdrew from the window and every thing was perfectly calm and still, which caused Buckingham and his companions to come from their hiding-places and pace backwards and forwards before the house, unnoticed as they imagined by their disguises—though Lawrence, with the eye of a hawk, was following every movement.

In the course of about half an hour, a heavy travelling coach rolled down Friday-street and stopped before the hosier's door. Servants immediately appeared at the door with torches, which gave Buckingham's party an opportunity of observing what was going on from across the street. Lawrence made himself very prominent giving orders and bearing a large torch, so that his person was instantly recognised by Buckingham as he led into the coach a young female and appeared to them to follow himself. The coach then departed, the doors of the house were closed, and the carriage rolled heavily along towards Cheapside, tracked in its wake by Buckingham, Blount, and Vincent Palmer.

They allowed the carriage to proceed as far as the open space behind Old Saint Paul's, when calling to the driver to stop, Blount held the horses and presented a pistol to his head if he refused. Paralysed with alarm, the man offered no resistance, and Buckingham assisted by Palmer forced open the doors and began to deal with the inmates.

"What's this for?" exclaimed a voice which sounded somewhat strange and peculiar to Buckingham, as he was lifting the female in his arms—"Are you robbers, or who are you!" and drawing a heavy cudgel from his belt, the questioner was about to enforce an answer, when the arm of Vincent held him back.

Dragging the female from the carriage, Buckingham darted down a narrow turning leading to the river; and Blount and Vincent having silenced the youth, who, of course, they supposed to be no other than Lawrence, and throwing a well-filled purse to the driver to ensure his silence, followed quietly after their leader.

Pursuing their way down to the Thames, they made for Blackfriars, where a boat was in readiness to receive them, and leaping into it Buckingham ordered the waterman to push off for Deptford.

Buckingham now turned to his fair partner, who lay quietly in his arms, but so wrapped up in the cloak which he had enveloped her with, that not a vestige of her features were visible.

"Constance," whispered Buckingham lowly in her ear, "look up and bless me with a smile—it is Arthur, your long-tried and constant adorer, who speaks to you."

"My name is not Constance, and the name of my adorer is not Arthur, but Scrubb; and I hope you have not hurt him, for master has promised us that we shall be married as soon as he gets settled in his country house," replied Pauline, artlessly.

"And who in God's name are you, then, if you are not Constance," demanded Buckingham of the astonished damsel, angrily.

"My name is Pauline," she answered meekly, "and I think you are the person who came to our house in the Old Jewry the day that my poor Scrubb got into disgrace with that old beldame Mother Sirloin. She's an old good-for-nothing wicked woman, that's what she is." And being left alone for a few moments in consequence of Buckingham's ruminating upon the mistake he had made and the decision he should meet with from his companions when he related the affair to them, Pauline ran on in a strain of unconnected trifling sentences till she was aroused by a loud conversation between Buckingham and his companions at the head of the boat.

17.

" Toast me for a cuckoldy knave," exclaimed the duke to Vincent Palmer, who with Blount were lolling in the bows of the boat as she glided rapidly down the pool,—"if I have not carried off the maid and let the mistress slip me!"

" I comprehend you not," replied Vincent.

' Why, the girl there—" answered Buckingham, pettishly—" it is a serving wench, and not Constance; I have been played a trick, and fell in a snare."

A long, loud and boisterous peal of laughter was the only reply made to this assertion by his companions; who seemed to relish the joke mightily, although they had participated in the dishonour of being trapped.

" What do you mean to do with the wench, Buck?" inquired Vincent Palmer eagerly.

" Oh pitch her overboard for what I care; I'd sooner have tramped fifty miles barefooted on sharp pebbles, than have been served such a trick—that mongrel 'prentice, too he must have participated in it—curse him I will lop his ears for him when next we meet.   It shall be his last joke to brag of!"

" She may be of service to you though," replied the Captain, anxious to put in a word to soothe the anger he saw rising in the duke's mind.   " No doubt she is clever enough to carry a message; and willing enough, no doubt, for a gold piece or two, to make herself useful in these matters.   Try what can be done with her.   Do you mean to take her down with you to Deptford?"

" Aye!" answered Buckingham doggedly.   " It is too late to return now; besides I am anxious to reach there, the girl can go back by the boat; but I must purchase her confidence, however dear it cost me," and addressing himself to Pauline, he thus interrogated her.

" Have you lived long with the family?"

" Not long, please your worship," replied Pauline, " but my dear Scrubb has lived with them ever since he was a boy."

" And what do you call him now?" said Blount impudently.

" Why, if master keeps his word and marries us the same time as he does Lawrence and Constance, I think I shall call him a man then.   I ought I think."

" Let us hope so, for your sake," remarked Vincent sneeringly.

" Enough of that!" growled Buckingham.   " I want to know all I can, while she is with us; keep your jests for the orange girls at the Globe Theatre, they will relish them best.   Do you mean to say that your master has promised to marry Constance to Lawrence," inquired Buckingham in a tone of great surprise.

" Scrubb told me so; at least when the plague is over; which I hope will not be long now."

" Too long, for most of us, I fear," replied Buckingham gloomily.   " You must excuse our rudeness this evening in taking you from your coach; but the truth is, that I wanted to speak with you.   I dare say you will not mind taking a letter to your mistress for me, or a message any time; and if I should by chance see you at any time you can always bring me any message your mistress may send.   This purse will buy you a new hood," he exclaimed, as he threw a well-filled silken purse into her lap.

" Oh I am sure I am heartily glad I met with you that I am; for I don't care whether I ride by water or by coach so as I reach master's new house before it is too late to get in."

" You won't reach it to-night then," replied Buckingham.

" Not to-night.   Why its more than my place is worth; I was ordered to sit up for Miss Constance and Dame Elliot; oh what shall I do, what shall I do!" and the poor little damsel gave utterance to a flood of tears.   " Cheer up," said Buckingham, " all will go well yet, put us ashore fellow," he called out to the waterman, who turned into a narrow creek just below Cuckold's point, and in another stroke of his oar, the boat's keel grated along the bank.

"And did your master intend sending Constance to Dulwich to night," inquired Buckingham anxiously.

"He did sir, she is now on her way there, accompanied by her mother and brother !"

"Who else !" inquired Buckingham.

"I dare say her father or Lawrence !"

"Fool, fool, that I am," muttered Buckingham, I have lost an excellent opportunity. And throwing a purse to the waterman, at the same time giving him direction to pull hard for London again with his fare, they all three leaped ashore, and struck off in a direction for the Kentish hills.

Wondering much at the suddenness of the adventure and wrapped in gloom by the stillness and darkness of the night, Pauline maintained a perfect silence. In about half an hour she was safely landed at Queenhithe and was soon after safely lodged at the hosier's in Friday-street.

CHAPTER XXI.

RELEASED from the grip of his assailants, Srubb stood bellowing like a child, not knowing which step to take, and it was not until he had been persuaded by his companion to return that he agreed to it, and accordingly the horses' heads were turned in the direction they had so recently left.

Arrived at Master Buckthorpe's, in Friday-street, he eagerly inquired if his master had departed, and being informed that he had not, but was now up stairs at supper with the hosier and his family, Scrubb made no hesitation in rushing at once up to him, but upon his arriving at the apartment in question he was met by Lawrence, who laughed loudly at him, and questioned him jeeringly about Pauline,

"You may laugh this time, Master Lawrence," replied Scrubb, "but I think if it had been your case, you would have had the whole city up in arms about it. But let me tell you my little Pauline is as dear to me as somebody else is that I know to you;" and he finished his reply by another loud burst of tears and lamentations.

"Fear not," exclaimed Lawrence, cheering him, "all will yet be well. I will help you to recover Pauline, but believe me she will not be detained. They have mistaken her for Constance, and as soon as they discover their error, she will be restored to liberty."

"But I must see master and tell him all about it."

"Nothing of the kind," interposed Lawrence peremptorily. "We expected as much when you set out. You have nothing to do but to order the coach to wait for us. We shall require it shortly, as we are to start for Dulwich to-night."

Proceeding to relate the circumstance of Scrubb's disaster to his master, Lawrence entered the room in which the families were assembled. Having informed them of all that had happened to Scrubb and Pauline, they all, with the exception of Constance, laughed heartily at the joke that had been practised on the duke and his companions, and it was arranged that Master Elliot and his family should prepare at once for their departure.

In the midst of their preparations, and when every thing was nearly completed for starting, they were much, though very agreeably, surprised by the return of Pauline, who having been landed by the waterman at Blackfriars, had made her way straight home. She related to them her adventures, which elicited nothing but mirth from all who heard it except Scrubb, who now in his turn with Lawrence was much enraged with Buckingham and his companions for the freedom they had taken with Pauline.

While Scrubb and two of the hosier's men were making the luggage and packing cases safe in the coach, Elliot and his family were busily engaged in taking leave of their worthy host, and there was one indeed of that same family to whom this separation was a bitter pang, a trial she fondly and ardently hoped would not have taken place, and which she put off from her resolution of entertaining from day to day, till at last it could be no longer put off, but had arrived with all those heart-rending emotions so incidental to the tearing away one's self from any beloved or esteemed object, and this one was Buckthorpe's daughter, who it has been mentioned had conceived a secret though ardent passion for Lawrence, unknown to him.

Watching an opportunity when Lawrence had entered a back apartment to procure articles of his own, Helen threw herself in his way.

" And so, Lawrence, you are really going to leave me—to leave us," she rejoined, checking herself.

" Yes, Helen, so it seems. Though I must candidly confess that the many pleasant hours I have spent since I have been here, assisted by yourself in your amusements and your studies, has rendered this the most pleasant and agreeable month I have passed for some time. But you are in tears, Helen. What has affected you so ?"

" Nothing—merely a thought," was the reply.

" Who will you procure, if I may be so bold as to ask the question," said Lawrence to the downcast maiden, taking her hand affectionately within his own, " as my successor in your drawing and music lessons, Helen ? Let him not, I pray you, examine any of my specimens and patterns, or he will think you had a sorry tutor indeed."

" Alas ! I shall require none now, Lawrence," sighed Helen in grief, " for indeed I do not think any one would take the trouble with me that you have done, and therefore I shall not give them the chance. But as we must part, Lawrence, here is a small and unworthy token which I must request you will keep for my remembrance, and if we ever do meet again you will answer me the question therein contained—nay, do not open it now, not until the morning when you shall have recovered from your journey, and have forgotten the friends you have left behind."

" Forgotten them !" exclaimed Lawrence with a strong emotion. " I trust, Helen, that will never be ; for without such benefactors we should all have been wanderers in this plague-stricken city. Whatever may be the contents of this packet, Helen, I will keep it while I have life, and while gratitude and memory holds a place within my bosom. I will not think of you, but I will pray for you, and was not my heart already—but I tarry ; my master is waiting. Helen, farewell ! may the great God who keeps all in his mercy and providence in the hour of danger ever be with you and protect you !"

Lawrence strained the maiden in his arms, and imprinting a tender and affectionate kiss upon her lips, hastily broke from her, and in a few moments he had joined his master's family, who had already occupied their seats in the coach, and taking his seat outside with the driver, armed with two heavy cavalry pistols, the cavalcade departed on its way to Dulwich. Scrubb also took his seat behind, armed with a cudgel and pistol, to protect the trunks and baggage, and to keep off any intruding visitors who might be more curious than welcome. The interior of the coach contained Master Elliot and his wife, his son and Constance, with Pauline and Dame Trivet, who were in high glee at the expected comforts, safety, and convenience they should experienco at their new abode.

Crossing London Bridge, between its rows of houses and shops, the coach proceeded at a jumbling trot through the Borough of Southwark, undisturbed by any noise save that of the distant pealing of the dead cart bell, which was always to be heard in any part of the city after nightfall. The high road of Newington once gained, they proceeded at a brisk rate through the little village of Walworth, and hastening on soon reached the hill at Brixton, which having surmounted and left behind they gradually gained upon the parish of Dulwich, which lay about five miles from London Bridge, and was at this time quite a rural country retreat for merchants and tradesmen of the first class, who were glad to avail themselves of some healthful retirement from the fatigues and danger of an infected city.

The villa which Master Elliot had taken for his family retreat was a complete suburban palace in miniature, having apartments of every description, and of the most convenient yet splendid appearance. The house was surrounded by beautiful lawns, gardens, and orchards; the front was enclosed from the high road by a low brick wall, which communicated with a pair of iron folding-gates with the road, and was surrounded by r wide ditch in the rear, which rendered it pretty safe from any nocturnal intrusions, as in these troublesome times, when both judge and criminal were hourly in fear of death from the plague, law was almost rendered useless, or at least regarded as harmless, by a desperate rabble, who, leaving the unwholesome confines of the city, obtained a wretched livelihood by prowling for plunder in the suburbs where the disease had not yet spread. Anticipating such visits, and acting on the preventive (ever a plan of Master Elliot's), he had arranged that Lawrence and Scrubb should guard the house by night at intervals, well armed, and having for a companion a huge Spanish mastiff, of a most ferocious nature. He had also laid in a plentiful stock of provisions, with the exception of a few necessaries; it being Elliot's intention to keep his household very select and reserve, allowing neither ingress or egress, except upon urgent occasions.

The morning after their arrival at their new residence, having refreshed themselves by a hearty meal, as well as they could from the effects of travelling all night, and the day being oppressively hot, the whole family, with the exception of Lawrence, proceeded to obtain a few hours' repose, and the apprentice, being in no mood for slumber, sought to beguile a few hours away by making a survey of the surrounding scenery and enclosures of the house, for he secretly anticipated a visit from the duke at some early opportunity, for he doubted not but that he would soon obtain information of the place of the family's retreat.

Happening by mere chance to have occasion to change his doublet for a lighter one, as he was in the act of casting it from him, he was surprised to see a blank packet drop from his girdle: it was closely sealed up, and fastened with a silken cord. For a moment he hesitated as to the propriety of his opening it, but after a few minutes' consultation within himself, not being able to tax his memory with any message or letter he had to deliver from any one, he at length ventured to break the seal, and hastily unfolding the paper by which it was enclosed, he ran his eye quickly down the side written upon to catch the signature attached, but to his surprise there was none to be seen. But if he was struck with amazement at finding the document to be anonymous, his astonishment was tenfold upon perusing the contents, which ran as follows :—

" From one who loves, but is not loved.

" How vain is the dictates and caprices of love. Those who seek its influence find its barb their woe. What is more poignant than unrequited love ?—(torture, thought Lawrence, when he considered of his attachment for Constance), and ten times more baneful is its effects when the object of our affection bestows the love we sigh for upon one who disregards and values not.   Love is not a language of the tongue, or the actions, but of the eyes. Think, then, O my heart's idol, of the return you receive ere you cast away such precious affections ; for if she upon whom you have set your heart slight the gift, remember that another passes hours, days, weeks, and perhaps even months, grieving for the loss of disregarded affection.   Ponder well ere you judge of this."

Lawrence was utterly confounded upon reading this epistle, and it was a long while before he fixed his suspicions upon any person who could have been the author of it ; till at length the image of Helen coming to his mind, he attributed it to her.   "I can but pity her," he reasoned to himself, "if she has really conceived a passion for me—wrung as my heart is by the return its affections have met with from Constance, no other woman has any attractions to me.   Still I can but pity her, and will strive to cause her no further uneasiness on the subject by keeping from her sight, which under my present circumstances will be no very difficult matter."   He then tore up the letter into a thousand pieces, and proceeded on his survey.

There were however more lovers in the family of Master Elliot than his apprentice and his daughter besides even the beautiful Helen herself, and these were Scrubb and Pauline, who had never fairly met to settle their difficulties since the night of her abduction.   Meeting however on this occasion more by chance than by appointment, though through a little of each, Scrubb pretended to be at first highly displeased, and commenced his addresses in a cold suspicious manner.

"The presence of Buckingham and his companions seems to have given you some pleasant grounds for reflection Pauline, and you seem to take pleasure in ever relating it, and speaking of them with a degree of satisfaction," said Scrubb taking her hand and leading her into a shrubbery adjoining the house.

"Why how can I help thinking about it, Scrubb, dear," replied the maiden innocently ; "I was never in company with such fine handsome looking men before, and then that Duke of Buckingham, oh ! he has such beautiful eyes, such teeth, and such a winning smile, I—"

"There ! 'tis as I said ! you are desperately in love with him, and if that be the case you had better go to him and live with him," exclaimed Scrubb, with emotion ; "and then me and Lawrence will fight a duel with him and kill him !"

"But if you should get killed Scrubb, dear, what should I do then ?" inquired Pauline, archly.   I do not think the duke would take the trouble to run away with me a second time, for when he found out I was not Constance, he was in such a mighty humour !   Lor bless me ! how he did stamp and curse and swear; and the two others who were with him only laughed at him.   Before that, it was all kindness, love and tenderness ; for you must know Scrubb, that taking me for Constance, he pressed my hand, encircled my waist with his arms, and he did whisper such sweet words in my ear. Oh, Scrubb, I wish you could make love in such a manner, how happy we should be !"

"I shall make love no more !—you may go back to the duke, and tell him I sent you as a present to him—as for me I will go and hang myself directly."

And with this intention Scrubb darted off with Pauline in his rear, screaming and calling upon him to stop.   The noise aroused Lawrence, who hastening to the spot and ascertaining the nature of the quarrel between the lovers, undertook to be their peace-maker, and with that intent led them both into the house, although Scrubb inwardly vowed to himself that he would either hang, drown, or go and catch the plague

CHAPTER XXII.

Tue day for the trial of Gowles and Mother Hagget having arrived on the charges of robbery and murder, at the instigation of the doctor, it had created such a sensation in the city, that long before the hour of commencing business, the Old Court of Justice was crowded to excess.

On the evening previous, however, Doctor Calder having availed himself of an excuse to visit the apartment of the late bell ringer, had secretly made his way to the stone vault, and in the dead of the night had removed the bodies of the two murdered vergers to some more secure spot—he was not particular where, so as he might confront the statement he had no doubt Hagget would make concerning the secreting of the bodies. This done, he was easy in his mind, and awaited the hour of trial with composure and defiance.

The form of trial was very different in the reign of Charles the Second to the present time; there was no counsel for prisoners and the judges were more prejudiced against the unfortunate criminal, than they were in favour of justice. After of a trial of four hours and a half, by the astounding weight of conclusive and circumstantial evidence Gowles and Hagget were both found guilty, and sentence was passed upon them. Mother Hagget was first arraigned;—and it having been proved that she caused the death of several of her patients, by violent measures, contrary to the usages of medicine and humanity, she was sentenced to be hanged at Tyburn. Gowles, who was only convicted as an accomplice in her crimes of death, but as principal participator in the robberies, was sentenced to solitary confinement for the term of his natural life; and thus did the law award its amends to these vile associates.

On the day appointed for the execution of Mother Hagget, the road leading from Newgate to Tyburn was thronged with people, and as the criminal was drawn thither upon a sledge, by a white horse, (according to the law when women were convicted of such heinous crimes as amounted to petty treason), she was received with yells, hootings, and groanings, and had it not been for the interference of the Yeomanry Guard, she would doubtless have fallen a victim to their indignation. Upon her arrival at Tyburn she maintained a gloomy silence, till the precise moment of her being fastened to the fatal beam, and as she was drawn under it upon a platform, she made signs to the multitude around her that she wished to address them; who feeling a desire to hear what such a wretch could possibly have to say, a general silence was soon obtained, as she delivered the following speech, which is still on record in the Jail documents at Newgate, or may be perused by consulting "The Old Chronicles of Newgate," vol 7, page 194.

Leaning forward as far as the bonds would permit her, Mother Hagget thus addressed the crowd :—

"Good people who have come to see me die!—you no doubt rejoice at my death, and think that I must be a wicked wretch to commit so many bad deeds. I have only a few words to say in vindication of myself. I was prompted and assisted to these wicked deeds by one who has since turned my accuser, I mean Doctor Thomas Calder, of Doctor's Commons; you may believe me, for these are the words of a dying and repentant woman. The phial found in my house, filled with poison, was made up expressly for me by that hateful man, but was never used by me. Likewise the deaths of the two vergers in Old Saint Paul's, as I swore upon my trial was also committed by him, and I was present and can testify it, he is a guilty wretch, and although at present out of the hands of the law, I trust Heaven will not long let him escape that vengeance so justly due to his villanies. Farewell! I have but one more word to say before I leave this world for ever, and that is about the plague which now rages through this country; it will last till it is either frozen out or burnt out; take this as a prophecy of one who has lived by its ravages; be just, be cleanly, be bold-hearted, but above all be a christian, and you may defy the plague!"

The platform, at her own signal, was drawn from under her, and Mother Hagget, the once renowned and dreaded plague nurse of the City of London, was no more.

Upon the termination of this ceremony, the whole of the assemblage, having gathered fresh fury in the words of Mother Hagget concerning Doctor Calder, loudly shouted for vengeance—" Death to the murderer!—let us root him out, and exterminate his name!—Down with him!—Death to the poisoner!" and uttering these exclamations, the concourse rushed away down the Oxford Road, across the Strand, towards Temple Bar, and stopped not till they had reached the scene of their rage and malice. The doctor's house was now besieged with loud clamours, but receiving no answers, already had the mob commenced battering in the doorway, and demolishing the windows in the front part of the house by pelting them with stones, crying out—" Bring forth the murderer!—the poisoner!—the hypocrite! bring him forth to our fury!"

Luckily for Doctor Calder a friend had out-ridden the mob and informed him of his danger, sufficiently early to enable him to pack up a few valuables ready for a speedy flight. The front door of his house was now forced; already had two or three ruffianly vagabonds made their entrance up the stairs, as Doctor Calder and his friend was descending, to make a speedy exit at the back of the house. Meeting on the stairs a deadly struggle took place between them—" Here he is! we have him—the murderer is in our hands!" exclaimed a stout built alsation as he rushed forwards to seize the doctor by the throat, who catching his arm, however, as he grasped at him, buried a short knife in the fellow's throat and leaped out at the window behind him, followed by his friend, and making for the Thames they speedily took a boat, crossed the water, landed at Greenwich, galloped on through Dartmouth to Rochester, where a Flemish captain was loading for Amsterdam, and on board of his ship did Doctor Calder embark, and the next morning wafted him from the shores of his native land, which he never after revisited; but becoming a dealer in silks and tobacco at Amsterdam, lived many years a wealthy, if not a happy man, and died at an advanced age, leaving his property to a Convent of Monks and Friars.

Gowles, who was banished for the remainder of his life to a new colony just rising into notice, which the government was now peopling with convicts and soldiers, followed Doctor Calder in his passage across the seas; but the horrors of solitary confinement prayed so much upon his mind that in less than six months from the time of his arrival he fell a victim to a raging disease at that time prevailing in the colony.

To return to London, however, the plague was raging with greater fury than ever, and although the summer was drawing to a close, still no decrease of the disease was visible. Churches were now converted into hospitals, and public divine worships either wholly neglected, or performed in the streets. Justice also seemed to have fled the land, accompanied with law, for crime was now committed with such impunity that none could be found either to arrest the criminals or to follow them to a Court of Justice to bear witness against them.

About this time the plague broke out in Newgate, and in the City Compter, the governor died, three of the principal turnkeys also died, and the control and discipline of the prisons being left to persons totally unacquainted with such an office, and equally regardless of anything like responsibility the plague now became a revolt. Those few wretched prisoners who had as yet escaped the disease, and knowing the state of the government of the prison, one night after a plan had been previously arranged, broke forth and having maltreated their superiors, set fire to the prison in several places, and during this confusion the sick and the hale, the furious and the lightheaded victims of the plague rushed forth into the streets, to breed fresh horrors by their contaminating presence.

Depredations and crime being now so prevalent, that law was looked upon as nothing. On the night of September the 2nd, a great fire broke out near Fish-street-hill, which raged with considerable fury all Sunday morning, but nothing of importance was attached to it; however, finding on the Monday it had increased nearly ten-fold, that the citizens began to be alarmed.

The fire had now spread along Gracechurch-street, Cornhill, and the Mansion House were now in one body of flame. On the southern side of Cheapside it had spread down Watling-street, Thornes-street, and carrying before it all the adjacent houses and alleys thereto. Reaching as far as Bow Church, the fire gained new strength from an unforeseen accident. Near Friday-street was situated a large gunpowder store and pitch manufactory, and this being attacked by the fire, soon blew up with tremendous destruction, carrying tiers of houses with it. By Wednesday the fire had passed Old Change and was fast spreading round the Cathedral itself, which the citizens were trying every effort to save from the impending destruction which awaited it. However, unfortunately a strong easterly wind blowing all Wednesday night, by daybreak on Thursday, the steeple and belfry were discovered to be on fire. In vain was hundreds upon hundreds of hands brought to lend in assistance upon it. No water could be procured nearer than the Thames with any effect, and then it would be utterly impossible to carry it to such a height. To pull down the steeple was therefore deemed the most prudent step to take and the one most likely to save the body of the cathedral. This was deemed a work of such peril that but few could be found who were willing to assist in such a task; and by the time the ladders were raised, the fire had reached the roof which being constructed of timber soon fell a victim to the devouring element. All further attempts to save the sacred edifice was now deemed useless. To rescue the property of the citizens which had been placed there as a place of safety was now the general endeavour, and to effect this upwards of fifteen hundred men assisted—but for what—only to place the furniture and warehouse goods in more imminent peril by the falling of surrounding embers, and by exposing them to the marauding gangs who were prowling about the city during this calamity for plunder and spoil.

On raged the fire, growing stronger with every destruction it occasioned. And three days after the sacred edifice of Old Saint Paul's had been attacked by the flames, it fell a victim to its fury, and nothing but the historian's pen was left to record its existence and place of erection.

All London was threatened to become a victim to the devouring element which was now spreading round in all quarters. The River Thames was now considered to be the only secure place for the secretion of property, and to effect this hundreds of boats and barges were constantly leaving their moorings with goods saved from the fire, which were conveyed to the shores of Essex and Kent, to await, when the excitement of the fire was over, the acknowledgment of their owners.

18.

At length the flames by dint of their own insatiableness were stayed. For having completely destroyed every thing that opposed them, they were at length lulled and defeated by having no more fuel to consume, and thus fell the famous and celebrated City of London, a victim to a ravaging disease, and perishing at last by the torch of the incendiary. By most persons of influence, however, and even to the present day, it is generally believed to have been the work of the government to eradicate the distemper, for the plague ended with the fire, and with the fire also fell the main object of our tale—the celebrated edifice of

Old Saint Paul's.

*   *   *   *   *   *   *   *   *   *   *

The fire having ceased, and the plague completely obliterated, our tale is soon told.

For two years from the fire, Master Elliot and his family passed their time in quiet retirement, even unmolested by the annoyances of the Duke of Buckingham and his party; for that nobleman having given much offence at court by his dissolute conduct fled to Holland, where he resided several years. Constance Elliot, the lovely heroine of our romance, at length fell a victim to the disorder that had long preyed upon her mind—a broken heart, and her grave was opened after a few months to receive the ashes of her mother. Lawrence and Helen were united, for Master Buckthorpe having died and made a will to the effect that his daughter should inherit all his property, on the condition that she married him; and they lived happily for many years and had a great family, which was the delight of Master Elliot's declining years, who in process of time went down to the grave honoured and esteemed by all.

THE END.

Carter, Commercial-road.

www.ingramcontent.com/pod-product-compliance
Lightning Source LLC
Chambersburg PA
CBHW082013170626
46817CB00009B/3076